Praise for *Shades of Mercy*

"Shades of Mercy transports you back to a simpler time, idyllic Maine backdrops, and all **the complications of racial tension and forbidden love. You'll cheer for the heroine and fall in love with the hero**—a perfect recipe for a sweet, enduring read."

—MARY DEMUTH, speaker and author of *The Muir House*

"A glorious coming-of-age tale that captures the scenic beauty of Maine as well as the ugly underbelly of racism. **I felt transported but saw a mirror of our current day.** You will adore this tenderly told love story—a love story expressed on many different levels."

—CHRIS FABRY, bestselling author and radio personality

"The human dynamics in a small town American community with a racially diverse population can be challenging. Some people walk with blinders on; others turn a cheek to the problem of social injustice. . . . Racism is often not easily identifiable or understood. *Shades of Mercy* **highlights problems of the past that in some cases still exist but also presents hope for a better future of understanding."**

—BRIAN REYNOLDS, Tribal Administrator, Houlton Band of Maliseet Indians

"Through the vivid lens of two lives set in small-town America, Anita and Caryn capture the heart of one of our biggest pieces of unfinished business: our relationship with First peoples. Anita and Caryn create with pitch-perfect detail the struggles and triumphs of the Maliseet people caught in a world of bigotry, suspicion, and ignorance—and just enough nobility to keep hope alive. **A book that both instructs and entertains, but above all inspires."**

—MARK BUCHANAN, author of *Your Church Is Too Safe*

"*Shades of Mercy* is a re-creation of small town America complete with its warmth and innocence and a frothy brew of secrets. **Tough moral and spiritual questions are faced head-on in this sweet tale of love and friendship."**

—DONNA VANLIERE, *NY Times* bestselling author of *The Good Dream*

"With an intimate, engaging voice, a budding young woman named Mercy extends compassion for the vestiges of the once proud Maine Maliseet, a Native American tribe short on resources yet long on wisdom and appreciation for beauty. **A heartwarming tale—of the real meaning of grace**—that stays with you. We need more stories about the intersection of Christianity and Native Americans, and this one is dignified and wonderful."

—LINDA S. CLARE, author of *The Fence My Father Built* and *A Sky without Stars*

SHADES OF MERCY

A MAINE CHRONICLE

ANITA LUSTREA
CARYN RIVADENEIRA

MOODY PUBLISHERS

CHICAGO

Scripture quotations are from the King James Version.

"Grief" in chapter 18 is taken from Emily Dickinson, *Selected Poems* (New York: Dover Thrift Editions, 1990), 25.

Published in association with ChristopherFerebee.com. Attorney and Literary Agent.

Edited by Pam Pugh
Interior design: Ragont Design
Cover design: Gilbert & Carlson Design LLC dba Studio Gearbox
Cover images: Veer images /AYP2903225; PHP2400038
Author photos: Anita Lustrea- Amy Paulson Photography
Caryn Rivadeneira-Connie Tameling

Library of Congress Cataloging-in-Publication Data

Lustrea, Anita.
    Shades of mercy / Anita Lustrea, Caryn Rivadeneira.
        p. cm.
    Summary: The world has changed from how it was in that special summer of 1954. Mercy tells her granddaughter what it was like for her to have fallen in love with a childhood playmate when that special young man is a Maliseet in small-town Maine. Illumined with the colors of fields of beautiful potato blossoms, enriched by well-rounded characters, and punctuated with the seasons of harvest and festivals, Shades of Mercy is a story that tells how a young couple challenged the prejudices of their day—provided by publisher.
    ISBN 978-0-8024-0968-3
    1. Interracial dating—Fiction. 2. Malecite Indians—Fiction. 3. Maine—Fiction.
I. Rivadeneira, Caryn Dahlstrand. II. Title.
PS3612.U795S53 2013
813'.6—dc23

                                                                    2013014295

We hope you enjoy this book from River North Fiction by Moody Publishers. Our goal is to provide high-quality, thought-provoking books and products that connect truth to your real needs and challenges. For more information on other books and products written and produced from a biblical perspective, go to www.moodypublishers.com or write to:

River North Fiction
Imprint of Moody Publishers
820 N. LaSalle Boulevard
Chicago, IL 60610

1 3 5 7 9 10 8 6 4 2

Printed in the United States of America

ANITA'S DEDICATION:
*To my family and friends from Maine. You have brought
my life so much joy and entertainment (especially
my favorite cousin) and I am forever indebted.*

CARYN'S DEDICATION:
*To my mom. Thanks for being a reader
and modeling a love of books and for every
single time you told me I could do anything.*

Contents

Remembering

The letter shook a bit in my hand. For a moment, I worried it was me, finally giving in to the "old age shakes," as Ellery used to call his tremors. But it wasn't me. It was only the breeze that had picked up, from somewhere. I looked up from my hand—and the letter it held—past the wrought-iron tables and plastic chairs of the coffee shop in which I sat and took in the stir of early morning Manhattan.

How good it would be to have Laurel joining me here. Tomorrow, already!

Though she had visited me in New York many times in the years since they moved to Los Angeles, this time would be different. Laurel was no longer content to take in Manhattan as a tourist. Laurel had no interest in Bergdorf's or the Frick. Nor did she care much about the Statue of Liberty or the Empire State Building. Certainly she's stopped caring about tossing bread to the ducks in Central Park. It almost hurt to think she was too grown to care about that.

No, Laurel had written—a real letter! on real paper!—to say she'd like to spend her time learning the New York her grandfather and I first lived in all those years ago, when her grandfather's graduate work brought us to Columbia University and the start of our lives together.

My fifteen-year-old granddaughter misses her grandfather. (So do I.) And she believes that being in New York and seeing the places where his ideas gained steam and his marvelous career took shape will reconnect her to him. And it will, I suppose.

But what I really want to tell Laurel, is that if she wants to understand her family and what makes our people great, we shouldn't be staying in the city. I should be picking her up at La Guardia, and we should be driving up the I-95, stopping at Mystic Seaport in Connecticut, circling the Portsmouth roundabout in New Hampshire, even taking in some of the beautiful sites on the coast of the fair state of Maine. Pemaquid Point, Rockland, Camden, picture postcard worthy, all of them. Yes, we should be going to Maine. To Watsonville, Maine. That's where Laurel's grandfather became the amazing man he was; that's where her great-grandfather wove *justice* into the DNA of this family; and that's where I lived the summer that would change the course of my life.

But Laurel arrives tomorrow. There's no time for a change of plans now.

Instead, as she and I walk past 606 West 114th St., the first apartment her grandfather and I lived in, as we pass the newsstands where her grandfather bought his morning paper, as we stop in at the hospital where her father was born, I'll tell her the story of that summer in Watsonville, all those years ago, when I was her age.

PART ONE

*"When you've been given much,
much is expected."*

Chapter One

I shoved *The Catcher in the Rye* between the mattress and box spring when I heard Mother yell up the stairs, although I probably needn't have. When I asked Mother for money to buy the book, she made it clear that it wasn't one Mr. Pop would condone. But she gave me the money anyway.

I figured a book tucked below the mattress, hidden by a stack of quilts and under a layer of ruffles, was one Mr. Pop would not find. And, therefore, could not disapprove of my reading.

"Mercy," Mother called again more insistently, this time from the landing, halfway up our staircase.

I cracked the door open—enough to poke my head out and let the cat in—never letting go of the glass knob. "Be right down."

"Please hurry. You need to get something in you. Your father wants you to go get Ansley and Mick."

I couldn't hide my smile.

My mother smiled back, shook her head, and waved her dishrag in the air. I watched her walk back down the stairs. Watched her graceful hand, still lovely after all that hard work, as it glided along the polished oak banister.

I closed the door and leaned for a moment against its dark panels. My smile spread wider across my face. Plenty of fifteen-year-olds would've balked at the idea of a drive into town, to where Ansley and Mick and all the Maliseet lived in the Flats, built over trash in our town dump. But not me. I'd go anywhere, do anything to be with Mick.

Though, of course, Mr. Pop didn't know this. He couldn't know this.

To him, sending me—"You're as good as any son, Mercy"—was simply prudent. I was a good driver, able to navigate the long road into town in any weather. And I was fearless. Unafraid of pounding on the plywood doors of the Flats, unafraid of pushing them open, stepping over and between bodies that huddled together or crisscrossed on the cold floors. Unafraid of clapping my hands, of announcing myself, even of shaking Ansley, Francis, Newell, and Clarence awake if I had to.

I suppose I should've been afraid, should've been more aware of the dangers that a teenaged girl stepping into a shack full of passed-out men might have presented. But these men wanted work, needed work. My presence was their manna. My knowledge of that kept me safe. Well, that and knowing Mick made these rounds with me.

I slid my nightgown off my shoulders and grabbed my shirt and blue jeans from the back of my desk chair. My flannel sleeve slid across the top of my desk and Lickers leapt toward it. She pinned the sleeve like she had a mouse's tail. Her claws dug into the slick-stained wood and dragged back.

"Lickers! No!" I swept my arm across the desk. Lickers leapt with a meow. *No.*

I ran my finger over the scratch and shook my head, tried not to cry as I thought back to what it took to get this. All last harvest, I'd worked for this desk. And even before with all the rock picking, clearing the fields of rock so the plows could ready the ground. Then I'd spent so many hours, days, weeks bent and sore picking potatoes out of the hard, dry earth. Filling the basket, emptying it into the barrel, filling the basket, emptying it into the barrel. On and on. The repetition might have made me lose my mind were it not for our farmhands Bud Drake and Ellery Burt and their encouraging banter.

But besides the long, hard hours, I got tired of being alone. Even though I was with a crew, no one else filled my barrels. When encouraging words failed to do the job, Bud's comments turned harsher toward us: "You're too far behind." "Your barrel isn't full enough." "Don't forget to put a ticket on your barrel when it's full."

You'd think we'd never done this before the way he nagged. Then again, Bud was only trying to please Mr. Pop. As was I.

Plus, I was focused on a goal: my new desk. So I put up with nagging and hard work and then the waiting—through the end of last October and first half of November—for the Sears truck to deliver this next piece of furniture to the farm. The one I'd longed for more than even the dresser or the bed, which I'd worked for the previous harvest.

The desk represented so much of what I'd wanted. A space to keep my pens, my journals, my books, and my sketch pads. And the mirror above it—the place I could sit and not only feel like me—the real me—but also *see* me: the young (was I also smart? Maybe even pretty?) woman looking back at me in that mirror. Instead of the sturdy farmhand Mr. Pop apparently saw.

So once again, I looked in that mirror and took a deep breath. Now wasn't the time to cry about a silly scratch. Not with Mother waiting to fill me with biscuits and eggs and fresh milk. Not with Mr. Pop waiting for me to bring back his workers. Not with Mick waiting just for me.

I put arms through sleeves and legs through pants. Pulled my hair back into a ponytail and gave Lickers a final glare. She licked her leg. She never noticed me.

✳ ✳ ✳

"Morning, Mercy," Bud said, scraping his fork against the plate. "Truck's all gassed up and ready for you."

"Thanks. And morning to you both." I latched my hand around the porch post and swung a bit as I balanced on the top step, like

15

I did every morning when I stopped to talk to Bud and Ellery, farmhands so trusted they were like family. Family that ate on the porch, that is.

I turned and raised an eyebrow at Ellery, wondering if his standard reply to Bud's greeting, usually some silly adage passed down through five generations of solid Maine stock, would make sense this morning.

"When all is said and done, Miss Mercy, don't let the door hit ya where the good Lord split ya."

Ellery shoved another biscuit into his mouth, and I laughed. This old chestnut even got a snicker out of Mr. Pop.

"So, Ellery, Mother put the last of last night's cheddar in those eggs this morning. What'd you think of it?"

Publicly, he'd eat anything. But privately, this man with the joke had quite the sophisticated palate. Sure, he'd eat anything. But knew what he liked.

"Wicked good," he said. "Butcha know, that creamy Kraft cheese melts smoother than the cheddar. Wonder if she might try that sometime."

I shrugged. Ellery slurped his milk and continued: "Hey, watcha think of them wax cartons they're puttin' the milk in these days? I want the glass bottles back. This'll be a fad, you just wait."

"I'll mention it to her next time she places her order with Mr. Callahan," I said. "You should've been a chef, Ellery. Could've been the new chef at Nelson's. I hear they're hiring."

"Nah," said Ellery, "I'd've missed all this."

I followed his arm as he waved it out across the farm. This place was beautiful. Not just the house and the porch that Mother had made so lovely and welcoming, with tidy and warm places for anyone and everyone to sit and feel at home. But the land. It wasn't an easy land to farm, with its hard-packed rocky soil and short growing season, but Mr. Pop always reminded us that it was the best. It was the very hardness of this place that made it so amazing, he said. The blessings of this place came right out of its trials.

Mother pushed open the screen door. "Mercy, honestly. Have you still not gone? Stop bothering Bud and Ellery and get on your way."

"She's no bother, ma'am," Ellery said and winked at me. "We're just talking about your delicious eggs."

Mother smiled, lowered her eyes, and stepped back inside. She let the screen door slap closed behind her.

"I'll see you in a bit then," I said and hopped down the stairs, landing hard on my sneakers. "Wait. Mr. Pop said to ask you where you'll be when I get back with the Maliseet workers."

"Oh, I suppose the three-acre field would be best to drop them off. If you manage more than five of them this morning, bring half down back and the others to the three acres, off the back road."

"All right. See you when I get back. Want me to feed the chickens and let the pigs out into their pen after that?"

"No, I'll send Bud out to tend to the animals this morning."

Mr. Pop loved his animals. He might act annoyed with Lickers, but he loved seeing her pounce on mice in the shed or in the barn. And the pigs, well, we only had four, but he had them named before they'd been in the pen ten minutes. There was Gracie, after the beautiful and elegant movie star Grace Kelly, then Dorothy, named after Uncle Roger's wife, Dot. I'm not sure how I'd feel having a pig named after me. Aunt Dot just laughed. I guess Mr. Pop knew she'd respond that way. Then there was Gertrude. Mr. Pop never said, but I always believed she was named after the most annoying woman on our party line, Mrs. Garritson. If you ever needed to place a call, you were almost guaranteed to be thwarted by Mrs. Garritson yapping on the phone. George rounded out the pigs, and no one knows where that name came from. Mr. Pop just pointed out that "He looks like a George!"

We had twenty laying hens that we simply referred to as the

"girls." Keep the girls fed, safe, and happy, and you'll always have plenty of eggs. That's what Mr. Pop said.

He always treated his farm animals well. They had names, a good place to live, and good food to nourish them. We all knew they'd be food on our table one day, and he wasn't afraid to slaughter them, but he treated them with dignity and respect all of their living days. I can't tell you how many times I heard Mr. Pop say, "Beware the farmer who treats his animals poorly. You could probably make a case that he doesn't treat his family all that well either."

The truck rumbled past the buttercups and clover down low on the roadside and the devil's paintbrushes and lupine in little patches here and there. I never tired of driving into town alone. It gave me time to think. Going the main road meant I could keep the windows wide-open and catch the breeze. The main road was one of the few paved ways to get into town. There was great beauty in the back way, either the Ridge Road or the Border Road, but the dust from the gravel made you close the cab up tight. Today I enjoyed the wind in my hair.

Mr. Pop had taught me to drive when I was eleven—four years before. It was standard practice for fathers to teach their sons to drive at that age or even younger. Teaching daughters was something of an anomaly. I'm sure plenty of the folks in town—and even on the surrounding farms—raised their eyebrows a bit when they first saw me at the wheel, bouncing and lurching down the back farm road as I learned to work the clutch on the old Ford potato truck. Who knows what they must've thought hearing those grinding gears halfway into town, watching me slide around corners in the muddy buildup at the end of the potato rows. However, the people of Watsonville, Maine, were plenty used to Mr. Pop telling them I was as "good as any son—if not better" and had been used to seeing me raised as the son he never had.

And certainly by now the sight of me, Paul's daughter, in that old potato truck was a regular one. I waved at Pastor Murphy and Mrs. Brown chatting in front of Fulton's on Main Street, knowing that the place I was headed, and what I was off to do, still offered plenty of fodder for gossip.

It had become clear enough by last summer when I was fourteen that I was no son. And that Mr. Pop still sent me and my "budding womanhood," Mother called it, to round up his Indian workers left many people shaking their heads and clucking their tongues.

If it had been any other father besides Paul Millar sending his daughter, it'd have been an uncontainable scandal, boiling over the entire town, through the farms, into the logging camps, and even across the border into New Brunswick. It'd happened with other stories.

But Paul Millar was a trusted, esteemed man. A true man of God and of honor. Although many folks questioned his decisions regarding me and the people he chose to hire, no one could question his heart and his mind. He was a good man. And everybody knew it. Everybody liked him.

Which meant that when Mother took me shopping in town—stepping into Fishman's and Woolworth's, our favorites for a chocolate soda and to look at magazines, pens, and diaries, or into the Chain Apparel and Boston Shoe Store for school clothes and shoes or browsing the beautiful dresses in Woodson's that sometimes made Mother tear up as she rubbed her fingers against the fabrics—no one dared ask the questions they were desperate to. When we stopped into the IGA Grocery Store, Miss Maude's checkout line would grow uncharacteristically quiet. She may have started her gossip about us the moment the bells jingled behind us, but at least she didn't pry for information. Not the way she did with other people.

✳ ✳ ✳

I slowed the truck.

"Molly! Molly Carmichael!" I yelled and waved out the truck window. But Molly just grimaced and waved me on. I stopped the truck midstreet to watch her kick off into a run. I hadn't gotten a chance to talk to Molly much since school let out a few weeks ago. And I missed that. Molly was the only one I could talk to about Mick, the only one who understood. Molly's older sister Marjorie and Glenn Socoby had been seeing each other on the sly since last Easter. Glenn was a Maliseet, like Mick. I was tempted to turn the truck to follow her, find out what was up, but Mr. Pop would've had my hide. I'd have to catch her another time. Mick, Ansley, and the others were waiting.

The truck croaked and lurched forward, causing heads to turn again on Main Street. But I kept my eyes on what lay ahead: the stately Second Baptist Church. I always wished we went there. Not just because our friends the Carmichaels were members, but because of its ivory steeple cutting into Maine skies, its creamy columns standing firm in front of scrubbed-each-summer clay bricks, and its English-born-and-bred preacher, Second Baptist breathed sophistication. Even though my family's First Baptist had beaten Second Baptist to the punch years ago and won the Baptist Church Naming War, somehow our little country church, tucked back among potato fields, seemed like the loser.

Especially since Second Baptist got its new sign—the one Ellery called a "braggin' sign." Today it read: "Sunday at 9 a.m. Love Thy Neighbor." I'd have to tell Mr. Pop this one. I knew what he'd say: "Better we love our neighbors all the time, Mercy. Not just nine o'clock on Sundays."

Chapter Two

The stench of rot and decay and animal waste hit before the sight of it.

But whenever the Flats came into view—after that bend just past town, after the buildings give way once again to the pines—the smell made sense. Because it isn't just the dump itself but the years of that putrid smell that clung to shack walls, if you call corrugated cardboard or tin (with tar paper stapled to it) walls. That gag-inducing odor steeped deep into old sofas and sunk down into chewed-through mattresses.

This is how and where Mick and the rest of the Maliseet lived. This is where our town had relegated them. But the proud Maliseet tried not to focus on the trash and the ugly; instead they set their eyes on the surrounding beauty. After all, here the rolling brook hugged the country road and sparkled as it ran over rocks and rapids. High white birch and tall pines peppered the landscape across and behind the dump. In fact, in many ways the mound of trash itself blended in. Were it not for the shacks, the rectangles of gray—the soiled mattresses that the Maliseet slept on under open sky—the stray, jutting bits of broken chairs, and piles of tin cans and cereal boxes that the people of Watsonville drove out and piled onto the heap every Saturday, one could be hard-pressed to distinguish this hill from the other ones that rolled their way out of town.

Mr. Pop had taught me to stay vigilant for the dangers that lurked along this inviting gravel-covered road: moose, deer, and bear could wander out at any moment. But as I drove out this day, the words of Second Baptist's braggin' sign reminded me of another danger Mr. Pop often warned me of. "Be careful," he would say, "when people fail to treat one another with dignity."

I hadn't always understood when he said this, but as I parked the truck at the base of the dump, a chill ran through me, suddenly understanding. I'd always figured the black bears that sniffed and poked around through the trash were the greatest danger here. Perhaps I was wrong.

"Hey! Hurry up!"

I jumped at the knock at the truck window. *Mick.*

"Come on. Before everyone's up." Mick jimmied the handle and opened the door for me, grabbing my hand as I stepped out. "Over here."

He looked around and pulled me toward a pair of smoke-streaked yellow cellar doors.

"Old Man Stringer dropped 'em off yesterday," Mick said. "He was too drunk to haul them up all the way. But wanted us to have 'em. 'They sure don't work for my shack, so I thought maybe they'd work for yours,' Old Man told me."

"So what are you going to do with them?" I asked, smiling and trying to resist reaching up to touch Mick's face. He didn't tower over me but had a good three or four inches on me. Mick's deep tanned skin and shiny-black, shoulder-length hair made me weak in the knees. His eyes almost squinted shut when he smiled at me, and his perfect creamy-white teeth usually made people take a second look. He was wearing the same red plaid shirt I'd seen him wear a hundred times, but it never seemed old.

"I'll show you. Help me move one." Mick smiled back at me and reached out to touch my face, running his finger over my smiling lips. "You must be the only person in town who smiles at the dump, you know that?"

"It's not the dump that makes me smile."

"Aw, shucks," Mick teased. "Come on. Grab one. Let's go."

I dragged my door until Mick scolded me. "You're making a

racket. You'll wake everybody up. Pick it up."

"I'm *supposed* to be waking everybody up," I said.

"And we will, in a minute. Trust me. Here."

Mick shifted his door under a trio of snuggled-tight pines, then took mine from me, kicking and tugging the doors into place.

"There," he said, wiping his hands on his jeans. "With the charred-side out, they can't see. Now, come here."

I followed him under the trees, ducking low to keep too many pine needles from dripping down into my shirt. Mick patted the brown ground and I sat beside him.

"Someday, we won't have to hide like this. We can have a real home. But for now. At least we have a place to be alone. Together."

Together. Someday. I breathed deep. Here, the smell of pine and sap tried to drown out the wretched odor that lurked behind it.

Mick wrapped an arm around me, snuck a kiss on my cheek. "Someday," he whispered. We sat for a moment, staring out into the forest.

"However," Mick said, suddenly antsy, "until someday, we've got to go wake everybody up. We can meet here again tomorrow. Come a little earlier."

"One minute," I said. "This is nice." I put my hand to his cheek, ran it back through his black-as-any-bear hair and kissed him right on the lips. This wasn't our first kiss—that had been last harvest. While everyone sat around on the porch and in the grass and dove into their peanut butter and jelly or cheese sandwiches, Mick and I stole behind the old shed and we snuck the first of many secret and dangerous kisses.

Mother had told me the stories of her and Mr. Pop—sneaking their own kisses when they were about my age. Later Mother caused a scandal of her own by skipping college and the future a girl of her "station" was entitled to so she could marry my dad.

"He's a good man, a good worker, and a good Christian, Geneva," my grandfather had told her before she married my dad at sixteen. "But he's a farmer's son. He can't give you the life I've given you."

I stared back into the trees, wondering what my own father would say now. Knowing, actually.

"Hey," Mick said, nudging me with his elbow. "Let's go get everybody."

I left first, and Mick met me in front of his shack. I had walked back around to where my truck sat, climbed the dump from that angle. Less suspicious—as always. Although as I passed the Indian women—sitting in their half circles, facing the road below and weaving ash wood into the potato baskets they would sell to local farmers along with the occasional tourist—their eyes followed my steps. They knew why I came. But I could never shake the sense they knew something else.

I smiled and offered my best "*tan kahk*," the Maliseet greeting. Mick heard me and jerked his head. Though I'd heard it all my life, this was the first time I said it. Well, except for in front of my bedroom mirror, where I practiced it and the other Maliseet phrases Mick'd taught me. I caught him in a small smile, before turning back to talk to his brother.

"Mercy," one of the women called out. I stepped toward the semicircle. It was Mick's mother. She leaned forward to stir the can of beans resting in the fire.

"Good morning, Miss Louise."

"Thank your father for the extra ash splints."

"No need. Mr. Pop says ash trees belong to God and the Maliseet."

Miss Louise smiled at me. "Yes, I know. He tells Ansley that. What I mean is, thank your father for *cutting* the ash. I had sent Joseph to do it. But—"

I glanced over to the shack where Mick and his younger brother Joseph now leaned. Mick's sixteen-year-old hand looked huge as it rested on Joe's thirteen-year-old and much-too-young-to-be-heaving chest. Bear and rusted spikes and people treated without dignity weren't the only dangers of living in this dump. Respiratory illnesses like Joseph's and the high incidence of diabetes ran rampant through this place. Once I'd heard Mr. Pop saying he wondered how much longer Joseph had. At the time, I didn't understand. As I watched Mick with his brother and saw Miss Louise's eyes tear, I knew. Even healthy Maliseet men typically lived only into their midforties.

"I'll tell him."

Miss Louise looked back at her work, without saying anything else. She pulled and tucked the strands of ash, weaving as if it were nothing, as if creating those intricate patterns for the colorful baskets were the only worry in her world.

By the time I got to Mick's shack, Mick had roused those ready to work and had pressed on to the next shacks. Joseph followed him—begging to be included, knowing he'd be refused. The work was too hard for a sickly thirteen-year-old, certainly one struggling even to breathe. Joseph tapped the maple trees in the spring, a much less strenuous job, and by the time harvest rolled around, he felt bored and invincible even if he wasn't.

I trotted over by Mick to help bang on doors, pushing them open if we had to, and call loudly, "There's work on the Millar farm. Truck leaves in five minutes. Mr. Millar's got work today. Get up and get going."

The men rambled out of doors, pulling up trousers, tucking in shirts—meaning we didn't need to go into any of the shacks. Always a relief.

Mick counted them off. "Looks like seven, plus me and Pop."

"And me," Joseph said with a deep breath, fingering the beaded Maliseet cap on his head. Ansley had given it to him during one of his lengthier respiratory episodes in the hospital.

"Sorry, kid." Mick gave Joseph a pat. "But one of these days, 'k?"

Joseph kicked a rock and rambled back over to the circle of

women. His mother pointed at a pile of ash splints and he reluctantly sat down to weave like the women were doing.

"He can't wait till sugaring season—so he can be off by himself, among the maples, instead of sitting there with all those women," Mick said. "He thinks it's not manly."

"He could always come, you know, feed the pigs and chickens," I said. "Ellery'd find something for him to do."

"He'd just take up space. They need to work. He doesn't. Just the way it is."

I stepped carefully over bits of rubbish, ears tuned for the growl of a bear as we headed back down the heap. After waking them up, I never said much to the men. We all just walked in silence—even me and Mick. Especially me and Mick, actually.

Mr. Ansley broke the silence with "In the back. Now," just as he said every day we reached the truck. A few of them reached out for another helping of beans and bacon from the women who'd met us at the truck. And as Ansley said this once again, so did the men follow—jumping over the back gate, their worn waffle stompers kicking up dust and grime as they landed. The same as they did every morning. At least, every morning I came to get them.

I used to wonder why Ansley needed to repeat these orders. Surely, the men knew they were to ride in back. But lately, his words were meant for only one: Mick in the back too. Actually the words were meant for two. For Mick. And me.

Picking rocks was worse than picking potatoes. After all, picking potatoes offered reward beyond the pay. It was true: eating those potatoes was sometimes pay enough. I loved those early golf-ball-sized cobblers with their white, mealy flesh soaked in butter, or with peas and cream added. Although, the Kennebec and Katahdin potatoes filled the bulk of harvest picking. It didn't matter. You could give me either variety baked and slathered with butter and sour cream, and I'd forget about the backbreaking work that got them to my table.

Rock picking—and its routine drudgery—offered little extra incentive. You came away with bruised knees, skinned knuckles, and sore backs. And they didn't make the supper table any better. But picking rock is what held the promise, Mr. Pop always said.

Maybe this was why we still worked so hard with those rocks—hope and promise aren't anything to sneeze at. So when I'd steal breaks—to stretch my back or legs—I'd scan the field for the other workers. Mick, Mr. Ansley, and the other Maliseet bent and crawled right alongside Mr. Pop, Bud, and Mr. Ellery. Right beside me. I'd wonder if this picture—of us all working together—wasn't part of that promise itself. Mr. Pop talked as if it were: men and women, boys and girls, Indians and white folks, Catholic and Protestant, rich and poor, all working together. All glorifying God together is what Mr. Pop would call it. It's what he'd said after reading about the U.S. Supreme Court's "good and godly" decision regarding *Brown vs. Board of Education* the month before.

"Back to work now, Mercy." I'd been caught. Mr. Pop had a keen sense of when my body started to slack and my mind started to wander. He said it sternly, but I caught his slight smile.

I smiled back. "Sorry, Mr. Pop. Just stretching."

I dusted my knees, took a step forward, and crouched back down on the rich, loamy soil. Such fertile soil, but winter frost forces the rocks to the surface every season. The colder the winter, the more rock picking in the summer. I resumed tossing rocks into my wagon. Mr. Pop had been doing this same work for nearly forty years. The way he tells it, his parents had him out picking rocks on this very farm by the age of ten. He let me know to understand just what a grace I'd been given by not starting till I was twelve.

Though he'd laugh when he'd tell me that, Mr. Pop's childhood hadn't been funny. He and his twelve siblings had been born on this farm. Only five of them lived to leave it. His father died of tuberculosis when Mr. Pop was ten, leaving his mother, him, his brother, and three sisters to run the farm and try to keep food on the table any way they could. Only Mr. Pop and his brother stayed in Maine. Their sisters, long tired of the hardscrabble life that Maine offered them, scattered. My aunts wrote occasionally. But I had cousins I'd never met.

But Mr. Pop's upbringing made him who he was. He knew what it was to be hungry, to be poor. He knew the humiliation and blessing of living off the kindness of neighbors, churchgoers, and strangers. He knew loss and desperation. He knew heartbreak. But he also knew second chances, hard work, and a good God, he would say.

"And," he'd tell me, "I know what I've got to do with what I know."

His friends tried to talk him out of this all the time. God couldn't really expect this from him. If God did, would He have made the Maliseet so different? Most people in town assumed God had meant Maliseet to be with Maliseet. The white folks to be with white folks. And French-Canadians to stick with French-Canadians. But Mr. Pop wouldn't accept that. At least, not on his fields.

So even now—I watched Old Man Stringer weave through the rock pickers and stagger up to Mr. Pop, eager for any work that would get him invited to our porch where we'd eat our sandwiches and have our fill of Mr. Pop's ice cold well water. And for any who forgot lunch, Mother always had a morsel or two ready. Mr. Stringer was counting on it. In less than an hour, I knew Mr. Pop would oblige him. After all, what others called "drunk," Mr. Pop called "wrestling demons." And that, he said, doesn't make you less of a man or less worthy of lunch.

*　*　*

Mr. Pop, Ellery, Bud, and I headed in to the bountiful table Mother set every dinnertime. A time to rest our bodies and replenish them, that's what farmhands needed at midday. A twinge of guilt passed through me as I eyed the beef roast, green beans that were canned from last harvest, and the pickled beets. Homemade bread capped off a dinner fit for royalty. Farm life was simple but abundant, at least last growing season was.

"Mercy, men, better be headin' out again," Mr. Pop said. "Lots to do before we knock off this afternoon. Need to finish the side field and start pickin' rocks down back." We followed his lead as Mr. Pop shoved his chair back from the dining table.

"How's your boy Glenn liking work at the mill?" Old Man Stringer asked. Maliseet conversation froze. Mick's eyes lifted across the room to meet mine. We'd built a friendship and started a romance based on our ability to read expressions undetectable to others. But I couldn't read this look.

Newell Socoby cleared his throat and brought the napkin to his mouth, preparing to answer.

Mr. Pop chimed in. "Nelson tells me Glenn's doing real well over there. Like he was born for mill work."

"Yes, sir. Glenn's doing well."

"Not just well," Mr. Pop said. "He got a promotion, I hear. We're real proud of him. Though we miss him here."

"We miss him too," Newell said. "Doesn't get home as much as we'd like. He's staying busy in Millinocket."

I smiled at Mr. Socoby and at Mr. Pop, then tried to catch Mick's eye. His head stayed bent. "Just hope Mick doesn't follow his footsteps," Mr. Pop said. "Would hate to lose another of my brightest young workers. Unless it's to a university, of course. Then I'll be happy to lose him."

Mick smiled and nodded at Mr. Pop. But this time I understood the expression I could read in Mick's eyes as they drifted, then landed on mine. It was something like horror.

✳ ✳ ✳

"Mick, wait!"

He stopped just shy of the truck and turned to me. I kicked my steps into a run to catch up to him before the others got there. Mick glanced to the wash bins. The men stood laughing and drying their hands and faces on rags Mother handed out with a smile. We had only seconds.

"We'll talk tomorrow," Mick said, turning back to the truck. "Come early. Meet me back at our spot."

I was relieved to hear the "our," but my heart beat faster as he jumped up into the truck bed.

"What's going on?"

Without glancing back, just knowing his father and uncle, Bud, Ellery, and my own father were just steps away, Mick said, "Tomorrow."

"Tomorrow, indeed!" Mr. Pop slapped Mick on the back as he walked toward the truck. "One last field to clear so we can get these seeds planted. Let's just keep our eye on that promise."

The rest of the men jumped back into the bed. Old Man Stringer tripped toward the cab and gave the door a hard yank. Mother stepped beside him with her basketful of rags and tugged it for him. She offered her hand as he stepped up.

"You okay, there?"

"Yes, ma'am," Old Man said. "Thank you. Another delicious lunch."

"Any time, Mr. Stringer."

Mother cleared his sleeve from the door's path and slammed it, tapping the door below the window to give Ellery the all clear. Then Mother waved me back around.

I couldn't move. I knew I had to get the other basket of rags, bring it around back to the shed. I knew they had to be scrubbed on the washboard, hung to dry on the line before I went in to wash up myself and help with dinner cleanup.

But as the truck rumbled away, fluffing up dust in its wake, I could only watch and wonder. As Mother passed by, placing her hand on the small of my back, I wondered if she could feel the small tremors that shook inside.

Chapter Three

The morning in most ways was the same as all the others. Mother called up the stairs for me, and my stomach growled as I imagined the food awaiting: a plate of biscuits, butter beside it along with boysenberry jelly; fried eggs, dusted with salt and pepper; bacon fried crispy, with a hint of maple. All spread across the claw-footed dining room table, covered in our breakfast linen.

And like every morning, I knew what else awaited: my father in the same olive wool-blend work shirt and work pants, sitting at the head of the table, his worn Bible cracked open to today's passage. His hands were calloused from hard work, and his slight frame had hands to match. Though they weren't big hands, they were stronger than most men's. I'd seen the potato barrel hoist fail once last year, and Mr. Pop grabbed the barrel with his bare hands, pulling it up onto the truck bed. I'd always thought Mr. Pop could do just about anything. After that I knew he could.

Mr. Pop would have already prayed that God would use those words to bless his family—to bless us. To bless our work. To bless the workers.

It was the unknown that awaited me, like whatever was going on with Mick that kept the tremors coming as I stepped into the dining room.

"Morning, Mr. Pop," I said, bending down to kiss his cheek.

"Mornin', Mercy," he said.

I sat to his left—my usual spot. He patted his Bible and breathed deep.

Mother pushed through the swinging door with her hip.

"Goodness, Mercy! Sitting there like the queen of Sheba. Come give me a hand with the rest of the dishes. Bud and Ellery are joining us in here this morning."

"For breakfast? In here?"

I looked at Mr. Pop. He nodded and went back to his Bible.

I rose from the table and followed Mother back into the kitchen, hoping she'd go all the way back near the door so I could ask her. I hated surprises. She stopped short at the stove.

"What's going on?" I whispered.

"Not now," she said. "You'll hear soon enough."

Her hands shook a bit as she handed me the baking dish wrapped in our old red-checkered kitchen towels.

She followed me back into the dining room and set a second plate of biscuits next to my dish of eggs. Bud and Ellery hesitated at the dining room door before Mother waved them in.

"Come. Sit. Please." She smiled at them, pointing to their chairs. No one did hospitality like Mother. You'd never know from her behavior that farmhands—even trusted, beloved ones like Bud Drake and Ellery Burt—had never sat for family breakfast with us.

They all rose again as Mother and I sat, so that we took our seats together. I wasn't used to the noise—the dish clattering and chair scooting. It sharpened the silence that followed.

We all looked to Mr. Pop, who stared back at his Bible, took two deep breaths, and said, "Lord, have mercy on us. Amen."

His sudden prayer caught us all off guard. As did its brevity.

"Please," Mr. Pop said, waving his hand across the dishes in front of us. "Eat."

As we passed plates and buttered biscuits, we made small talk. Bud asked me, rather awkwardly, about Molly. In the last year Molly had grown into a shapely beauty like her sister. Where our friendship had once been easy conversation between adults and me, now men stammered over mention of her name.

I opened the conversation. "I bet Molly'll follow her sister's footsteps and enter the Potato Blossom Queen pageant this summer."

Mr. Pop cleared his throat. Mother smiled and offered more eggs.

"I think she'd do well," I went on. "She's prettier than anyone."

"Also, it'd be nice for her to get to go to that fancy hotel with that bathroom," Bud said.

The way Mr. Pop shifted in his chair, I thought he might respond. When he didn't, I simply said, "Indeed. That sounded like some place."

When Molly's sister, Marjorie, won last summer, Marjorie got to go to Bangor and stay overnight at the Bangor House Hotel. Ellery called it a "grand old palace of a place" and told me of the special guests like Teddy Roosevelt and Gene Autry who had stayed there through the years. According to Marjorie, the hotel had a bellman who carried your bags and a maid who did up your bed and brought fresh towels. But her favorite part—the part that amazed us all really—were the bathrooms. Each room in the hotel had its own toilet and tub and sink. Marjorie's bathroom had been painted blue like the Maine sky, trimmed in white tile squares. When she came back and sat on the front porch telling us about it, Bud's eyes were like saucers. For a man who had never traveled outside Watsonville, for this man who scrubbed himself clean with cold water in a galvanized metal tub set smack-dab in the middle of his one-room cabin, this luxury must have sounded like heaven. "You know that you're always welcome to use our tub, Bud," Mother said. "It'd be no trouble."

"Thanks for the offer. But I could never accept, Mrs. Millar. Just doesn't seem right. Besides, I hate to wait in lines."

We all laughed. Mr. Pop too—though he kept his eyes on his plate.

"You all do Henry Ford proud," Ellery said. "Assembly-line bathing every Saturday night."

We all laughed again except, this time, for my father. "When you've been given much," he said instead, "much is expected."

We had heard that passage recited by him about almost everything over the years. About our need to share our money, our food, our fields, and our indoor plumbing—something many people in Watsonville still went without. So if someone needed a warm bath, we could share that, as we often did.

"Much is expected," he repeated. Then cleared his throat and shifted again. "Which is why I've asked you to join us for breakfast before Mercy leaves to get the men."

"Paul," Mother whispered, "are you sure that's a good idea? Considering?" Mother rarely questioned her husband, certainly not on farm matters. But he nodded along with her question.

"I'm not sure if it's a good idea. But I'm sure it's the right thing."

Mother looked down. And no one met my gaze. We all just put down our forks and waited for Mr. Pop to continue.

"Frankie Carmichael stopped by last night. Perhaps you heard him." He finally looked at me now. I had heard Mr. Carmichael, but it didn't strike me as unusual. Folks came by our farm to visit any old time.

"The man was a mess," Mr. Pop said. "Broken apart. Seems his Marjorie has run off."

"Run off?" I asked. "I don't . . ."

"With Glenn Socoby."

I gasped and brought my hand to my throat. Now it was Mother's turn to look straight at me. My mind went back to Molly scurrying away from my truck, ignoring my calls, and to Mick, doing the same. They had known, of course. Why couldn't they have told me? Bud wiped his face with his napkin and shook his head. "Poor Frankie. Poor girl. Is she . . . um . . . ?" He wouldn't go on, not with Mother and me in the room. But I knew what remained unspoken. If she wasn't . . . um . . . why else would she go off with a Maliseet?

"Frankie doesn't know," Mr. Pop said. "But whether or not she's with child doesn't seem to matter as much as what people are saying."

"So what does this mean for us?" Bud asked. "For the workers?"

"This is what I wanted you to hear: It means very little. It means that Mercy is still going to leave after breakfast to pick up Ansley and Newell and Mick and whoever else wants to come and work. It just means people around here are not going to like this. Even more than usual. But I've been praying all night about this, and God doesn't seem to have changed His mind about how we're to treat our Maliseet neighbors."

That morning, I drove the potato truck down one of the back roads. In my years of picking up Maliseet in the early mornings, Mr. Pop had me keep to the main road, Main Street, actually, and head straight through town. For one, he'd say, traveling back roads looks like you've got something to hide. No shame in giving people work, according to him. And for another, the back road, the border road, with its tight turns that wound and wove up and around the farthest outskirts of town, past the Meduxnekeag River, past the woods where the hobos camped out, was as treacherous as it was alluring. Bud once told me that the back road wasn't the sort of place a young lady wanted to get stranded, if the truck were to break down.

"I'm not afraid of the bears *or* the moose," I had joked back.

But Bud hadn't been joking. "It's not the animals you need to worry about there, Miss Mercy. It's the hobos jumpin' trains. Not all of them are out for adventure. Some are out runnin' from the law."

Indeed, this was the road lying just a quarter mile from the Canadian border, that the sort who wanted to roam from country to country, province-to-state, town-to-town without being seen or heard or would travel down in search of quick food or drink or another night out of jail. The one murder the town of Watsonville had ever counted happened on that road, right there, where Mt. Katahdin first comes into view, rising up from the trees, stretching into the clouds.

But still, today, Mr. Pop decided this road was safer than the border. Main Street. Molly and the Carmichaels had no choice but to take Main Street everywhere. Their house, a beautiful, white clapboard Victorian with a big wraparound porch, sat just off it. The Carmichaels took Main Street to school, to church, to the shops, to visit friends. Marjorie had probably gone down Main when she ran off with Glenn, probably ran right past Fulton's, her father's hardware store, spreading her shame.

Mr. Pop hadn't said much about Marjorie and Glenn. But he didn't need to. I could figure in the rest. I'd seen this sort of thing before. Once news spread—and the gossip had surely trailed behind Mr. Carmichael even as he drove out to our farm last night—I knew what this meant for our community; I knew what it meant for the Carmichaels and for Molly and the Maliseet, and for Mr. Pop.

And I knew what it meant for Mick and me.

* * *

Mick was waiting for me, not at our spot but at the base of the dump. When he saw the direction my truck came from, his jaw tightened. He turned his head back up to the Flats and then ran over toward my truck as I slowed and pulled over.

"You took the border road?" Mick asked. It always surprised me to hear him call it this as the Maliseet hated that we called this a border road, as the Maliseet border was nowhere near here. The Maliseet spread into Canada without any acknowledgment of crossing a border.

"Yes."

"So you know?"

"I do."

"Your pop told you?"

"Yes," I said. "This morning. He told me. But *you* should've. When did you find out?" I hadn't come to accuse. I hadn't even known I was angry at Mick. But I was. Together we kept our own secret, but it didn't seem right we should be keeping other people's from each other.

"I wanted to, but when could I have?" Mick asked sharply. "I only found out yesterday in the truck on the way to the farm. And I didn't know much. Just that Old Man Stringer saw Glenn's car the night before. He saw Newell Socoby at the tavern and asked about him, thinking he was here. Next morning, Mr. Socoby heard Marjorie was gone. She left a note, I guess. Old Man Stringer told us that too. Came back here to warn Mr. Socoby."

"A note?" Of course, there'd have been a note. But I was stunned. I hadn't figured that. I realized then how few questions I'd asked Mr. Pop. How little I knew, and how much I wanted to know. I wondered who found it. Molly? Marjorie would've left it on their bureau. Molly would've had to deliver that news. A wave of nausea rushed through me. Poor Molly. I wanted to sit—or throw up. But instead I just stood there, staring at Mick.

Mick held his head straight, high. His thick black hair dipped behind his shoulders. His arms hung stiff at this sides, hands clenched into fists. I realized how much I wanted to reach for him, to run my hand along the plaid of his shirt, to feel the strength of his arms before weaving my fingers through his. But I couldn't. The tears started when I realized I may never be able to again.

"I'm sorry," I said, shaking my head. "I'm being stupid."

Mick's body softened. His hands unclenched, and he took a step toward me before stopping.

Though his cursing was mumbled, I still heard.

"Mick!"

"No, forget it." Mick breathed in. "Meet me." Then he took off running, side-stepping tin cans and hurdling logs as he disappeared into the forest.

I waited a bit, then ducked under branches to reach our spot, and snuggled in beside Mick on the ground he had cleared free of brambles and loose dirt and pinecones. For me. Mick's arm felt heavier than I remembered; his hand pressed tighter into my arm.

"Why'd you take the border road?" he asked after several minutes of our sniffly silence.

"Mr. Pop said I could. I always jump at the chance."

"Your pop said you could or should?"

"Should, I guess."

"'Cause everybody knows now?"

"I suppose."

"Right. So your pop thought it'd be better for you to be killed by a moose or a tramp than to be seen coming to get us."

I pulled back and looked straight at him. I had been prepared to set him straight, but the glistening in his brown eyes and the terrified boy shining through the man he was trying to be dissipated any anger.

"I just wish you'd have told me *something* yesterday," I told him.

"I told you: no time. I couldn't. When'd you find out?"

"Mr. Pop told us over breakfast. I knew something was up, seeing Bud and Ellery at the table."

"At the table!" Mick laughed. "Must've been some sight. Those hillbillies eating off your grandmother's breakfast china."

I smiled. It had been a sight. Though it hadn't occured to me until now.

"You know, even Bud and Ellery told Mr. Pop I shouldn't come today. But Mr. Pop thought different. This hasn't changed *his* feelings about Maliseet."

Mick shook his head.

"It might not change his feelings about having us work still, Mercy. But it sure as—it sure changes his feelings about his daughter marrying one."

I smiled at his determination to keep his language clean as I ran a finger through the dirt.

"Marrying one?"

Mick laughed. "Mercy, what'd you think all our 'someday' talk meant? I had it all planned out."

I raised my eyebrows.

"Stay secret through harvest. But your pop would be so impressed with my work and the seventy-five barrels a day picked this fall, he was going to write me into the will. *I* would be the true son he'd never had."

I laughed.

"But then he'd feel bad that he cut you out, so he'd suggest you and I start—you know—seeing a bit more of each other. Then we'd officially and publicly fall in love. And folks would ooh and aah and we'd get married once you turned sixteen. Your pop would walk you right down the aisle at First Baptist. I'd kiss the bride right in front of the altar and the whole town would give us their blessing."

I laughed again and leaned in to kiss him right there.

"*This* is how you imagined it?" I asked. "You think I want to get married at sixteen—like Mother?"

"My ma was married at fifteen."

I made a face at Mick. He leaned in for a kiss.

"This is 1954, Mick, not 1934. I'm not getting married at sixteen. Besides, one of the benefits of being the son he never had is that Mr. Pop has promised he'll send me to college. What about college? What about *you* going to college?"

"I'd've waited. Or gone when you went. We'd go together. Or you'd've gone and I'd've worked. But we can do it all together. Or we could've. Maybe."

"And you really think people would've ever blessed the marriage of Mr. Paul Millar's only daughter to a Maliseet?"

"Well," he said. "I was hoping. But now, no more. Because of Glenn. I could kill him."

"Don't say that. He's your friend."

"He's ruined our lives. That's what he's done. He's made it so we can't be together, even like this."

"Please," I said. "Stop. Things are *changing*. Mr. Pop says black and white kids will *have* to go to school together because of the Supreme Court. My cousins live in Alabama. My aunt's not happy about the integration. She says there'll be trouble for all the kids. But Mr. Pop says that this is *God*'s way and that we can't act out of fear of 'trouble.' Maybe it's like that for us too. Maybe there *is* some trouble for Glenn and Marjorie. But maybe they'll make it easier for us to be together. Maybe Mr. Pop will see this as God's way too."

Mick shook his head.

"For a smart girl, you don't understand much about the world, do you?" Mick asked. "There's a world of difference between thinking it's okay for Blacks and Whites to share a classroom and thinking Maliseet and girls like you should be holding hands on Main Street. Centuries' worth of fear over 'the Indians coming for our women!' will boil up faster than your mother's teakettle. That's what Glenn and Marjorie have roiled up. That's what we're up against."

I stared at Mick, fearing the words that might come next. Mick grabbed a stick and drew lines in the dirt and bramble.

"Here's you." He pointed to one line. "Here's me." He pointed to another. "And this is the gulf that's come between us." His stick drew the lines bigger and bigger.

I swallowed.

"We can't just *stop* this. Not how we feel. At least, I can't. I can't just write you off. We have too much." I waved my arm toward our lean-to doors. "We've built too many forts together."

Mick laughed. Though this fort we sat in was our first romantic hideaway, it was far from our first fort. In our early rock-picking years, Mick and I became master crafters of stone forts. Not for us. But tiny ones for the the field mice and chipmunks and woodchucks. Back then, when we were grade-schoolers constructing rock homes for various Northwoods rodents, people found our friendship adorable. Pastor Murphy even once used us in a sermon about building your house on the rock. "Not the rock like the ones Mercy and her little Maliseet friend make," he said to much laughter.

"People got used to us back then," I said. "People were okay with it. We can just keep meeting like *this*. Stay secret for longer. It's bound to cool down."

Mick sighed.

"It's not going to, Mercy. It's not. My dad and the tribal leaders have been talking. They're ready to petition the government for land of our own. They're tired of how we've been treated. It's time for things to change. For us to have land of our own and get off this dump."

"Well, of course. You know Mr. Pop supports that for you."

"In theory, yes. But when it comes down to him giving up his land? To his friends giving up theirs? I think Old Mr. Pop may change his tune. Especially if he finds out about us."

"No. You're wrong, Mick. That'll make him understand more."

"It won't, Mercy. It won't."

"So what are you saying? This is all over?"

Mick breathed deep and stared ahead into the dark forest. Then he turned back and held his hand to my face. I thought Mick would kiss me, hold me, but instead he stood—crouched, really—back bent under the limbs, hands perched on his knees, ready to go.

"No, no. Not saying that. Just . . . I dunno."

I reached toward him, offered my hand.

"We could lie low, just take what we've got a bit more underground or something. Like field mice or woodchucks."

"Woodchucks?" Mick asked. "Tunneling?"

"Yes."

Mick smiled. "Yeah. Maybe," he said. "C'mon. We have men to wake up. Work to do." And he took off running, forgetting to kiss me.

Chapter Four

Unlike most nights when the dark of night and the light of day bow to one another and agree to a friendly swap, tonight the dark forced its way across the sky as the band of gray clouds crowded out a glistening summer evening.

"My ma used to tell me . . ."

I jumped.

"Sorry, Miss Mercy," Ellery said. "Didn't mean to startle you."

"It's all right, Ellery. Was lost in my thoughts."

"Bet you were. Was just sayin', my ma used to tell me when I was little, on her knee and whatnot, that clouds could tell us something about God's moods. Not sure if she was right or not."

I smiled. "Sounds like something Ansley'd say."

"My ma always liked the Maliseet. Maybe that's where she got it. Still. I wonder if she was right. What'd'ya you think?"

"I'm not sure. But I know that my mother says you move like a cat," I said. "And she's right. You're quiet."

"I am. But *you* usually notice me. Like you do everything. You're like me. Mind if I sit and wait with you?"

I patted the step next to me.

"I taught you how to tie a fishing line right here. Right on these porch steps. Crazy place to teach a girl to fish."

"That was just after Tommy Birger almost drowned in the Meduxnekeag and Mother was too scared to let me go down there. Even with you."

"That Tommy. What hasn't he almost died doin'? That's what I want to know."

I laughed. Inside, some light pushed back against my own darkness.

"Molly told me his horse threw him just last week."

Ellery's laugh rang out to compete with the thunder.

"Musta been pushing that horse something hard. Trying to outrun all Molly's chasing."

"For the life of me, I don't know why he runs from her at all. I mean, it's *Molly*. What boy wouldn't be thrilled by her attention?"

"Miss Mercy, I'd guess the kind of boy who wished he had *your* attention."

I rolled my eyes.

"Tommy Birger does not want *my* attention."

"If you say so."

"I say so."

I turned to Ellery with my "doubtin' look," which Ellery said I'd been giving him since before I could talk. "You've never believed me, but you've always adored me," Ellery liked to tease. And he was right. Though I believed him more than I ever gave him credit for.

Our weary laughter faded as our stares fixed on the road that stretched across the front of the farm. Before I was old enough to work the farm with Mr. Pop, I'd sit for hours on the front lawn overlooking the main road. I loved that the big road, the main way into town, was practically outside our front door. I used to count the cars. I tried to make the logging trucks honk their horns as they drove past. Because our farm was at the crest of the hill, I could see for miles. Out beyond the old outhouse, I could see Mother's garden. Mr. Pop might be the resident farmer, but Mother had a green thumb to rival any farmer in Watsonville. Her rhubarb patch, just to the north of the flower garden, yielded some of the sweetest in the county. The fact that it was on the north side of the old outhouse might have had something to do with it. Then to the south of the flower garden, which was filled with beautiful gladiolas of all colors along with a small patch of pansies, marigolds, and snapdragons, was the truck garden. This garden filled our table and enabled generosity toward others, as the Spirit led, all summer and on into fall. Besides her famous broccoli, she grew cauliflower, peas, lettuce, kale, corn, scallions, and my favorite, beet greens. Only thing better than beet greens were fiddleheads in the spring.

On the crest of the hill, I could see almost to the Canadian border to the north. To the east I could even see the top of the old Carmichael farm, where Mr. Carmichael grew up. He decided a long time ago that town life was more appealing than farm life. The only farming his girls ever knew was when they were visiting me. They thought picking raspberries or cutting cucumbers from the vine was fun work. But they knew nothing of doing that kind of back-bending work for ten hours straight. No, Marjorie and Molly had grown up townies.

Truth was, I envied them. I didn't want to be the girl that was "better than any son." All I could think of when I heard Mr. Pop say that was the story of Hannah in the Bible when her husband Elkanah said, "Aren't I worth more than ten sons?" I didn't want to be as good as ten sons or one son. I wanted to be a girl, a woman. I wanted to be somebody's girl. And I was. I was Mick's girl, or I would be if I could hold on for "someday."

"You think they're really going to come?" I asked, breaking into our thoughts.

"If Mr. Carmichael tells your father he'll be here, then he'll be here. No doubtin' looks for that, Miss Mercy."

I smiled and we both breathed deep when we saw the red of the Carmichaels' sleek Buick Riviera cut across the gray, rumbly twilight. I loved that car. No new cars on the farm for the last eight years or so. Owning a store in town certainly had its perks. A new car every couple of years was one of them. That Buick was a real beauty.

What I wouldn't give to get behind that wheel. As we stood up to greet them as the car turned into the drive, the heavens opened and the rain began.

* * *

"Mercy, you and Molly take your cobbler and milk upstairs," Mother said, pushing me out of the kitchen and into the hall.

"Upstairs?" I asked. Even when I was at my sickest, Mother resisted allowing food in my bedroom. Lickers had offered us enough gifts through the years to prove that Mother was right to worry that even bread and soup for a sick soul was only giving mice a chance to find snatches of crumbs and bring more disease and pestilence in where we slept. So Mother allowed food to be eaten in only two places: at the corner kitchen table, tucked into the bay window Mr. Pop had added as a wedding gift, or at the dining room table that had held the "fine food and fancies of generations of Millars," as Ellery said.

"That's right. You girls go enjoy your dessert. Maybe you can show Molly your new book. Now scoot."

Mother swept her fingers at Molly and me and jerked her head toward the stairs. When Mother pushed the oak-paneled door back into the kitchen, I shrugged at Molly.

"Guess we aren't invited to the discussion."

"It's okay," said Molly. "I've had enough discussion for a lifetime."

As we started up the stairs, I craned to see the living room. Mrs. Carmichael still sat in there on the sofa, staring at her shoes while she fiddled with the clasp on her handbag. I'd never known her not to help Mother in the kitchen. I wondered if Mother had refused her help or if Mrs. Carmichael hadn't offered. Neither way made any sense.

But Muriel Carmichael wasn't the one I really wondered about. It was her husband. We all knew Muriel would fret and fidget over her lost daughter. But Mr. Carmichael? None of us knew. This was what Ellery and I had sat on the porch wondering. Why we stayed in the rain as they stepped out onto the gravel. Would he collapse into despair? Lash out in fury? Both were equally likely from this man Mr. Pop considered as close as his own brother, from this man I should have loved like an uncle but who remained distant and remote.

"Girls, I said scoot!" Mother sat another full pan of cobbler on the table and turned toward the stairs. "If I don't hear the click of your door on the count of seven, Miss Lickers will be getting that cobbler and milk you're holding." I took one more look at the living room and then we double-timed it up the stairs.

The door clicked closed at the count of six.

We set our desserts and milk on the desk and smiled briefly at each other. It was good to see Molly's face lighten, even if for a moment. We hadn't gotten time to talk, and I didn't know when we would. Because now we would discuss neither the secret life of Holden Caufield nor the secret life of Marjorie Carmichael, who maybe now was Mrs. Glenn Socoby. We were here to do one thing—what we'd do ever since we were old enough to get shooed upstairs. With the synchronization that only a lifetime of friend-ship and practice can bring about, Molly and I knelt on the floor, rolled back the rug to reveal the register. Whether it was the stress, desperate for release, or our conspiracy, our teamwork, or just doing the thing we'd always done, our stone-cold serious eyes met and brought laughs from somewhere deep in each of us.

"Ssssh," I warned, but my shushing only made us giggle more. It felt too good. But I managed to add: "If we can hear them, then they can hear us." This shut us both up as we lowered our ears to the heating grate on the floor. This was better than any gossip sec-tion of the *Watsonville Chronicle*. This grate was how Molly and I learned of the big news, the difficult marriages, the troubled chil-dren, the struggling farms, the heretical deacons, and now . . . the truth about runaway sisters and distraught parents.

But it stayed quiet in the living room below us. We heard only mumbles and murmurs and clanking of forks and clinking of coffee cups from the more distant dining room. "Maybe we should head to the bathroom?" Molly suggested. That register, as we both knew, fed into the dining room.

"Too risky. Mother is on to us, you know. She's got one ear in the dining room and another to the stairs, just waiting for the door to creak and Lickers to escape."

We both looked back at the cat who sat hunched at the door, alternately mewing to be released from this room and tending to something on her paw. If we opened that door even a crack, Lickers would make a run for it. She'd head downstairs and be the tattletale we didn't need.

"Maybe she'd stay for some cobbler and milk," was Molly's idea.

I smiled. "Maybe she would." But as I contemplated setting our dishes down for the cat, a chair scraped across the floor below. Our ears moved back to the grate as though pulled.

"I'm sorry, Geneva. I just can't eat."

It was Mr. Carmichael. And it was his feet that stomped back into the living room, followed by a plea from Molly's mother.

"Frankie, please."

Then Mr. Pop said something, presumably to Mother and Mrs. Carmichael. I imagined words of comfort, of assuring Mrs. Carmichael that he would take care of it, that everything would be fine. Those were the words Mr. Pop always gave, and he was always right. He always took care of everything and everything was always fine. Then his chair eased back, gently, not wanting to scrape the wood floors he'd so carefully sanded and stained not two winters ago and took his usual steady and sturdy steps toward his friend.

Molly and I looked at each other. Lickers wouldn't get her cobbler-bribe after all. We both gulped. I brought a finger to my lips. Things were about to get interesting right below us.

* * *

"Frankie," Mr. Pop said.

"What'd that general used to say? 'Only good Indian is a dead

Indian'? That man knew what he was talking about."

"Frankie," Mr. Pop said again. Slower and softer this time. The sofa squeaked. Mr. Pop must've moved to sit beside his friend. I never knew Mr. Pop to sit anywhere but in his chair, but I also never knew Mr. Pop to move away from a person in need.

"If Glenn Socoby comes back to Watsonville, he'll be good *and* dead."

"Even if Marjorie is carrying his child?"

"If Marjorie is carrying his child, I'll kill him. And that goes for his—" Mr. Carmichael snorted—"offspring as well."

Molly's head shot up from the grate, her hand covered her mouth. I thought maybe she'd need to run to the bathroom after all. But she eased her head down at the sound of her mother's voice.

"Franklin Carmichael!" Mrs. Carmichael yelled. Two chairs scraped and scooted across the floor, followed by two sets of heels running into the kitchen.

Molly's eyes glazed over and sniffles began. I reached my hand toward her and set my hand on her back.

"I don't mean that," Mr. Carmichael said. Mr. Pop stayed silent. "Not about killing the baby. Though I've thought about, about sending her to one of those doctors in Nova Scotia. Montreal, maybe? Children are a gift from God, but not Indian children. They're straight from the devil."

Still Mr. Pop said nothing.

"But even still. There's probably some ignorant couple out there—a Negro couple maybe—longing for a child, so desperate that they won't care what sort of mother and heathen father that baby has. Someone out there won't care about the alcohol running through its veins. The Catholics have places to send those kind of mothers. I'm going to find out about it."

I waited for Mr. Pop to say something, to defend Glenn or the baby or Marjorie, to tell Mr. Carmichael that everything would be fine. But he said none of that.

Instead, we heard Mr. Pop say: "God in heaven already knows the right couple for that baby . . . if there is one. We don't rightly know yet."

✳ ✳ ✳

I turned to Molly. I opened my mouth to speak but nothing came out. I tried again, still nothing. I couldn't imagine Mr. Pop giving in like that, especially if there was a child concerned. Two children: Marjorie and her baby. But they didn't even know for sure if there was a baby. I knew my creased eyebrows and shifting eyes betrayed the number of questions that filled me. But I hoped my sigh and smile and my outreached hand would conceal what I worried about for what felt like the first time in my young life. I hoped that Molly couldn't see that for the first time I didn't know if everything would really be all right.

Once we were sure the talking below had stopped, or at least moved out of range of our ears, Molly and I lifted ourselves up from the floor. Molly was the first to speak, not in the careful whisper I imagined would come out but in full voice.

"Dad's been like that since yesterday. He hasn't calmed down at all. Mom's tried to get him to ease up. But he won't."

"So there was a note? From Marjorie, I mean."

Molly nodded. "But it just said she was leaving and that she'd write later and explain. She said she loved me and to tell Mom and Dad she loved them."

"She left the note for you?"

"On our dresser. I found it when I woke up yesterday morning. I can't believe it's only been since yesterday."

Molly walked toward the window and pulled back the poof of curtain to look out. "Marjorie could be anywhere, with anyone," she said.

"But if with *anyone*, what's all this talk about being with Glenn and about babies?" I asked.

"Because Old Man Stringer saw Glenn Socoby in town two nights ago. At the Old Pine Inn," Molly said. "And because—" her sobs choked off her words.

I walked up behind her and put my hand on her back, rested my chin on her shoulder. Two heads looking out my perfectly paned window to the world.

"And because I told Mom about her and Glenn. About how they were in love. And about how Marjorie was worried about what Dad might do to him if he knew. But they don't believe me that Marjorie loved him. They don't believe me that she was desperate to marry him and start a new life as his wife. Dad says she'd only run off if she was scared about a baby. I've told them they're wrong, but I've made a mess of everything."

Molly turned to me and grabbed my hands. "What if I'm wrong?" she asked, her eyes now more crazed than crying. "I mean, Marjorie didn't tell me for sure that they were going to run off. And she made me swear not to tell. I was just so scared. I thought it'd help them find her if they knew. But now Dad's—"

Molly's panic settled back into sobs. I let her cry it out until she calmed down. I was hugging her so close neither of us heard the knock at the door.

"Girls," Mother was saying. "The Carmichaels are leaving now. Molly, dear. It's time to go."

Molly nodded into my shoulder, and Mother asked if she might wrap her cobbler up for her to take home. Somehow, Molly and I both laughed. We both knew the only thing my mother approved of less than eating in my room was taking food into the car.

"No, ma'am. Thank you, though." Molly pulled away to wipe her eyes and share a smile. "I'm sorry we didn't eat it."

"No one did," Mother said. "Come on down now. Mercy, you too."

Mother turned, her skirt swishing with a grace that betrayed her farm-wife status, that gave vision to the society girl she could've been. Lickers followed her out.

Molly stepped forward, but then stopped short. "I don't know when we're going to see each other next. So I need to tell you this now."

Molly's face alarmed me. But I forced a smile, hoping to capture some of our past, brief moments of laughter, hoping I could lighten her mood. I didn't.

"Glenn isn't the only one Dad's been talking about killing. He says that if the rumors are true, if he sees Mick so much as look at you funny, he's going to kill him too."

I couldn't breathe. I felt dizzy. I leaned against my desk to steady myself. Had Molly betrayed me?

"Molly, what did you tell them?" I whispered this, but the softness of my words only punctuated my rage.

"Nothing!" Molly said, stepping toward me. I shrugged away from her outreached arm. "I didn't tell. But someone must've told."

Molly walked out as Mother called us down again. I stood to follow her, taking steps as though in a trance. The Carmichaels waited for us at the bottom of the stairs, where Mr. Carmichael's eyes stayed trained on mine. Behind his eyes were hate and vengeance like I'd never seen, but as soon as I met his glance, Mr. Carmichael turned to Mr. Pop.

"You be careful with that girl of yours, Paul," he said. And the Carmichaels walked out.

Chapter Five

Time ticked by. Two weeks later Mr. Pop was still sending for the Maliseet to come work the fields—rock picking had wrapped up, and now in mid-June, planting was in full swing—but I was no longer the one who went to get them. Ellery would take the truck, sometimes traveling down the main road, sometimes the border road, depending on what sort of talk was coming from town, or specifically, what Frankie Carmichael had been stirring up at the potlucks after church or telling hardware store customers. Those who came into Fulton's thought they would simply get the new hammer or skillet or bit of sandpaper they needed, maybe a grub hoe, new spade, or a mattock, but instead they'd hear the story of how his oldest daughter, last year's Potato Blossom Queen, Miss Marjorie Carmichael, had been stolen by Glenn Socoby, the Maliseet, and how this was typical for that dirty and disgusting tribe.

When folks asked if the authorities had been notified, Mr. Carmichael would tell them the truth: they had. But the authorities contended that Marjorie was eighteen, so legal, and that the postcards she had sent home from New York were proof enough that she ran away of her own free will. Add to that the flood of Micmac crossing the border for planting during a time when newspapers were all too keen to let *Brown vs. Board of Education* highlight race issues even in the deep north of Maine, the last thing the Maine State Police needed was to deal with a pesky family dispute and rile up the Indians over on Hungry Hill.

So they did nothing. Mr. Carmichael might tell them that he had driven around the state—heading down to Millinocket, where the paper mill was and where Glenn had most recently worked, on down to Skowhegan and over to Fredericton, New Brunswick, but didn't make much headway. So he had come back home to pray. Specifically, to pray that God would take a mighty vengeance on the Maliseet for raising such evil beings.

I spent these weeks out planting just as I always had, although now I took my dinner inside at the table with Mr. Pop and Mother, with Bud and Ellery. Only. No longer did I linger over lunch on the porch with the Maliseet workers, as we often did during the heat of planting season. Instead, after dropping their lunch in baskets on long tables under the shade of our maples, Mother called me in.

Mr. Pop had me riding the back of the tractor while he or Bud drove it. I watched the potato planter making sure it ran smoothly and didn't malfunction. The seed potatoes dropped like clockwork into the soil, then got covered over and hilled up. Watching, focusing on the planter was tedious but necessary work. My body jarred to the bone as we rode over acre upon acre across bumpy farm terrain. Mother's garden tending was a welcome relief to riding that bucking bronco Ford tractor. I was all for walking the rows instead of riding them. The joy of drawing sketches of the garden, sitting side by side with Mother, was always a favorite time for me, dreaming of the kinds of vegetables we'd be enjoying on our table. Looking at the newest varieties Burpee had to offer in their annual seed catalogue was a highlight of the process. Planning Mother's garden caused my imagination to go straight beyond harvesttime to sitting down to a cornucopia of flavors. I was already living in September. Fact is, I wished it were harvesttime already, so maybe all of this mess would be smoothed out by then.

I tried to catch Mick's eye as he worked down the row from me in the fields, but I'd become a ghost to him. Some days I wandered through my life, through the fields, through my house, through church, and sometimes town, like Holden Caulfield had wandered Manhattan, wondering who were the phonies and who was real.

✳   ✳   ✳

Mother stopped me in the kitchen.

"Mercy, before you head back out, could you help me with something?"

I nodded and followed her into the pantry. The pantry was large, even for farmhouse standards, but even then I understood what a master organizer my mother was. No one's shelves could touch hers. The top two shelves housed rows of red raspberry and black raspberry jams. Then came the jellies: apple, boysenberry, chokecherry, and cranberry. The canned vegetables came next. Beets, corn, green and yellow string beans, as well as boxes of Cream of Wheat, oatmeal, cornstarch, baking soda, baking powder, along with salt and sugar in big tins to keep the moisture out.

It took two shelves to hold all the spices needed for everything from baking various flavored pies, cookies, cakes, and dough-nuts, to the ones used for pickling. I could always count on find-ing pickles in the pantry. Some weeks it was dill, other times it was sweet, or bread and butter pickles. On the bottom shelf was the large crock where Mother kept the cream. She let it stay there until it soured, and once a week she'd churn it into butter. Oh, how Mr. Pop loved this weekly ritual. He had a sixth sense about when Mother was churning butter. About halfway through the process, Mr. Pop would show up. He could have been clear down on the back acreage, but he knew butter was in the making. This meant buttermilk. Mr. Pop would come into the kitchen and make a bee-line for Mother. He'd uncork the churn and have a glass ready. He'd drink it down, let out a sigh, and exclaim, "That was wicked good!" and head right back to the field.

Any good pantry had noodles. Mother shelved box after box of macaroni, mostly for casseroles and macaroni 'n cheese and chili mac. Jars of honey, thanks to Mr. Pop's bees; molasses; and Karo, were situated and mentally catalogued according to purpose and frequency of use. Her pans and plates, measuring cups and mixing bowls, the same.

But she walked me past all this toward the one snag in her system, the one fault in her genius: the corner, The place just beyond the big flour barrel filled with twenty-five pounds of Robin Hood flour, and just behind the heating vent where Mother stored her baskets. Baskets that were seldom used, but often purchased. The ash baskets she'd traded Maliseet women for more times than she could count, simply so that they could have vegetables from her garden. Mother would have gladly given them away, but the women did not want charity. So Mother gladly accepted the baskets. She had a collection of baskets, the kind used to gather potatoes in the field during fall harvest. There were small jewelry boxes woven from brown ash and dyed with indigo, a basket woven over the top of a B & M Baked Bean jar, all kinds of sewing baskets, and woven pin cushions. All of the baskets, including her favorites, sat tilted and pressed together inside a medium-sized skillfully woven but plain looking laundry basket, filling the corner in a haphazard array of color.

Her least favorites held turnips, butternut squash, parsnips, spaghetti squash, and all kinds of other root vegetables in the cellar.

Mother led me to the baskets and pointed to a new stack I hadn't seen. "Ellery brought these back this morning. Mrs. Polchies wanted beets and onions and, of course, wouldn't simply *take* them, so she had Mick get these out to give to me."

My heart nearly stopped.

"They're lovely, of course, but they're going to take over the house. Can you sort through these? Figure out where to put them?" Mother lifted up the top basket and raised an eyebrow. I looked into the basket and gasped. Mother simply put the basket down and turned. As she walked out, she said, "You can see that you need to be very careful with these, my dear."

When the door clicked closed, I knelt beside the stack of baskets, running my hand along the edges before reaching in to pull out the piece of paper. On it, an image I'd know anywhere: a stone fort with a field mouse tucked inside and a woodchuck tunneling toward it.

I smiled for a moment before dissolving into tears.

✳ ✳ ✳

Mother was sitting at the kitchen table as I walked out of the pantry, a stack of baskets in my left arm, the note from Mick folded and tucked in my pocket. I stopped as soon as I saw her. Mother never just sat. But there she was, with a cup of tea in front of her but nothing else. No needlework, no paperwork, no labels.

Mother took a sip of her tea and said, "Could you join me a minute?"

Just moments before, as I had sat on the floor, weeping with Mick's note pressed to my face, hoping to catch his scent or a sense of his presence, I thought I'd found an ally in Mother. She would be someone who would keep my secret, not just about books I read but about loves I held secret. I thought she'd be the one to stand up for me and for Mick in a way I now doubted Mr. Pop would, at least since that night with the Carmichaels. I had swelled with love for Mother just moments ago. Now worry swelled instead, sinking my stomach as I stepped toward the table.

"You can set the baskets on the floor," Mother said. So I did before sliding up next to her on the bench she had patted for me.

I wanted to thank her for letting me see the note, but instead I just swallowed hard.

"I want you to know that you never need to run away from us," she said.

"Run away?"

"You know that your father and I have money aside for you to go to college. And that's only a few years away. You can stay here, do your work, and then fly off."

"Fly off?"

"To go see the world, meet new people, study grand ideas, become the woman you're meant to be."

At this, tears filled her eyes. I wrapped an arm around her and rested my head on her shoulder.

"Mother, I'm not going to run off."

Mother dabbed her handkerchief to her eyes, sniffed, and straightened her back. She smoothed her skirt before wriggling beneath my arm and turning to me.

"I can see the way you look at each other. I've seen it for months. The change, I mean. I'm not blind. And I wasn't born yesterday. I've known this would happen, for years. You and Mick have always been two peas. But . . ."

The screen squealed open, and Mother and I looked up to see Mr. Pop in the kitchen.

"Well, this is a sight for weary eyes," Mr. Pop said. "Don't usually catch you two just chatting."

"No, I suppose you don't," Mother said. "But sometimes ladies just need a minute to catch up. To talk about women things."

At this, Mr. Pop blushed. "In that case, I'll fill my water from the faucet out back."

Mother winked at me as he walked right back out the door.

"Does Mr. Pop know?"

"Heavens, no! You think he'd be this calm if he did? He thinks I'm giving you the 'talk.' I've never had the heart to tell him you and I had *that* conversation years ago."

We both laughed. Years ago, when I was maybe eight, I had caught Lickers in a "romantic mood" with Saucy, one of Ellery's barn cats. I was in the potato house breathing in the scent of the dirt mixed with the seed potatoes, a smell that always made me smile and think of planting again. But then I saw Lickers and Saucy. I had run in terror to Mother and Ellery. Ellery, fixing a loose floorboard on the porch, immediately said, "Well butter my

bottom and call me a biscuit! Mercy, what are you goin' on about?"
I was screaming that Saucy was trying to kill Lickers, that he had
grabbed her from behind and was shaking the life right out of
her. Mother, in the middle of doing the wash on the front porch,
stopped everything to listen to me. She never believed in obscur-
ing the truth, so she had told it straight to a slack-jawed me that
day. Of course, when I was eight she only told it true about *farm*
animals. It took till I was eleven and learning a little more about
life from Marjorie and Molly that I gathered up the nerve to ask
Mother if farm animals and farm *people* were made the same way.
Once again, Mother didn't hide the truth. Well, maybe she hid a
bit of the truth. At least, that's what I was figuring out from those
stolen kisses with Mick.

"Although," Mother continued, "with all that's gone on, I think
Mr. Pop would be relieved knowing that you're not naive about
these matters. And that you've always known you could come to
me with anything. That you don't need to hide things."

I took a deep breath, knowing there was no use in hiding any
of this from her any longer.

"Well, you know then," I started. "You *have* known that Mick
and I are really, um, *fond* of each other."

"Fond? Is that what you call it these days?"

I smiled. "No, ma'am. I guess I'd call it in love. Or *would* have
called it. But now . . ."

"Now is no different than before, Mercy."

I scooted back on the bench, not able to hide my surprise.
"How can you say that?"

"It's as unacceptable and as dangerous for you and Mick to be
in love today as it was three weeks ago. Nothing has changed."

"Of course, it's changed!" I said. "Everything has changed.
Before I had—I had—"

"Had what?"

"Hope! Before I had hope."

"Hope?"

"Hope! That Mr. Pop would accept us. That you would be fine with it. That this stupid town was maybe changing. I've never even once thought about running off. You didn't have to remind me of that. I've always known where I was going and what I wanted to do. I had just hoped I'd be able to decide who I wanted to go with me."

Mother took another sip of her tea and stared out the window above the sink. Normally, seeing the plain white plates with a couple of bright Fiestaware serving bowls stacked in the deep, double-wide porcelain sink would be enough to compel her to stop chatting and get to her chores. But she stayed seated.

"I met your father when I was about your age, you know."

"And you married him at sixteen. Grandpa hated him."

"*Hated* is a bit strong, I think."

"But Grandpa didn't like Mr. Pop. Said he was beneath you and that you were ruining your life for marrying him."

"He did."

"And Grandpa changed. Just before he died, he wrote that letter to Mr. Pop, saying what a strong man of God he was, how proud he was to have him as a son-in-law, how glad he was that you married him. All of that."

"He did. My dad grew to love Paul. But—"

"But what?"

"But your father wasn't Maliseet. Your grandpa was simply worried that I wouldn't be *amply* provided for, that I wouldn't be happy without new dresses from New York and without summers on the coast or without a woman to help clean. He wasn't worried that I'd be shunned from society or that my life or my husband's or my children's lives would be in danger."

"And is that still what's going on? Does Mr. Carmichael still want to kill Glenn?"

"Mercy! What a thing to say!" Mother wiped a drop of the tea that had seeped out of her mouth when she tried to sneak in a sip. "Mr. Carmichael is a God-fearing man! He's a distressed man, rightfully so, I might add, but a Christian man. Where did you get an idea like that?"

"Because I heard him say it."

Now Mother scooted back a bit. Somehow we'd found a way to face each other on the hard, dark kitchen bench Ellery had built to sit under this window.

"You heard him? Where?"

"That night," I confessed. "When the Carmichaels came over. When you sent me and Molly to my room. We heard."

"But how?"

"The registers. You know. The same registers that allow you to hear my music *too loud* let me hear living room conversations."

"Of course," she said. "I just had no idea he said that."

Mother's eyes drifted back out the window as she held the small, gold cross that she wore round her neck, the one her father had given her when she'd been baptized in the Meduxnekeag River back when she was fourteen. The party her parents had thrown her was the stuff legends were made of. Folks still talked about Mother's party.

"If Northwoods Baptists had debutante balls," Ellery had once said, "Geneva Weaver would've been Deb a' the Year." Of course, he wasn't there. But Ellery'd heard enough news about Presque Isle from the local paper. "Everything I need to know about life and this world I can read about in that Bellyache," Ellery'd say. And mean it.

After all, the Bellyache, the *Watsonville Chronicle, had* covered news of the parties of the Presque Isle elite right alongside news of Herbert Hoover's financial policies and editorials about trouble brewing in Germany. Even before Mr. Pop and Mother met, folks in Watsonville knew about the general goings-on about their more interesting neighbors to the north and the specific goings-on about things like Miss Weaver's post-baptismal gown, about the food and decorations at the party, and even about the string quartet hired to play hymns but who shockingly snuck in "Over the Rainbow." The real scandal wasn't the song itself, but instead, the number of good Baptists who found themselves humming along, revealing themselves as moviegoers. Mother laughed every time she remembered that the following Sunday's sermon focused on the evils of Hollywood and the need to resist the temptation of the movie house in town.

I wished she would laugh now. But her face stayed solemn. I reached over to hug her. "I'm sorry I listened in," I said. "I just wanted to know. I hate all these secrets."

"So do I," Mother said. "There's so much of this I don't even understand. Not fully. But what I do know is that Frankie Carmichael is not a bad man; he's just a scared man. There's a difference."

Chapter Six

I felt less and less like going to church those days. All the whisperings about Marjorie and Glenn—only speculation and gossip, really—and there at church of all places. Somehow, I felt eyes heavy on me. Probably because both Molly and Marjorie were my friends, but sometimes I thought people knew. I wondered if Mother had told even one person to unload the pressure. I questioned Mother's promise to keep Mick's note to me as well as our relationship secret if I promised to take it no further. "At least—at *least*," Mother had warned, "until all this passes. Until we hear more from Marjorie. Until we can figure out how to talk to your father about this." But I hoped, as I brought up my offering, that in fact they were not wondering when I too would run off. I hoped I was just imagining things. That they were really just thinking about Jesus. But I was probably wrong. And if I was, I just prayed they'd keep their thoughts to themselves. The last thing I needed was for Mr. Pop to hear rumors. Though Mr. Pop never paid them any mind. "Gossip is as big an evil as anything," he always told me.

Naturally, Mr. Pop insisted that we dress our best on Sundays. He had one suit, dark gray, almost black, with a white dress shirt and a black and gray, paisley-print tie. He was proud of that suit and his title of deacon at First Baptist. Not proud in a sinful way, I liked to think, but full of pride that he could serve God, and that his farming had provided for us to dress well on Sunday.

I'd grown up at First Baptist walking the aisle in my nicest dress with my Sunday school money to put in the little church bank like every other kid in the church. Even at fifteen, I still took my change up front and dropped it in while everyone sang, "Come to Sunday school, bring someone with you," sung to the tune of "Bringing in the Sheaves," one of Mr. Pop's favorites.

I'd hear this sung and would dream of the "someday" when I could bring someone with me—and that someone was Mick, of course.

Sometimes I'd heard Mr. Pop, dressed in his dark suit and tie and looking more like a preacher than a farmer, ask folks gathered for potluck if we were "serious about the gospel." Or he'd demand to know, "Is God's Word about loving the world only for white folk?" The many times I'd heard him say this, I thought him a hero. But in these past few weeks since Marjorie and Glenn ran off and had sent so few postcards home, I didn't hear Mr. Pop talk like this much. I wondered if he'd changed his mind.

That said, I knew Mr. Pop was scared too. Not as scared as Mr. Carmichael or some of the others with teenaged daughters but still scared.

Of course, it didn't take a genius to see that whole thing with Marjorie and Glenn was way bigger than some teenagers running off and eloping. And it was bigger even than the tribal land grant matters that popped up in conversation with increasing frequency. These were issues at the heart of our Christian faith that no one was talking about. Not on Sunday mornings, not at Wednesday night potlucks, and not at the Sunday night fellowship times at Randolph and Cleo Henderson's place either.

We almost always gathered at the Hendersons' for an after-meeting supper, both Wednesday and Sunday nights, but those gatherings were less frequent recently. I couldn't help but wonder if it was for fear Mr. Pop would launch out about some of the issues at hand that might not make for our usual pleasant conversation.

Though Mr. Pop was a man of slight build, probably all of 5 feet 9 inches, he was sturdy of character and strong of opinion. His round wire-framed glasses made him look studious despite having dropped out of high school. But Mr. Pop always said he had enough education to know how to read his Bible and run his farm, and that was good enough. He especially loved to sit and read his Bible. When Mr. Pop got wound up at a potluck, he'd run his fingers through his brown, wiry hair, and before meeting's end he had the appearance of a mad professor.

Through the years, I'd come to love these suppers. Usually it was the church at its best. All were invited, even the quirky folks and the disgruntled ones you sometimes thought you were better off without. Everyone in the church was considered part of these fellowship times. If Randolph and Cleo didn't want everyone, they hid it well.

Not many came empty-handed either. The basic sandwich fillings, along with the bread, was provided by Cleo. The prep was assembly line, but every other essential item walked in the door with someone. The Browns brought their famous chocolate chip cake. Bud could stuff celery with peanut butter and cream cheese like no one else. Someone almost always brought potato salad. Mother and Mr. Pop alternated what they would bring. Tonight it was Mr. Pop's famous molasses cookies, my favorite. Everyone in Watsonville knew Mr. Pop as both a farmer and a baker, for as long as I could remember, certain baked goods were his specialty. Mrs. Johnson always brought her delicious bread-and-butter pickles, and Cleo usually had ten to fifteen hard-boiled eggs ready in the refrigerator, or a stack of canned water-packed tuna. When it was boiled eggs, as it was that evening, three or four of us started cracking and peeling, while a couple of others slathered butter on the bread. Another one or two grabbed bowls to start mixing and mashing the eggs along with the mayonnaise. Someone would slice and dice pickles for half the sandwiches, leaving the rest plain.

The hum of voices around the room was a comforting sound. I knew that as long as people talked in small conversation groups, we were safe. If someone spoke up to start the larger community dialogue, I knew it could get rough. My heart always swelled with pride as I looked at farmers and farmhands sitting together laughing and talking about yesterday's work and tomorrow's challenges. Store owners, a gas station attendant, and a banker rounded out another part of the room. Joke telling was an art form at these suppers. When things stayed light, I felt carefree and warm inside. As long as the preparations were under way, no serious tone emerged. Once it was time to pray, all turned quiet.

When Mark Simms, attendant at the Texaco station in town, offered to give the blessing, my heart sank. He didn't even take a breath after saying "Amen." He kept right on going, posing the question I dreaded, but that was not unexpected: "So what are we gonna do about Glenn and the rest of those Maliseet? We've heard mumbling but no real action. When are we gonna do something? Before another daughter gets stolen away?"

All eyes stayed on Mr. Simms, but I was sure thoughts were turning toward me. Normally, I loved conversation on the issues and debates of the day. But this one I dreaded. I knew folks couldn't keep the conversations about Glenn and Marjorie contained in their own homes or to "prayer" at the Wednesday night prayer meetings forever. But now that the conversation was finally happening out in the open, I felt like I was living one of Ellery's humorous sayings, only there was no humor in it at all, just truth: "I'm up to my neck in alligators and the dam just broke!"

I could be thankful that I wasn't expected to join the conversation, but I felt helpless sitting off to the side picking at my supper.

"You okay?"

I looked up into Tommy Birger's face. I hadn't seen the Birgers arrive. I'd hoped they'd just gone home after church. Some days it was better *not* to have anyone to talk to.

"Sure," I said. "Why wouldn't I be?" I pointed to my potato salad with my fork and nodded.

"That's my mom's," Tommy said.

"Really? It's delicious. I'll have to tell her. I always think I'm so

68

sick of the stuff, but sometimes someone makes a batch that makes me forget I've eaten potato something four times already today."

Tommy laughed. I scooted over on the piano bench, making room for him.

"Thanks," he said, staring across the room where a small group of men were speaking with Mr. Simms. Mr. Simms cackled at someone's point, and then the group splintered apart. The women had already turned away from those conversations, as had Pastor Murphy. Maybe this dam break was only more of a leak. I looked around for Mr. Pop and saw no sign. I wondered where he'd gone off to. It wasn't like him to flee the scene of a fiery debate. But if things got too bad in here, someone would go get him. Folks always did when his soothing, calming influence was needed.

Tommy cleared his throat. "When I asked if you were okay, I didn't mean all general-like. I meant, because of all this stuff."

"Oh."

"So are you?"

"Well, I'm worried about Marjorie, of course. And feeling sick for Molly. This is all so difficult for their family."

I'd never spoken faster in my life. I sounded like Mother when she was back in her society girl days of trying-not-to-lie, polite-at-any-cost.

I heard a snort from Tommy's nose. He shook his head and stared out across the room. When Tommy and I were little, we played castle on the Hendersons' curving staircase. I wondered if he remembered that.

"You know that's not what I mean," Tommy said. "I'm asking if *you* are okay. You must be nervous about"—Tommy shifted his head around and leaned toward me and whispered, "you and Mick."

I breathed in, not sure if I'd have the strength to breathe back out. So I closed my eyes a second and did what Mr. Pop taught me to do. *"Call on the name of Jesus,"* Mr. Pop often said. *"For whyever, for whenever, for whatever, for whomever, for however."*

Jesus, I prayed. *Jesus.*

"Nobody else knows, Mercy, and I'm not going to say anything."

"Nobody else knows what?"

"About you and Mick.

"What about us?"

Tommy laughed. "You're just being cagey now."

"I am not. What does everybody know? That Mick and I have been friends since we were tiny, since we were out picking rocks and building forts as *toddlers.* Because, yes, as it turns out, everybody *does* know about that."

"About that, yes. About that, your Pop's been sending you out to pick up drunken Indians and their boys since you were just a girl, yes. Everybody knows that."

I rolled my eyes, a technique I'd developed long ago to mask the ire that boiled whenever people spoke of my rides to the Flats or of the Maliseet in those tones.

"So what don't they know?" I asked.

"That you love Mick," Tommy said. "That Mick loves you. That you hold hands. That you kiss. Should I go on?"

I rolled my eyes again but wondered if it was too much. Nerves were taking over. *Jesus, Jesus, Jesus. Help me, Jesus.*

"Of *course,* I love Mick. Of course he loves me. Do we need to revisit that we've-been-friends-since-we-could-toddle-around-the-fields bit?"

"Oh, well, so then you must love me too. Right? Because I was toddling with you too. Playing castle with you. Fishing with you. Swimming with you. Just never got to sit beneath the pine trees holding your hand or kissing you, that's all."

I folded my hands. They had started to shake, on top of their sweating, and I needed that to stop.

Jesus. Jesus.

I rubbed my tongue across the top of my teeth, hoping to calm the anger and find the words. Just as I opened my mouth to speak, I heard a familiar voice. My mother was standing now addressing the group. Her back shook as she spoke.

"We're pointing the finger at the wrong person, the wrong people," Mother was saying. "Whoever you're blaming, and I think for most it's Glenn Socoby, you're wrong! We have ourselves to blame. We've pushed them to this point. Sure, we like their cheap labor on our farms. We're happy to round them up and bring them to pick rocks, to help plant, to help weed, and to help harvest." Mother was definitely warming to her subject. She went on.

"But every day we take them back to the same horrible living conditions. How many of us ride down by Hungry Hill and look over the Flats and think, 'what a lovely place to live'? Really, how many of us even care for anything more than what's under our own roof? You know we pushed them off our land. We point fingers at the government, but we influenced those decisions. We need to be pointing fingers at ourselves."

Mother threw a napkin she had been wringing down on the coffee table. But she had worked herself up. This was a rarity, not just for *my* mother to speak up in public, but for any woman to speak out, let alone stand up and say her piece. As Mother looked from person to person, hoping to find a nod of approval or at least some eye contact, she was emotional enough to be almost on the verge of tears. My throat swelled, and my eyes filled too. But I wasn't about to cry, not with Tommy Birger next to me, not after what he'd just said.

The level of surprise at Mother's comments was palpable. People were startled and restless, but no one else ventured a comment to the entire gathering. Instead, conversations restarted gradually, moving the talk away from the controversial and back to comfortable topics like farm life. Cleo moved toward the kitchen for cleanup and started what usually was a trickle of folks heading toward the door. It was a rushing brook tonight.

"Tommy, time to go!" We didn't see his mother call but could hear her clear enough from wherever she was.

Tommy stood and looked down at me.

"Nice chatting with you, Mercy. Can we do it again sometime? Soon?"

I was too stunned—from him, from Mother—to say anything more than, "Yeah, sure."

Mother and I were the last to go, still wondering where Mr. Pop was, why he hadn't even eaten. As we headed toward the door, Mr. Simms grabbed Mother's elbow, startling her.

"I don't agree with one word you said, Geneva," he said. "But unlike the rest of these folks, you had the guts to say something. And I appreciate that. We can't just push this under the rug and let Frankie Carmichael stir up his own hornet's nest of vigilante justice that's going to do no one any good. We've got to discuss this as a community. No matter where we stand. It's not easy, but we got to."

Mother laid a hand on his arm, surprising Mr. Simms perhaps only more than me. I'd never see Mother so much as shake hands with another man besides my uncle or grandfather.

"I agree," Mother whispered, her words intended only for his ear. "Thank you." And together we stepped out onto the porch. Mr. Simms was first to spot Mr. Pop sitting in the car.

"I guess he missed your tirade," Mr. Simms said, while we all stared ahead at the car. "Darn shame. If you were my wife, I'd'a been proud. I'd'a thought you were wrong, mind you, but I'd'a been proud."

Mother laughed and then grabbed my hand. "Mercy, say goodbye to Mr. Simms."

As Mother tugged me toward the car, I turned and waved at Mr. Simms. People were complicated, I was figuring out.

"Goodbye to you too, Miss Mercy," he said. "Be careful."

These warnings were getting to me.

Mr. Pop got out of the car to open the door for Mother. She slid into her seat without a word. Mr. Pop opened my door too. But I stood outside it for a moment to wave goodbye to the Birgers. Tommy's father slowed the car as they passed on the gravel.

Tommy leaned out of the window and said, "Thanks again, Mercy."

I could feel eyes once again on me—Mr. Simms's, Mr. Pop's, Mother's, the Birgers', and the Hendersons' farmhand—as I walked toward the Birgers' car. But this time I wasn't afraid of their eyes. They would be my and Mick's saviors.

I smiled at Tommy, a smile just like Molly had told me about, the kind Marjorie had said was enough to make any boy "your slave for life."

"Come by the farm, sometime," I heard myself say. "I've perfected a boysenberry pie. You'd love it." I could've thrown up with each word as I felt my eyes brighten and eyelids bat. But what the heck, I figured. Molly wasn't allowed to go out, not even to my place. And without Mick either, life was getting a bit lonely. Maybe a new boyfriend would be the just the thing to let me see my old one.

Chapter Seven

I could hardly sleep. It didn't matter that the hard work of weeding with the hoe, and hilling up the potatoes until the dirt was
packed up high around them wore me out down to the core or how
desperately I needed sleep to energize my body for the work that
lay ahead. I spent my nights tossing and turning, finding the only
consolation of anxious nights to be the gorgeous sunrises I'd wit-
ness when morning finally dawned.

The controversy over where the sun shines first in the whole
United States was always funny to me. I know the sun kisses the top
of Mars Hill, Maine, before any other spot. The rest of the country
has given in, but it's remained an argument among Mainers. Those
on the coast say it's Cadillac Mountain, a few say Lubec, but I know
it's Mars Hill, and my sleepless nights and early mornings solidi-
fied that for me.

So many mornings, when sleep wouldn't come, I'd dress and
head down to the woods off the back field. I did my best thinking
and hoping there. These woods were thick with alders, and the
pines jutted majestically into the sky. The forget-me-nots hung like
clouds barely suspended above the earth and the moss lay like a
beautiful blanket, making my steps stealthy. A big, old bull moose
hung around this part of the woods but not even he could hear
me coming thanks to the green moss cushion. I'd find my favorite
rock, the one I'd been coming to for as long as I could remember.
Whenever I needed some space to think or just wanted time alone
to dream, I'd head for the big rock next to the little creek running
through the back end of the farm.

That morning, I headed out to think and pray and hope that tensions would dissolve, that issues would come to some kind of resolution. And that I'd find a way for Mick to start talking to me again. Since Mick had sent that note—that picture of the woodchuck tunneling toward the fort—I'd hoped it meant he was somehow "tunneling" toward me, that he was looking for ways to see me, to talk to me, or to connect with me somehow. But it'd been three weeks since Mother had led me to the note in the basket and since then, nothing. Mick still came to the farm with the other Maliseet, and he still planted in the fields not far from me, but without even a glance from him, it became agonizing.

It'd been two weeks since Mother spoke up at the Hendersons' and two weeks since any of us spoke of that at all. Mother seemed different, rather distant, at least from Mr. Pop. I'd never known my parents to not speak around mealtimes or to let their anger seep deep enough into them that it pulled their smiles down and turned their eyes glossy. I wasn't sure if they had discussed his not being around when she spoke out or if Mother ever asked him about Mr. Carmichael's threats toward Glenn or if she told him about Mick and me, but I knew something had changed. And I hated it. I hated all of this.

A twig snapped behind me. I swung around, startled. "Sorry," he said. "I scare ya?" It was Old Man Stringer, steadying himself on an alder.

"Thought you were the moose."

"If I were a moose, I'd make a lot more noise that this. You'd have heard me huffin' at ya."

I laughed. "And you'd have heard me screaming and running."

"Some people do scream and run from me," he said.

"That they do. But only 'cause they don't know you."

"That's where you're wrong, Miss Mercy. They scream and run because they *do* know me."

I had to laugh. He was right. His smell, his torn, plaid flannel, his dirty and cracked bare feet scared people. That Old Man Stringer committed the sin of drinking so flagrantly only left people to speculate on what other sins he was up to privately.

Figuring my quiet time on the rock was over, I stood and offered Old Man a hand.

"Here," I said. "Let me help you up to the house. Mother'll have some biscuits for you."

"If you don't think she'd mind," he said as he swaggered a bit toward me.

"You know she won't and that's what you're doing out here."

"Oh, you got me, Miss Mercy. Always so smart."

I wove my arm through his elbow and patted his arm before aiming for the house.

"Not *so* smart," I said, as we started walking together. "I can't figure out why you'd have been coming up this way and not across the fields this morning. Whatcha been doing in the woods?"

"Ain't been doin' nothin'," he said. "Just hoping to find you here."

"Oh, I see," I said, laughing again. "To find me?"

"Yup."

"This isn't just about biscuits?" I teased.

"Nope. I'm on a mission."

"And what, may I ask, is your mission this morning?"

Another reason folks ran from Old Man Stringer was to avoid getting caught up in one of his gin-fueled fantasies. Through the years, he'd been known to bust through tavern doors, announcing that he'd been recruited by the government to go fight the Communists, and to stagger into church to warn everyone about the hurricane that was set to barrel through and drown the woods in the middle of winter. But I liked Old Man's stories. And he never ceased to surprise me with them.

"Ma'am," he said with dignity, "I am here to warn you to be on the lookout for moose and old drunks prowling these parts." Old

Man Stringer snorted and slapped his leg as he laughed, nearly falling over in the process.

I laughed along, but grabbed his elbow again and started walking, this time faster, toward the house.

"All right then," I said. "Consider me warned. Let's go."

Old Man Stringer tried to stifle his laughter but every five or so steps would stumble again and burst into giggles. It was like walking with a two-year-old. When we could see the peaks of the house above the ridge, Old Man Stringer stopped and sniffed hard, still trying to stop cackling.

"No," he said, shaking his head, as if that would shake the drunk from his brain. "This is serious. I did come to find you. It's a very important errand," he added, carefully pronouncing the words distinctly. "At least, that's what Mick called it."

I stopped, nearly tripping myself in the process, and pulled my arm from Old Man's elbow. I looked around to make sure no farmhands were in the back field.

"Mick sent you?" I asked.

Old Man nodded and began rummaging through his pockets.

My eyes widened as he thrust his hand into his ratty jeans pocket, pulling it out empty before tapping his chest.

"Ah, this one," he said as he pulled out a folded slip of paper. Old Man Stringer held the paper toward me like a king presenting a pardon.

"For you, madam."

I took the paper from his hand and started to unfold it.

"Don't read it *here*," he said. "Wait till I get my biscuits."

Old Man's few moments of solemnity had been broken. We both smiled.

I quickly folded the note, shoved it into my pocket, and pulled Old Man Stringer toward the house, now hurrying. I had a million questions for Old Man, but I didn't want those answers as much as I wanted to know what Mick sent to me.

After getting Old Man settled with a plate of biscuits and a tin cup of coffee on the front porch I skipped steps up to my room. Mother called after me to remember that I still had a breakfast table to set, and I called back that I'd be down in a minute.

I ran into the bathroom, figuring this place would buy me the most time. I perched on the edge of our claw-foot tub and unfolded Mick's note. My hands trembled a bit. Maybe Old Man's shaky hands were catching.

The note was addressed to no one and signed by no one. Mick was smart to avoid writing names down, but my heart sank a bit not seeing my name and his together on a page. Still, I knew Mick's handwriting and I knew his intention. There was no denying this really was from Mick, for me.

Tommy? Really? You're lucky I've hunted with you enough to know you're an expert at throwing off a scent. Otherwise I'd be pummeling your new boyfriend every time he drove up to the house. Hardee-har-har.

I miss you. Still tunneling toward. Someday. Somehow.

I didn't know whether to laugh or cry. So I did both. Smiling as I thought of how well Mick knew me; that he understood Tommy's frequent presence at the farm. That he understood was the best news I could've gotten.

Tommy had taken me up on my invitation for boysenberry pie, just a day after I'd extended it. I knew he would but thought it might take a bit of time, wished it would've. I was glad farmwork goes on, so Tommy helped out weeding and hoeing to hill up the potatoes. He even followed me into Mother's garden to help me do some work there. He followed me around like a loyal dog hopeful for a treat. I struggled to keep up appearances with Tommy. Insincerity wasn't my strong suit. Perhaps batting my eyes now and then blinded Tommy to my true agenda, but I was starting to like myself less and less.

Mick's note helped me stomach my own behavior a bit easier,

but I couldn't keep this up for long. I couldn't purposely keep leading Tommy on. I was pretty sure a fifteen-year-old's life was not
meant to be this complicated.

Mother called for me again from downstairs. I sniffed hard
and cleared my throat, trying to rein in the cry-laughing the note
brought out in me, before I answered back with, "One minute.
Funny stomach!"

"I'll get the Pepto-Bismol," she said before her steps moved
away from the base of the stairs toward the kitchen.

I read the note a third time and clutched it to my chest. I was
tempted to smell it but knew any scent would hail from Old Man's
pocket, not from Mick. So I folded the note again, using the exact
same creases Mick had made. I didn't want to change anything
about it. Though, for all I knew, Old Man had creased the note. Mick
could've had it in an envelope. And who knew how long Old Man
had the note. I'd have to find him later to ask. I'd also probably have
to guarantee his silence with more than biscuits. I figured Mick had
worked out a way to keep him quiet. More than once Old Man had
stumbled to the Flats sick with need for a drink when the shops and
bars in town had colluded to stop selling to him. But the Maliseet understood Old Man's predicament. It was easy for the good Christian
townsfolk to shake their heads at a man's desperation for the evils of
alcohol. But though Old Man wasn't Maliseet, the Maliseet understood when it was less of a devil and more of a savior.

Somehow, one of these times, when Old Man had been shaking and begging for a drink, it'd been Mick to run to town to get
it for him. Mr. Thibodeau at the liquor store would've never sold
anything to a white sixteen-year-old, but he'd sell to Indians at any
age. The only time I ever knew Mr. Pop to go into Thibodeau's
Food and Liquor was to confront Mr. Thibodeau when Mr. Pop got
wind of his selling to Maliseet children.

Mother called me again. "I've got the Pepto when you're ready,
Mercy. I'll go ahead and set the table."

I shook my head. A funny stomach was the one surefire way to get out of chores in this house. Both Mr. Pop and Mother would keep working with broken legs and limbs, pounding headaches, stuffed noses and coughed-out lungs, and expect others to do so also. But digestion issues were another matter. They required tender care and lots of space and, of course, the pepperminty pink liquid. My mother had been traumatized by reading of cholera epidemics as a child and became convinced any slight disruption in digestion could signal another outbreak waiting in the wings.

For me, it was just a handy excuse. I always asked God to forgive me for lying, but somehow I imagined He understood. Mr. Pop had told me every Sunday for my whole life that we didn't work on Sunday because "rest was God's idea, not mine, Mercy." So I figured if God invented rest, He might not mind if sometimes I snuck a bit extra in. Even if I had to come by it dishonestly.

I flushed the toilet and ran the water in the sink, knowing that wasting water for a faked illness would get me in more trouble than the fake illness itself. With my parents as well as with God. But I couldn't worry about that now. Not with Mick still tunneling toward me and me needing to throw people off our trail.

✳ ✳ ✳

"Well," Mother said as I pulled my chair to the table. "Your color seems fine."

She put her hand to my head. "And you don't feel warm. Or cool." Mother stepped back and looked at me quizzically. I looked across at Mr. Pop, who also studied my face.

"No, actually I feel fine now," I said. "The Pepto is already working."

"Think you're coming down with something?" Mr. Pop asked, eyes scrunched.

"No," I said, smiling first at Mother who moved the box of cornflakes closer to my bowl. The price to pay for my lies was not getting any biscuits, eggs, and bacon. So I figured I might as well continue. "I *might* have splashed some of the creek on my face this morning . . ."

Finally Mr. Pop smiled back at me.

"For goodness' sake, Mercy!" Mother said, throwing up her hands. No matter how long Mother lived on this farm, she could not shake her disgust at the little creek that ran through the back field. Although the glacial water came crystal clear to us from the heights of Mt. Katahdin, Mother was convinced it was nothing more than a sewer for the tramps who passed through these parts. To her the creek positively sparkled with disease.

"I think I just saw a moose use it the other day," Mr. Pop said and winked at me.

"You two will be the death of me, I swear," Mother said.

"Better death by us than by funny tummies," I said, winking back at Mr. Pop.

For a moment it felt like old times. My parents happy. Me laughing. Mr. Pop opening the Bible to read morning Scripture and then following up in prayer. But as Mr. Pop closed his prayer by asking for God's "hand and guidance and wisdom" for the Indian Rights Council meeting coming up, I realized we had returned to the very new times we all now lived in.

I wasted no time after the amens. "What Indian Rights Council?"

"Mercy," Mother said, passing a plate of biscuits to Mr. Pop. "Let your father get some food on his plate first, please."

I shook the cornflakes into my bowl, reaching farther than Mother would like for the milk. Mr. Pop didn't seem to be in any hurry. He gently pulled his biscuit apart and spread the butter, pausing only to ask Mother for the jam. He lifted two pieces of bacon off the plate in front of him and spooned a bit of egg before looking around the table.

"Is the pepper out here?"

"Goodness," Mother said. "Forgot. Be right back."

Mr. Pop nodded at Mother, and then I noticed Mother's empty plate. A ruse if there ever was one. My stomach fluttered as I feared what was coming.

Sure enough, as soon as Mother could be heard opening drawers and cabinets in the kitchen as though she'd hadn't kept the pepper mill in the same spot for twenty years, Mr. Pop answered my question.

"The mayor has asked for an Indian Rights Council to look into some of these new concerns with the Maliseet."

"New concerns?" I asked.

"Well, maybe new situations that bring to light old concerns is a better way of putting it."

"Like Glenn and Marjorie."

"Yes," Mr. Pop said. "For instance, like Glenn and Marjorie. But also like all this land settlement talk coming from the Maliseet and even how the Supreme Court's school ruling for the Negroes in Topeka affects us up here."

"But the Maliseet already go to school with us. No one objects to that."

"Yes, they go to school with you. And I'm glad for that. But it's not true that no one objects. Plenty of folks have thought the Maliseet children should be sent to their own school. Some have claimed the Maliseet influence on our children would be damaging. But up until now, *most* of us have argued that this was a terrible idea. Although, it's gained popularity."

"Because of Glenn and Marjorie," I said.

Mr. Pop nodded at me. "Because of Glenn and Marjorie," he said. "But, really. Just because we haven't segregated schools doesn't mean we've accepted the Maliseet into our lives."

"You have," I said.

He breathed in deeply. "To some degree. Maybe."

I spooned some cornflakes and gave them a couple chews

before asking, "So what do you think? What's going to happen?"

A few months ago, I would've felt certain of Mr. Pop's answer. Today, of course, I wondered. Having heard nothing but Mr. Pop's silence when Mr. Carmichael raged about killing Glenn and having seen him sitting in the car while my mother defended the rights of the Maliseet showed that Mr. Pop might be coming around. The widespread community fear caused by Glenn and Marjorie had gotten to Mr. Pop and changed his heart and his mind.

"What I think," Mr. Pop said, "would be best answered while you and I ride to pick up the men."

He didn't have to ask twice.

* * *

In the weeks before harvest when the fields showed off in their purple-flowered glory, the Maliseet came to the farm to work odd jobs with Mr. Pop and Ellery and Bud. Mr. Pop had mentioned something about needing a bigger potato house, but I wasn't sure. And I didn't want to ask, to throw him off the subject. Not that he was talking yet.

Instead, Mr. Pop was enjoying the beauty of the fields. It was hard not to. Potato fields in full bloom in July might be the most exquisite sight on a farm. Even though they signal backbreaking work of potato picking just around the bend, the grace and elegance of the flowing rows of blooms focuses all eyes on the joy of the present, not the work of the future. Purple blossoms up against the rich, dark green leaves are a striking sight. The creamy yellow blossoms look antique. The beauty came when, like patchwork, different varieties of potatoes grew in fields side by side. The delicate cream color echoes the hue of the tuber just below the surface of the rich brown dirt.

While folks in Augusta or Portland might have rolled their eyes at the idea of our holding a festival and crowning a Maine Potato Blossom Queen, well, if they'd just look at the soft waving

fields, they'd agree it was only right to celebrate this bit of alluring
and inviting brilliance in the midst of our otherwise rough and
rugged landscape and life.

I wondered what this year's Potato Blossom Festival, which was
starting in less than a week, would be like. Certainly, it wouldn't be
anywhere near as fun as last year's. It was hard to believe it'd been
just last year when Mick and I first caught each other's glances, and
something changed in each of us. From childhood friends to whatever we were now: secret boyfriend-girlfriend? Or woodchucks,
like Mick said.

It was hard to believe it was just last year that Marjorie
Carmichael won the Maine Potato Blossom Queen title and had
gotten to go to the Bangor Hotel. Of course, Molly had hoped
to enter this year but her family put a quick stop to that. Mr.
Carmichael was actually pushing the festival committee to put an
end to the Potato Blossom Queen Pageant altogether. He credited
it with driving the Indians wild with lust, and accused the pageant
of being nothing more than a public peep show of sorts.

"So, the Indian Rights Council." Mr. Pop's words jarred me
back to the present, to this truck, to the fields, to where we were
headed. To Mick. "The mayor asked me to serve on it."

"You're on it?"

"I felt it important to say yes, especially now. We'll meet in Fort
Fairfield the weekend the Potato Blossom Festival begins."

"But that's next week!" I was surprised they were moving
ahead so quickly. "Why now? Why not wait until after harvest?"

"I think the rumblings and speculations and anger seething
under the surface has barely been held at bay. You were at the
Hendersons' after church that night. I might not have been inside,
but I knew it was some hot supper of a meeting. Your mother is
like a pot of beans simmering on the stove all day. When troubles
bubble and boil inside, it doesn't take long at all before the lid is
pushed from the pot and her righteous anger rises to the top. With

most people it's just anger, but with your mother you can count on it being righteous anger—that's why she made a speech. She's always been a barometer I watch closely. It's one of the things I love about her."

"You love this about her?"

"Of course I do. How can you ask that?"

"Because it sure didn't look like love when you were sitting in the car. At least, not to Mother."

Mr. Pop sighed heavily. He clenched the steering wheel tighter, steadied his breathing, then relaxed his grip. "Your mother and I have talked about this. I apologized. Well, I apologized to her for not being there. I would've stayed had I known the pot of beans was about to boil over."

Mr. Pop glanced over my way, hoping I'd crack a smile. I gave in.

"So you weren't avoiding her speech?"

"Not at all. But I was avoiding everyone else's."

"But you *never* run from stuff like this!"

"I wasn't running, Mercy. Just sitting it out. There's a differ-ence. None of us has to get involved in every little thing, every little conversation, every big fight no matter how much we care about it."

"But you weren't inside. She had no one to back her up."

Mr. Pop clenched the wheel again. "She had *you*, Mercy. Did you back her up?"

I stared out the window. Of course, I hadn't said a word to defend Mother. Until now, it hadn't even occurred to me to do so.

"I'm sorry, Mercy. Wasn't your job to back her up. Would've made it awkward for you. I know that."

I turned to Mr. Pop as the car slowed at the stop sign, ready to roll into town. "You know what?" I asked.

"I know you're worried about how people see you. I know you're wondering what everyone thinks about you and Mick."

I answered too quickly: "Mick and I are friends. Why would I worry what everyone thinks?"

Mr. Pop tried to hide a wry grin. "Your Mother and you think I don't know anything. You think I've got my head buried deeper than the potatoes. You girls think I can't see."

I picked at my thumbnail and stared straight ahead at Second Baptist's steeple coming up behind town. I was too nervous to say anything. I knew Mr. Pop could see. I just didn't know what he *had* seen.

"Mick's a nice boy, Mercy. He's smart and a hard worker. In many ways, I've loved him like a son. So all I'm saying is . . . land sakes, what's going on up there?"

My eyes shifted from the church's steeple to the sidewalk just ahead where a crowd had gathered in front of Fulton's. Mr. Carmichael was yelling and pointing.

Mr. Pop pulled the truck over and we both jumped out. Though, Mr. Pop raced far ahead of my more dazed steps. Somehow, as I drifted toward the crowd, I knew. Though I couldn't hear his words, I recognized the fury of Mr. Carmichael's voice.

Then a path cleared among the people, and I could see: Mick standing in the direct line of Mr. Carmichael's finger above Old Man Stringer. Mr. Carmichael's words rang clear to my ears now as well as he yelled to my father just what he had seen.

"He killed him, Paul! I saw him through the window. That boy struck Old Man. Cold blood. He's dead."

Mr. Carmichael swung around to the crowd, his eyes flashing, his hands waving. "It's like I've been telling you people. Maliseet aren't simply pagan. They're monsters." Mr. Carmichael lunged toward Mick. The crowd gasped as Mr. Pop grabbed Mr. Carmichael, restraining him.

And then something overtook me. I pressed through the crowd, stepped over Old Man and Dr. Benson, who someone had run to get, and grabbed Mick, wrapping my arms around him as though we were back in our fort, as though we were alone, as though not all eyes were on us.

I never heard the sirens or the commands for Mick to let go of me and go with them. I didn't hear Mr. Pop urging me to let go. I never heard his words of assurances that all would be fine, that he'd sort this out. All I heard was Mick whispering "someday" before being pulled away and then Mr. Pop thrusting the keys into my hand and grabbing my shoulders.

"Go right back home. Tell your mother to call Uncle Roger. Now!"

I nodded and stepped backward toward the truck. People spilled out from the brick facades along Main Street, bunching together, at first staring and then turning toward each other to start churning the rumor mill. Then a few folks splintered off, running toward Dr. Benson's office, following his pointed finger and clipped demands. While I walked backward, the scene ahead of me blurred, the bricks of the buildings and clear glass of the doors and height of the steeple at Second Baptist and the cross of St. Mary of the Visitation faded and whirled together in the terror of my mind.

I had lost sight of Mick, of the police who led him away, and of Mr. Pop. But as I stepped up onto the running board of the truck, I saw three figures walking up the steps of the jail, each with their hands on the boy in the center. Two police officers grasped Mick's elbows, leading him ever forward, toward who-knew-what future. Mr. Pop rested one hand on Mick's back and raised his other toward heaven, toward the One who knew that future.

PART TWO

"But what doth the Lord require of thee?"

Chapter Eight

MID-JULY 1954

Dear Mom and Dad,

Sorry it's been so long since I wrote. Just wasn't ready, I guess. Well, I want you to know you can be at peace. What you've almost certainly thought about me isn't true: Glenn did not take advantage of me or force me to do anything I didn't want to.

But the truth is so much different and so much better. Yes, we're married. After we left Watsonville, we drove to New Hampshire and got married by a justice of the peace there. So don't worry. I'm Mrs. Glenn Socoby and have been for six wonderful weeks.

The point is . . . Glenn is a good man and a gentleman, even, and made sure we did things right. I know you'll never see this as right—the running off and all—but what else could we have done? I love Glenn. I wanted to be his wife. Glenn wanted to go to you and ask for my hand, but I knew Dad would sooner kill him than give us your blessing.

Besides, I knew I wanted to build a life away from Watsonville. And I knew I'd never get your blessing for that either.

I wish it could've been different, but I didn't see any other way. Not after hearing Dad night after night talking about how the Maliseet were evil and filthy and responsible for all the crime and corruption in town. How could I tell you I loved a man whose entire tribe Dad wanted to see "sent off to camps like the Japs"? How could I tell you I wanted to spend my life with a man you'd rather see sent away?

I couldn't. So I left instead. Well, I want you to know now that Glenn got a job at Royal Lace Paper Works, Inc. here in Brooklyn. Yes, maybe you saw the postmark that I'm writing from New York!

Mr. Booker at Great Northern sent Glenn's new boss a stellar recommendation. Within three weeks of starting, Glenn got a promotion. From mill worker to supervising ten men. He got a raise too.

I'm taking a correspondence course to learn shorthand. We don't need the money right now, but one day I'd like a job in one of those glittering towers in Manhattan. Mom, you wouldn't believe them if you saw them! Some buildings are taller than Mt. Katahdin, I swear! And the women who head in and out. Ah, so glamorous.

Life isn't as glamorous in Brooklyn as it is in Manhattan, but it's wonderful. Really, I thought life would be so much different in Brooklyn than it was in Watsonville; I was scared that Glenn wouldn't be as accepted at the mill in Brooklyn as he had been in Millinocket. I thought the people would be mean and the neighbors uncaring. That's the way Dad had painted the world outside Watsonville.

It was because of Watsonville's unusual purity and safety that Dad said we needed to move the Maliseet. Always made it sound like Watsonville was safe and holy and the Maliseet were a corrupting influence.

But when Mrs. Franza from downstairs helps me carry my groceries up our five flights or when Glenn's boss takes us out for a fancy steak supper at DeVito's to celebrate his promotion, I realized, Dad, you're wrong about people. Just like you are wrong about the Maliseet.

In whatever ways you might be worried about me, you don't need to worry about me in this: People in New York are just as nice as they are in Watsonville. Our neighbors look out for us. Jenny from two floors down even invited us to her church.

And now for the news you thought you already knew: it's early days yet, but I'm almost sure—okay, very sure—that there's a baby on the way! Please know and believe me when I tell you that he or she was conceived the "right" way—in marriage.

Well, Glenn will be home soon and will be hungry. I need to get supper started. Mrs. Franza taught me how to make lasagna—

something we never had in Maine, right?—her mother's recipe from Italy! I made a pan this morning and need to close now and get it in to bake.

I hope you can forgive me and maybe even come to visit. I hear New York is beautiful in the spring. And the baby will be beautiful too, I just know. Oh, and if it's a boy, we'll name him after you, Dad.

Your sweetheart,

Marjorie

Mr. Carmichael had torn Marjorie's letter right open on the steps of the post office and read it quickly, no doubt hoping it would tell him the whole thing was a mistake, and she was on her way home.

But in a few simple sentences, Marjorie had delivered the news Mr. Carmichael had most feared: a baby. At least, probably.

While most folks would have been relieved that a coming grandchild was legitimate and that no sins were committed, to Mr. Carmichael this had to be worse. There could be no rescuing and rushing Marjorie off to one of those homes for unwed girls. I'm sure he had imagined storming into her Brooklyn apartment, convincing her of her sin. Then Marjorie would confess and together they would board the train to St. Andreas Home for Unwed Mothers in Biddeford, where Mr. Carmichael would hug his repentant daughter goodbye, promising to return in the spring. By then, town gossip would have died down. They could return to their normal lives. Marjorie could find and marry a nice boy, a lawyer's son, perhaps from Bangor.

And then the letter came, shattering Mr. Carmichael's plans and heaping all kinds of new evil. It would be that much harder to convince her to give up the baby now since they were married, and divorce would have to enter the picture for them to break up, another evil. And now that she was settling down happily in New York, it could only get worse.

He looked lost somewhere in his thoughts when Mrs. Carmichael walked out of Mildred's Bakery and up two steps and sat beside her husband.

He thrust the letter at his wife without a word. As she read the letter, Mrs. Carmichael's face grew from concern to delight.

"Her very countenance beamed," Mildred from the bakery would later say. But Mr. Carmichael tore the letter out of her hands, ripping it in half while Mrs. Carmichael begged him to stop.

"His face was stone," Mildred said later. "Then he walked into his store."

The bells at the top of the door jangled wildly as he slammed the door behind him.

I figure Mr. Carmichael must've decided that his own personal agony had been getting lonely. Which was why he decided to drag Mick down into it with him. And it was too easy. Mr. Carmichael had been looking for any opportunity to discredit the Maliseet in Watsonville, and he hadn't planned on being choosy. All of them had a hand in Marjorie's choices and in her demise.

And then a plum opportunity for revenge fell right into his lap. As he wrote up an order for roofing nails, he looked out the front window of Fulton's and saw Mick. From Mr. Carmichael's vantage point and mental state, Mick was clearly up to no good. Old Man Stringer was just to the left of the front entrance to the store, and Mick was toe-to-toe with him. He had Old Man's face in his hands. A person in a better mind would've seen Mick trying to help Old Man stand up, to help steady him in his drunken stupor. That person would've seen Mick smack his face, trying to help him focus and become more alert.

And ordinarily ten people would've attested to that. This time was different. Frankie Carmichael was on the accusing end, and most right-minded people had a long line of credit at Fulton's. They couldn't afford to pay up and stay current with their account, and the whole scenario made them a bit nervous. What if

Mr. Carmichael cut them off, took their credit line away? Besides, when push comes to shove, people stick with their own kind. If Mr. Carmichael said he saw Old Man drop to the sidewalk after Mick accosted him, it must be so. When so much hate fills your heart, you can make a leap to any conclusion. You don't need the truth because you are above the truth. You create the truth.

✳   ✳   ✳

Mother was waiting for me on the porch, one hand grasping the porch rail, the other jammed into the pocket of her skirt. Mother wore this skirt every day, but as the truck rolled up on the gravel, for the first time I noticed the blue of it. Not dingy at all as I'd come to see it but crisp and cool like the summer sky, like her.

When I opened the truck door, Mother rushed forward, as though she knew those steps toward the house would be impossible for me to take alone. And she was right. My body went limp against her as soon as she wrapped her arms around me and pulled my head onto her shoulder.

"Sweetheart, sweetheart," Mother whispered, smoothing my hair. "It'll be all right. It'll be all right."

I shook my head as she tightened her grip on me.

"It won't be. Mr. Carmichael says Mick killed Old Man Stringer. He says he killed him."

Mother took a step back and helped me stand straighter. "I heard. Your father phoned me from the bakery. Let's go into the house," she said.

I nodded. "I've got to call Uncle Roger."

"I've already called him. He's calling Judge Dodd today and then he's heading up first thing day after tomorrow."

"Two days? No! He's got to come now."

"Mercy, let's get inside."

Mother helped me up the porch steps and into the house. She turned my elbow into the front parlor and released me at the sofa, whose cushions she pounded and pillows she fluffed.

"Lie down," she said. "I'm going to get you water. When I get back, we'll talk."

I lay down and tried to clear my mind of what had just happened. I realized this might be the first time I'd ever lain on that sofa. "Sofas are for sitting on; beds are for lying in." I wasn't sure how many times Mother had told me that, but it was enough that the very act of bringing my feet up and resting my head on its gold and green flowers and leaves felt like breaking a commandment. Usually Mother kept the French doors to the living room shut tight, as if that would keep the dust out. I loved sneaking in and sitting in the overstuffed platform rocker. I did some good reading and thinking in that chair. When I could talk Mr. Pop into letting me turn on the Zenith console radio, I did some secret dancing in that room, pretty good if I say so myself. I loved searching, rolling the dial to find the best music stations.

Then there was the big, black robot dial front and center on the console. Mother kept the mahogany finish shining all the time. I could hardly wait for new episodes of *Dragnet*. We'd sit around listening, waiting for the announcer with the "voice." His opening lines are indelibly etched on my mind. "Ladies and Gentlemen: the story you are about to hear is true. Only the names have been changed to protect the innocent." Mother would be knitting and I'd be rocking away in my favorite chair while Mr. Pop would just sit and listen. How I wished we were back in that moment, and not living our own police drama.

Again, I tried to push it out of my mind. From my lying-down vantage point, I could see Aunt Dot's painting of Mt. Katahdin. For as long as I can remember, I loved to sit and stare at it. Always the naturalist, Aunt Dot had set up her easel and canvas in some of the most beautiful spots in Aroostook County, hoping to capture what she saw. Aunt Dot had always praised my sketches and had promised to teach me to paint one day, but when she and Uncle

Roger moved to Bangor, I figured it wouldn't happen. Not that it mattered to me now. By the time Mother returned with a glass of water set neatly next to a plate of Saltines on the wicker tray, my body shook the cushions.

"Sweetheart, here. Sit, drink."

I didn't want to sit up. Even as parched as I was.

"Uncle Roger will sort things out," Mother was saying. Then she told me to rest, to try not to think about all this. As Mother shuffled back into the kitchen, I thought about my uncle Roger—pushing out thoughts of him not being here until the day after tomorrow—memories of him. He was my favorite uncle and not just because he always brought me a gift when he came for a visit but because he was a man of character.

Uncle Roger and Mr. Pop were given a choice of farming or college. After their father died, Grandma Millar never had much money, but she was willing to put what she had toward college for either of her boys. Her daughters, of course, were expected to marry, which they all did before they turned sixteen. They hadn't been expected to move so far from home, but they each did that too.

Instead, Mr. Pop chose farmwork, and Uncle Roger headed downstate to Brunswick to attend Bowdoin College and then worked two jobs to pay his way through Harvard Law School. Uncle Roger had been courted by some fancy Boston and New York law firms that had been around as long as this country, but his dream was to practice law in his "own home, great state of Maine."

But though he moved back to his home state, Uncle Roger steered clear of his hometown, choosing Bangor, with its symphony and visiting ballets and plays, with its art museums, with its interesting dinner party guests. All things one finds in a university town and all things key to wooing a woman like Aunt Dot.

I suppose that every family has a bright, shining star. Uncle Roger was ours. And not even Aunt Dot, who hailed from one of Maine's oldest families, could resist Uncle Roger's shine. Even when Aunt Dot's family worried about his prominent role with Indian affairs, they couldn't help but beam along with the rest of us as Uncle Roger rose in stature in state government.

Where Mayor Crawford asked Mr. Pop to sit on the Indian Rights Council for our local area, it was Governor Cross who requested that Uncle Roger join the effort to work on Indian rights for the whole the state of Maine. It was interesting that both brothers were working toward the same goals from different places and in different ways. Sometimes I wondered if Mr. Pop ever got sick of having a brother that shone so. But I doubted it, since Uncle Roger's shine helped illuminate Mr. Pop's causes as well.

Last Christmas when Uncle Roger and Aunt Dot stayed with us for a few days, Uncle Roger expounded about issues the council was taking on.

"It'll be a long fight," Uncle Roger had said. "There's plenty of opposition, especially at the state level. I think the Passamaquoddy and the Penobscot will be able to vote in the next national election, but I don't think it looks good for the Maliseet or Micmacs."

Uncle Roger had looked at Mr. Pop. Both of them sighed and looked weary, or like they were recalling a shared, held-back secret.

"Some days I'm not sure if it's worth the fight," Uncle Roger said to Mr. Pop. "Except I keep thinking of Father's description of a good man, a godly man, and what is required of him. He would always quote Micah 6:8."

At this Mr. Pop had smiled, nodded his head, and joined Uncle Roger in his recitation: "He hath shewed thee, O man, what is good," they said together, chanting like the eight- and ten-year-olds they'd been thirty-some years before, "and what doth the Lord require of thee, but to do justly, and to love mercy, and to walk humbly with thy God?"

Then Mr. Pop had said, "If working for the benefit of the Indians isn't to do justly, then I don't know what is. I don't understand why more people don't see this."

Just yesterday I might have thought Mr. Pop had forgotten this definition of "to do justly"; today he remembered. But now all I could think about was the day after tomorrow, the day Uncle Roger would arrive, a day I was most anxious for, a day that felt like it would never come.

My stomach churned with a queasiness I felt rise into my throat. I pictured Mick sitting in jail, hungry and cold. I wondered if Mr. Pop got to be near him or if Mick could at least see or hear that Mr. Pop was trying to help. I wondered if anyone had sent for Mick's parents, Ansley and Miss Louise, yet. I wondered if anyone remembered that Mick wasn't legally an adult yet. Could you even put a sixteen-year-old in jail? Would they have if it would've been Tommy Birger or another white boy standing over Old Man Stringer? Wouldn't they have at least stopped to ask him questions before they dragged him off?

For the first time, I began to see the stark reality of being born Maliseet. Mick's reality for sixteen years. Being Maliseet in the Maine Northwoods was more than living on a dump or being ridiculed on the playground. It was more than going hungry or becoming desperate for a drink. Being Maliseet was about being seen as less than human. At least, by too many folks. We'd learned in school that in this country a man was innocent until proven guilty; I readied myself for the reality of how that played out when Maliseet weren't considered men.

Chapter Nine

I didn't remember falling asleep. For the first moments after my eyes blinked open and my shoulders stretched themselves up toward my head, I had no idea where I was or why. As the room came into focus around me, so did my memory. While I would've loved to have luxuriated in the belief, even for a few moments, that what my mind was reminding me of had only been a dream, I wouldn't give in to that. Especially not with the plate of Saltines and glass of water resting on the lace doily.

I started to swing my legs off the sofa when Mother's and Mr. Pop's murmurs rumbled out of the dining room. I settled back into the sofa, closed my eyes, and concentrated on hearing their words. I'd get more information if they thought I couldn't hear.

"I don't know, Geneva. Must've been ten people inside Fulton's and on that sidewalk saying exactly what Frankie says he saw."

"But you know as well as I do that they're afraid to contradict him!"

"Of course. And Sheriff Cain knows that too, but . . ."

"But what, Paul? But what? But he'll do nothing. Just like no one else here will do anything to help that poor boy."

"*We're* doing something, Geneva. Roger's making calls and then heading up. He told you that he'll even call the governor if he has to. Believe me, Governor Cross is not going to want this made into a big issue, especially with the election coming up."

"Honey, is that you?"

Mother had heard me clear my throat. There was only so long I could look at that glass of water without realizing how parched I was. After sitting up and taking a sip, I answered her.

"If you're feeling up to it," Mr. Pop called, "why don't you come in here. Join us for a sandwich. I can fill you in."

I decided not to pretend I hadn't heard and began my questions before I even reached the table. "So everyone believes Mr. Carmichael? That Mick killed Old Man?"

"Yes and no," Mr. Pop said with a small smile. "Folks seem to believe that Mick *tried* to kill Old Man. But since Old Man was taken to the hospital, with a heart still beating, no one actually believes that Mick's a murderer."

"Not yet," Mother snapped.

"True enough, Geneva. Not yet. Old Man's heart was still beating. But he's not in good health and he was out cold, enough to make him seem dead at first glance."

A wild hope soared within me. "So are they going to let Mick out of jail?" I asked.

"Well, we've got to see where Judge Dodd sets bail. It'll be at least tomorrow until he can get released at all. Uncle Roger will have to sort through that."

"But when Old Man himself was arrested last year, he was released within the hour. You said they decided it didn't need to go further than scaring him a little."

"That's right," Mr. Pop said. "But this is different. We aren't talking about public intoxication; we're talking about attempted murder. That's what the sheriff is calling it, at least."

"It's also different," Mother said, staring straight at the cold bean sandwich on her plate, "because we're talking about a Maliseet."

Mr. Pop nodded. "It's true. This is all different. Which is why we need to pray. Hard. But we also need to sit tight, and not do or say anything rash, and wait until your uncle Roger gets here."

"So we're just supposed to stay *here* and do nothing, just pray, 'Oh, God, let Uncle Roger fix this'?" I asked. "Has anyone even gotten Ansley and Miss Louise? What about Joseph? Can I go get him?"

Mr. Pop shook his head slowly and looked toward Mother until finally saying, "They already got Ansley. Found him at McGillicuddy's Tavern actually. He passed out there last night. Never made it home."

"So Ansley got to see Mick, then. He's there with him?"

"Not exactly. The sheriff decided Ansley wasn't fit to see Mick yet. Sent him back to the Flats to rest and pull himself together."

"Pull himself together? For jail?" I looked at Mother who was still staring at the cold bean sandwich on her plate.

"So Mick's alone there now?" I asked. "Then I need to get back there. I need to go!"

I pushed my chair back from the table and slammed my hands on the table. The plate of sandwiches rattled along with the silverware.

"Mercy, please sit," Mr. Pop said. "You are going nowhere. *I,* however, am. Bud and I are heading out to the Flats right now. I need to ask how they feel about Roger coming to represent Mick. Plus, we've got broccoli and cauliflower to cut besides two or three rows of peas that need picking. I promised your mother I'd get some weeding done in her garden and I thought maybe Joseph could lend a hand today, actually."

I hadn't cried yet. Not for Mick sitting alone in jail, not with the fury toward Mr. Carmichael bubbling up inside. But the thought of Joseph, struggling to breathe in his terror, finally pushed the tears out.

"You think Louise'll let him come?" Mother asked. "She's got one boy in jail; you think she'll let another one out of her sight?"

"I don't know," Mr. Pop said. "But I *do* know that when I was praying with the deputy on the ride back to the farm, God put his name on my heart and in my mind. That boy's got an anger that's burned in him since he was born blue. It was like his first gasps and wheezes into this world were fueled by an inborn knowledge of his lot in life. I'm worried about what he might take it in his head to do."

Mother nodded. "It's a miracle if they aren't all as mad as that boy. Certainly, they have every right to be."

"But what about Mick?" I asked. "Sure, Joe's going to be mad, but shouldn't we be figuring out how to help Mick and not just how to soothe Joseph?"

"Right now," Mr. Pop said, "I'd venture to guess that soothing Joseph is the best way to help Mick. Not much more we can do until tomorrow. Well, except pray."

Mr. Pop reached his hand across the table toward mine. I grabbed it and reached my own hand toward Mother's. Together, our arms formed an unfinished triangle on the dining room table as we lowered our heads together.

"Dear heavenly Father," Mr. Pop began, "help us in our hour of need. Emotions are running high, and we pray for the safety of all involved. Please put Thy hand of protection on Mick as he waits in jail. Help him to not despair. Please, Lord, help Frankie's anger to simmer down. Keep him from saying things he'll come to regret. Please keep Ansley and others in the Flats from drinking their pain away, and help Miss Louise, and all of us, hold on to hope. I pray this in Jesus' precious name."

Before he said amen, Mr. Pop invited us to share our words. Mother prayed for peace. I prayed for a miracle. I prayed that God would soften Mr. Carmichael's heart toward Mick and that the others would be brave enough to tell the truth. At least, I prayed for this out loud. Secretly, silently, I prayed just for Mick. That he would be okay. That Uncle Roger could get him released. And for the first time, I prayed that God would help Mick and me escape this place. I prayed that someday we could live in peace, up five flights of stairs, with lasagna-making neighbors. Just like Marjorie and Glenn.

A knock, followed by the squeak of the front screen door, became our "amen."

"Who on earth?" Mother asked as she rose, smoothing her

apron as she stepped away from the table.

Mr. Pop and I sat in silence, each listening to her heels click on the wood floors, each fearing what this knock might bring. We both let our breath out and gave each other weary smiles when we heard, "Tommy! What a pleasant surprise. We're just finishing our bean sandwiches, but I'd be happy to fetch you one if you're hungry."

"No, ma'am," Tommy said. "I'm fine. Thank you."

I stood to greet Tommy as he now stepped under the thick-trimmed doorjamb. I tried to smile at him, as though I was happy to see him, as though, perhaps, he was just the person I needed to see. But my eyes, quickly brimming with tears, betrayed me.

His small, sad smile coupled with a tiny tilt of his head told me he understood perfectly. Too perfectly.

"I heard about Mick," Tommy said. "And I know he's your friend. I'm so sorry."

"Thank you," was all I could say as Mr. Pop patted Tommy on the back, offering his own hello before announcing he was off again. This time finishing the trip to the Flats we'd aborted.

Mother shooed Tommy and me back onto the porch with promises of milk and the freshly baked date cookies she'd made that morning. When I first smelled them after waking from my nap, I understood the stress Mother felt with this news. While Mother could fix lunch fit for kings and presidents and serve it up for twenty-odd farmhands without batting an eye, and while she could summon flowers from the rough Maine ground pretty enough to glory-up the Lord's Table every Sunday, cookies—particularly her own grandmother's date cookies—got baked only when Mother needed her mind on something else. She wrestled with the recipe, silently cursed the stick-and-goo of the dough and the trouble of rolling them out, then fretted about them turning out right.

The few times in my life I'd known Mother and Mr. Pop to be in a bit of a marital pickle was from the sudden presence of these cookies. Mother had baked a lot of them this summer.

Tommy sat down on our swing without being directed. I leaned against the porch rail, hoping he understood I couldn't sit next to him. Not anymore. Not like I had these past three weeks when I'd feigned interest. When I'd done my best to sigh and coo, and sometimes even giggle, when I'd see him at church, or when Tommy would stop by on his way to fish. That little game was up. I hoped he understood this.

"Listen," Tommy said. "I know you never really liked me. I get that. I had just . . ."

I scrunched my eyebrows at him, suddenly curious about this Tommy I'd never actually noticed.

"I had just hoped that maybe I could *make* you like me. You know, like you like *him*."

"Like I like Mick? Like a friend?"

Tommy laughed and then looked down. He closed his eyes and took a deep breath before going on.

"Not like a friend, Mercy. Let's just stop that, okay? I mean, look at you. If Mick was just your friend, you wouldn't look like that!"

"Like what? How do I look?"

"Like—like your heart was just hammered to bits. If *I* were in jail . . . heck, if *Molly* were in jail, you wouldn't look like this."

"You or Molly wouldn't *be* in jail. So that works out."

"That's true. We're not the murdering sort."

I felt the blood drain from my face, and yet instead of feeling faint, all I could think of was decking Tommy Birger. I stared at his face, feeling my own expression harden and wondered if I could time a punch right, and clock him good, while matching my own swing to the rhythm of the porch swing.

"I meant that you and Molly wouldn't be in jail because you're not Maliseet. Because nobody'd ever believe Mr. Birger's son could ever hurt a fly, let alone kill a drunk."

Tommy started to respond but then shook his head and stomped his feet to the ground, stopping the swing.

"Listen, Mercy. I'm sorry. This isn't how I meant this to go. I came here to tell you it was okay. That I knew you don't like me that way. That I knew you don't really want to go to the festival with me. And that I won't tell anybody how you feel about Mick."

I felt my face soften, but I continued my glare.

"Regardless of how you feel about me," Tommy said, "I really like you. I always have. You may never want to be my sweetheart, but I'm not going to treat you any different because of that. I'll be your friend. Or I'll keep my distance. Or I'll be or do whatever you need me to be. Lots of folks are going to be saying stuff about you, and I wanted you to know that I won't be one of them."

For the third time that day, tears flooded my eyes. I tried to tell him thanks, but the words wouldn't form. Where just moments before I'd wanted to slug him, now I could've hugged him. *Grace*, Mr. Pop would've attributed this to.

I saw what Molly had for so long seen in him. A kind boy whose wild streak skirted carefully just under his quiet exterior and good manners and popped out occasionally in a flash of his eyes or a pull of his lips.

"You know, Tommy, you're pretty smart, but you don't know everything."

"No? But I'm close, right?"

"Yes. Very close. Except I would actually like to go to the festival with you very much."

"You would?"

I nodded. "I would. But so would Molly. I wonder if . . ."

"I could take you *and* Molly?"

Our eyes met and we both laughed.

"It won't kill you," I said.

"No." Tommy shook his head. "It won't. But do you think Mr. Carmichael is going to take his family to the festival and let his daughter out of his sight for even a moment? Seems unlikely to me."

Tommy had a point. I shrugged. "I don't know," I said. "But if she goes, I promise: she won't walk around staring at you all dewey-eyed like she does in class."

"Promise?"

"Besides, this is *Molly* we're talking about. Beautiful Molly!"

"She's beautiful Molly all right," Tommy said. "It's just that I'm doing this for beautiful Mercy."

Both of us turned as Mother pushed open the screen door, and set down a plate of date cookies and two cups of milk perched on an ash-woven tray. Tommy and I both stared at the tray as we thanked Mother. We stayed quiet, studying the platters' intricate designs for the first moments after Mother went back inside, then each chewing the date cookies and sipping our milk dutifully.

Tommy bit into another date cookie and then broke the silence. "What do you see in him, anyway?"

"What do you mean?"

"I mean, what does Mick have that I don't?"

"I'm not sure that's a fair question," I said. "Or, at least, I don't think it's the *right* question. Because, honestly, Mick doesn't have anything that you don't have."

"Except you."

I laughed. "Oh yeah. Right, except me."

I tilted my head back and counted the lines in the blue wainscoted porch ceiling, while I searched for words to express out loud what it was I loved about Mick. I'd never done this before. Molly knew I loved Mick, but she didn't know why. She just figured the obvious: Mick was dreamy. No way around that. Mick's face, perfectly sculpted and framed by the shine of his shoulder-length black hair, rivaled that of any Hollywood leading man. A life of work on the farm and of play in the forest had given him a physique that Molly once said would stop traffic in Times Square.

Neither of us knew anything about Times Square traffic firsthand, but it sounded about right. I don't remember when he changed from being a rough-and-tumble boy full of bruises and brambles and awkward angles to the man he'd become: one of strength. And not just physical strength but strength of character, as Mr. Pop called it. The boy Mick who loved running through the woods and splashing in streams and digging in dirt hadn't left the man Mick had become. Yet somehow, they'd all deepened, shaped the core of who he was as they shaped the twists and ridges, the rises and falls of his form.

I looked a moment at Tommy, still trying to figure out how to answer his question. What *did* Mick have that Tommy didn't? Tommy had many of Mick's physical qualities. Though Tommy's hair was as wispy and fair as Mick's was sleek and dark and though Tommy's skin was as pale and freckled as Mick's was tan and even, both enjoyed their share of second looks and secret glances from girls of all ages. Certainly, farmwork and endless hours on the baseball fields and swimming in the Meduxnekeag River had transformed Tommy's chubby-cheeked, baby-fattened self into a young man who'd probably stop a car or two in Times Square himself. He certainly did on Main Street.

But it was more than the physical I saw in Mick. Because at fifteen I loved him for the things I'd loved about him when I was five and he was all of six. I loved him for his love of this world, for the way this world was so part of who he was and all he hoped to be. I loved him for the way he saw himself—and me, with him—in this world, how he recognized that his every movement, every moment rippled through the rest of nature. Though Mick had yet to acknowledge the Creator behind the creation he loved, my hope was that one day he would.

But I didn't tell Tommy Birger any of this. I gave him the best answer that I could: "It's not that Mick *has* anything you don't. In fact, I think most of us would agree that he's got an awful lot less."

Tommy looked bewildered but said nothing.

"Mick lives on a *dump*, in a shack, for Pete's sake! You live on a farm in a beautiful home with shutters and flower boxes. You sleep alone—in your own bed, in your own room."

Tommy smirked. "So, you're saying somebody's sharing Mick's bed?"

I slapped his shoulder, feigned anger but then smiled. "You are terrible, Tommy. If Mr. Pop or even Ellery hears you with that fresh mouth, that'll be your last date cookie on this porch."

Tommy laughed too. "I'm sorry. I really am. And sheesh, I've seen the Flats. I know how they live. I hear how folks talk about them. And honestly, I hate how they'll be talking about Mick. He's a nice enough kid. If he weren't Maliseet, we'd be friends. We'd have been horsing around in the Meduxnekeag and playing catch in the front yard. But with all he doesn't have, all I can see is what he does have: you. You seem like a nice prize for having to grow up on a dump."

"And how about for sitting in a jail cell, all alone, because Mr. Carmichael hates Maliseet? Am I a good prize for that too? How about we move you out there this winter and see how you feel about it then?" Though the prize talk hinted at flattery, it settled into pure anger in my soul.

Tommy lifted his foot up to the swing and retied his shoe, buying time, it seemed.

"Can we just start over?" he asked.

"Start what over?"

"Today. The reason I came over."

I shrugged.

Tommy grabbed my hand and looked straight into my eyes. I froze, terrified to think what might come next.

"Mercy, the thing is, I like you. I care about you a lot. I wish you were my girlfriend. But I know you can't be. Or that you won't be. But I still like you and I'll always care about you and I want to help you." Tommy stared ahead, out across the farm and made a decision. "Even if it means helping Mick."

"You want to help Mick?" My eyes widened.

"No. I want to help *you*. And if helping Mick helps you, I'll do it. Whatever I can do, just tell me. I'll do it."

I smiled and asked, "Ever visit anybody in jail?"

Chapter Ten

J oseph stepped out of the car. As he looked around, took in the fields and the house and the woods beyond it all, I realized this moment was one he'd waited for, wished for, for such a long time.

The circumstances, however, were completely unwelcome.

For the dream to play out like Joseph had imagined, Mick would be with him along with his dad and Mr. Socoby and Clarence and some of the other men. This was not the scenario Joseph had wanted. I could see that Mr. Pop was right to get Joseph to come help on the farm. I saw his eyes flash as he got out of the car, anger seething just below the surface.

When Mr. Pop had visited the Flats the day before, he told me about how he'd been met with the same kind of anger. Though the Maliseet understood Mr. Pop to be on their side when sides were drawn, when he arrived at the Flats, Mr. Socoby and Ansley had met him by the road and warned him away.

"The women are upset," Ansley had said coldly, his jaw twitching. So Mr. Pop had told them quickly that Roger was on his way, that Roger had influence and ability to get Mick not only released but the charges dropped. Mr. Pop told them that if they wanted, Roger was willing to do this *pro bono*. He reminded them that this was the same Roger they'd run with as boys, the same one who'd splashed with them in the Meduxnekeag, who'd spent afternoons tracking moose and bear and who'd laughed all the way home with them after they'd found that moose, and Roger'd nearly peed his pants with them. Mr. Socoby reminded Mr. Pop that Frankie Carmichael had run with them too in those days. Much had changed. Now they didn't know if they could trust Roger, whom they hadn't seen since he left for college over two decades earlier.

Mr. Pop understood that they could choose their own lawyers, that they might want to hire someone with no ties to the community, but Mr. Pop wanted them to know Roger would work *for* them on this very local, very personal level just as he was working for them and the Micmacs as well as the Passamaquoddy and Penobscot tribes that claimed Maine land with his work on the council for the governor.

They had agreed to think about it and to at least see Roger when he arrived the day after next. Mr. Socoby and Ansley had also agreed that Joseph should come to the farm, that he needed something besides weaving to keep him busy and out of trouble. So when Mr. Pop left them, saying Ellery would be back the next morning to fetch only Joseph, Mr. Socoby and Ansley had nodded slowly, their jaw muscles looser but their eyes still steeled by a rage and hurt Mr. Pop told me he realized he could never fully understand.

I hopped up from the porch swing and jogged to the car, grabbed Joseph and linked arms with him, like I'd done with him whenever I'd picked up men, Mick too, at the Flats. It was my attempt to cheer him up. It never worked, but I never stopped.

I'd woken up cheerier than I expected to. The call we'd gotten from Uncle Roger after dinner, telling us that he'd talked to a colleague in Presque Isle who'd come down today to talk to Judge Dodd before Uncle Roger would arrive tomorrow, shored up my faith and brightened my mood. All would be back to normal before we knew it. I was certain.

"Joe, thanks for coming," I said. "You're a sight for sore eyes."

Joseph gave no response, so my nerves kept talking, desperately trying to lighten the mood.

"I thought I'd have to cut all the broccoli by myself," I said. "I'm tired of being the only one with green fingernails and fingertips. I could use some help picking peas too. We're all out at the roadside stand."

My ball of nerves pushed out the words a mile a minute. But when once again, Joseph said nothing, I paused to look at him. Somehow, as I looked into his face, his own dark eyes and slick hair, Joseph's presence calmed me. There was no mistaking that he was Mick's brother. It felt like a little piece of Mick was standing in front of me. Before, I'd only ever seen this boy's weaknesses and his illness and his bitterness, but now I could see his strength and his promise. The same every other thirteen-year-old should brim with. I pulled him forward.

"Let's head to the shed and grab the linoleum knives for cutting broccoli and head back toward the northeast field," I said, still unable to slow my speed of speech. "I'll grab a bushel basket for the peas, and we can both work at filling it. Mr. Pop said he'd be happy if we got one bushel between us to bring back up to the road stand. The field of peas is adjacent to the broccoli field. If we get fifteen head of broccoli that's good enough, then we can get to picking the peas. Sound good? I'll grab some chicken feed from the shed, too, and drop it off in the coop on the way by."

As Joseph mumbled a "sounds fine," I realized I really didn't want to leave room for him to talk, at least not until we headed down the farm road and gotten a few more paces between us and the shed. I didn't know what or how much he would say about any of this, but somehow I knew it wasn't stuff I wanted others to be able to hear. Not even Mr. Pop.

But Joseph said nothing. Not as we walked to the field with our knives and bushels. Not as I knelt on the dirt, slicing heads of broccoli from the ground, before passing them to Joseph who lumped them into their baskets. And not as we lifted the bushels together and waddled them over to the stand, arranging them so they "flowered up and over" the rim, just as Mother had taught me.

As we headed to the field of peas, I could no longer wait.

"Joe," I said. "I know Mr. Pop came to the Flats yesterday to talk about my uncle Roger getting involved. I'm dying to hear. What did your mom and dad say?"

Joseph snorted and knelt down toward the peas. He plucked a few and dropped them into the basket before shaking his head and answering. "What'd'ya think they said? They know just as well as you or me or your Mr. Pop or your uncle Roger or that stinkin' Mr. Carmichael that nothin'll happen unless a white man gets involved. Same old story. I mean, do you think we'd just let Mick rot in jail? Your uncle Roger is our *only* option. Of course *Maliseet* can't take care of our own."

This sarcastic tone was a side of Joseph I rarely saw. Sometimes, when Mick had said no to him for the umpteenth time he'd asked to come work on the farm, it'd show, but this time it had an angry edge. His attitude put me on guard.

"Mr. Pop doesn't think you *can't* take care of Mick."

"Oh, right. Sorry. He just thinks we *won't*."

I snapped off another few peapods and stood up, towering above Joseph.

"Mr. Pop thinks *no such thing*! You need to apologize this minute."

"For what?"

"For insulting a man who's trying to help you. He's worried sick for you and for Mick and for your family and for everyone."

Joseph stood up as well. Though I had a couple inches on him, with his shoulders pulled back and his chin up, he was bigger than ever before. Only his uneven breaths diminished the power he tried so hard to convey.

"He's worried *now* but has he been so worried before? It's not like Mick being in jail is the worst thing that's ever happened to him. Or to me. Or to any of us."

I stepped backward, nearly tripping over the plants. "What do you mean?" I asked.

Joseph shook his head and then nodded toward the road. "Car," he said.

I rushed over and pulled out two heads of broccoli for the customer who had just driven up to our farm stand. I told her I could have a sack of peas for her in five minutes if she was willing to wait.

The woman agreed and then looked over at Joseph picking the peas and tossing them into the basket. "If he speaks English," she said, "tell that Indian boy to go easy on my peas."

I nodded my head at the woman and stepped over to the already picked peas. I'd always hoped the attitude toward the Maliseet was just a local thing. I'd dreamed that elsewhere in this state, in this country even, nobody would care about a person based on when or how you got to this land, but this woman, whose very comment betrayed that she was from away, proved how wrong I was.

But I smiled as I handed her the bag of peas and as I took her money, just as Mr. Pop had taught me to. Some customers will be rude, he had told me, but we never would be. I turned to join Joseph in the pea field when I saw Ellery nearly running toward me.

"Just got a call from Nelson's in town," Ellery said. "They told your mother they got some big order for their broccoli salad. The chef—the honest-to-goodness chef himself that Nelson's just hired—is coming over in person to check the quality. Needs fifteen head. You and Joseph need a hand?"

I looked at Joseph, steady at work in the fields, pulling pod after pod from their stems, giving each one a little look before tossing it into the bushel. I had cut the broccoli myself, thinking his eyes and hand wouldn't be keen enough to pick the best ones and cut them with the love Mother claimed they needed. But as I watched him with the peas, I knew I'd been wrong.

"Nope," I said. "We'll get it. Tell Mother not to worry."

"Sure thing, Miss Mercy. Your mother would have me tell you to not be goofing off and pounding sand out there. If your mother can make this hotshot chef happy, maybe he'll spread the word and she can pick up some business. She deserves to be Broccoli Queen of Maine. Dontcha think?"

I didn't. If Broccoli Queen would be anything like Potato Blossom Queen, I figured it'd only cause more trouble than it's worth.

"All right, then, back to work," Ellery called, as he ran toward the house.

I walked over to Joseph.

"Was he checking up on me? Making sure I wasn't pocketing any peas?"

"Ellery? Hardly. We need to cut some more broccoli. The new chef from Nelson's." Joseph looked blank. "He needs broccoli for some salad or something. I'm going to need your help this time."

Joseph nodded and pulled one more pod before standing. "Leave this here then?"

I looked into the bushel. He'd worked fast, filling it nearly a third of the way with farm-stand perfect peas while I'd talked to Ellery.

"Let's put this out at the stand, actually," I said. "Then people can look at your perfect peas while we make our way up there."

"They aren't *my* peas," Joseph reminded me. "Your mother's. Nothing is mine."

"Well, the work is. Mr. Pop says all we can control or really own is the effort we give something. He'd say you owned this. He'd say it's like you've been doing this all your life."

Joseph sniffed. "Easy for your Mr. Pop to say. I'm pretty sure he won't think I *owned* these peas when it comes time to pay me. He'll keep the profit. Give us a little bit and keep the rest. Just like you all do."

"We're not all so bad, Joseph. Not like you think. Mr. Pop is a good man. And if he didn't make a profit, there'd be no work to hire out. Think about it."

"He's better than the rest," Joseph conceded. "But *good*? I dunno. Do good people live like this while letting other folks live on dumps?"

I sighed as we reached the broccoli field and set down the knives we'd carried over. I'd forgotten that we needed to get the bushel basket from the farm stand.

"Walk with me, Joe." I grabbed his hand and pulled him toward the road, forcing him to walk faster than he might have liked to. As we emptied the bushel of the picked broccoli and arranged it on the farm stand's green linoleum-covered counter, I said, "I understand, Joseph. I really do. How all this is so frustrating for you. How all this looks. How *wrong* all this feels."

"Oh, you understand, do you?" Joseph asked.

"Ugh. Okay. I get your point. I know how the system works, but Mr. Pop wanted to be respectful of your parents. That's why he asked first and didn't just have my uncle Roger show up at the courthouse."

Joseph laughed as I looked down the road to make sure no cars were coming before we headed back to the broccoli field.

"Merce, you *don't* get it. You *don't* understand and you never will. You can't. Because you're from here. Because you live like this." His eyes swept across the farm, taking in our house and the fields. "Because you think everything you do is an act of charity, of being good to the poor Maliseet. You think you can offer a little work and make it all fine. Make it okay that your great-great-great-whatevers *stole* our land and have made life a living you-know-what for us ever since."

I drew breath in quickly. "Joseph, that's not true! I do know. I *do* understand. Mick told me."

"Oh, right. *Mick* told you." Joseph laughed again. "You and Mick love to meet in that little fort you made. And he tells you *everything*."

"He does! Well, he did. But how did you know about our fort?"

"Everyone at the Flats knows about it. And about how you feel about each other. And everyone knows what you want is impossible." I felt myself sinking at his words. He went on. "If you were a different kind of girl, maybe. But you're Mr. Millar's daughter. Your father is one of the most respected men in Watsonville, heck, in all of Aroostook County. It can't work. Everyone knows that but you and Mick."

"Not true!"

"Why don't you just back off? You two are making everything worse, just like Glenn and Marjorie. All for your precious love." He singsonged the word. "Go ahead and let the mighty Uncle Roger step in like a great white hero. But leave Mick alone after that. If you care about him at all, you would."

I jerked back, stung by Joseph's words. Though not just because they were cutting and mean, but because somehow I knew they were what I needed to hear. The truth was, what Mick and I had—or the sweet, secret romance I'd once seen it as and maybe wished back—was all over. I couldn't face the fact that it might need to end.

But Joseph was right. If I cared about Mick or Joseph or the Maliseet at all, I had to give it up.

Chapter Eleven

We walked on in silence. I'd been taught in Sunday school that all people were created in the image of our Creator God, which made us equal and equally loved by God. I also knew it was an easier message for me to accept when I went to bed every night in a house that had indoor plumbing, a woodstove to keep me warm, and a soft bed with clean sheets and blankets, not to mention a full refrigerator.

But Mr. Pop hadn't always had these things. He'd known hunger and hardship. He understood that doing good was more than dropping money into the offering plate on Sunday morning.

"You could be right about me and Mick," I said. "Maybe that does need to end. Maybe it has made things worse. But you're not right about me or Mr. Pop or even Uncle Roger. They're trying to make things *better*. To change things. They're fighting for Indian rights, and that includes the Maliseet."

"Because we can't do that ourselves."

I gave up. I wasn't sure why Mick and I had always been able to talk so easily about this stuff, but Joseph and I were at odds. I handed him his knife back at the field, never more grateful for work that would keep our hands busy and the conversation on what we were doing.

"Watch me a minute," I said. "We need to leave about a six-inch stalk on the broccoli when you cut it. Keeps it fresh longer."

My instructions were curt, to the point. Joseph nodded.

"And make sure to cut any heads that look like the flower could open. Tight heads are preferable, but we want to make sure we grab anything that might soon go bad. Let's count out loud, so we know who's cut how many and that way we won't cut more than fifteen."

"Okay." Joseph gave a minimal response. He knew my reaction to his words wasn't positive. Although I'd just conceded that he might be right about Mick and me, I was backpedaling, at least in my mind. Maybe I was a bit naive, but my feelings for Mick went beyond a teenage crush or physical attraction. I was drawn to Mick rather than Tommy because of Mick's vision for a better future. And not just a better future for his people. He knew that if Maliseet and Whites could be treated as equals, it would transform the Maine we both loved. He didn't like that Glenn and Marjorie had run away. Mick knew that wasn't the way to do things, by running. Yet he understood why they did it. After all, we both wanted what Glenn and Marjorie now had: a new life in a new place with mutual respect from neighbors and equal opportunity from employers. That was a future worth working toward and praying for.

"But what if you're wrong?" I asked.

"I just cut number seven," Joe said.

"I have eight and nine," I said back to him. "What if Glenn and Marjorie and me and Mick make things *better* ultimately?"

Joseph paused in his cutting of the broccoli but said nothing, before continuing on.

"If Mick and I can't—if we ended our friendship, doesn't Mr. Carmichael win?"

Joseph crawled over to the basket with two heads in his hands. "Ten and eleven," he said, before crawling back.

"Two more each. Then we're done. Ready for Monsieur le Chef?" I tried to pronounce it with a French accent to amuse Joe. It didn't.

"Looks like he's here." Joseph lifted his chin toward the road and I stood up. Joseph handed me his last two heads and we headed over to the chef, whose big smile and outstretched hand greeted us before any words. He'd pulled up in a 1945 Plymouth

Deluxe Coupe with nothing at all deluxe about it. His happy de-
meanor didn't match the road-weary vehicle.

"Salvatore Barone," he said as I shook his hand. Oops, I
thought. Not French.

"I'm Mercy. This is Joseph."

Joseph hesitated a bit when the chef's hand reached for his, but
after Chef said, "You think I bite? Food is what I bite. People, I love!"
even Joseph couldn't resist, offering both a smile and his hand.

"Now," said Chef Barone, "where is this superb broccoli my
customers have been asking for?"

Joseph turned around and pulled the basket off the counter.
Chef Barone picked two off the top, turning them over and lifting
one head to his nose.

I made a face.

"What?" Chef asked. "You don't smell your broccoli?"

"I barely want to eat it," I said.

Chef laughed, almost drowning out Joseph, who spoke suddenly. "I smelled them," he said. "After I cut them from the ground."

Chef Barone stared a moment at Joseph, who stepped back.
When the chef didn't appear jolly, his face settled into a grimace
that, when taken in with his height and girth, made him terrifying.
Until his smile broke again.

"Wonderful! Wonderful, my boy!" Chef said. "And what did
they smell like?"

Joseph looked across the road, over the fields, and up toward
Mt. Katahdin as he thought. "Smells like the trees. After the rain."
Joseph smiled again. "If a moose has pooped nearby."

Chef Barone's sharp, hard laugh made me jump in my boots.

"Joseph, you are something else. And dead-on. I've always
thought broccoli smelled like wet trees, but I knew I was missing
something else. Moose poop it is! Though I come from New York,
and not too many moose in Brooklyn, so who can blame me?"

"Rat poop, maybe, then?" Joseph asked, desperate for more

laughter at his jokes. I wondered where this personable boy came from and where the sullen one had gone.

Chef obliged Joseph, offering a hearty laugh before saying, "No rat poop. That's one of the many things I will not miss about New York. Right up there with the crime and the crowds. Moose poop is a small price to pay for the second chance Hiram Nelson is giving me. Speaking of which, I'm looking for someone who could help with prep work in the kitchen. If your parents agree, would you be interested in giving it a shot?" He looked directly at Joseph when he said this. Joseph made no response and Chef Barone spoke again. "I know your smell is something else, but how's your hearing young man? I was talking to you."

Joseph continued to stare at the chef, stunned. I can't say I wasn't stunned myself. Chef Barone continued. "I can't leave a boy who cares about broccoli enough to *smell* it out here in these fields." He stared at Joseph for a moment, then said, "I think quick and I act quick. I have decided—a love of food like that can't be taught. I need your nose in my kitchen. Will you come?"

Chef Barone spoke in full animation, his hands punctuating each of his words.

Joseph had practically been rendered mute.

"Joe," I said, with a poke to his ribs, "answer Mr. Barone."

I saw Joseph's chest heaving a bit. His breathing had come so easy all morning, even as we rushed between the stand and the fields. After one deep breath, Joseph finally squeaked out a few words. "Sir, I'm here through the afternoon. I live near town and can come by the restaurant tomorrow if that's okay."

"Perfect! How about 10 a.m.? You can help prep for lunch, which is what I must now be off to do. I'm in a rush today. Two of my workers could not be here and we're short-staffed."

With one smooth motion for such a large man, Chef Barone was in his car, broccoli nicely bagged and in his backseat. He honked and waved as he drove away.

Joseph and I stood with our eyes watching the car disappear down the road.

"What just happened, Joseph?"

"I'm not really sure, but I think I just got a reason to leave the Flats every day."

"I think you did," I said. "But if we don't get at least a bushel of peas to sell, Mr. Pop might not let you leave here. Ever."

I laughed at my own attempt at a joke, hoping Joseph's mood would carry over. But it didn't. Joseph just turned and walked toward the pea field. I followed, eager to get back to the work, hoping Joe would talk more once we were set in the peace and rhythm of the middle of a row of peas. Molly and I had spent hours in conversation in this very place: unlike broccoli, picking peas meant no numbers to shout out, no precision cutting required. Just sitting across from each other picking and tossing the peas into the bushel basket.

"Mercy, you don't understand," Joseph said, surprising me. Sullen Joseph had returned. "As much as you think you do, you can't understand. You've never woken up in the morning to find your father passed out drunk on the kitchen floor or on the lawn outside or didn't even come home at night and you wondered where he was or what'd happened to him."

"But—"

"Wait. There are some things you need to know if you can't be talked into walking away from Mick."

"Okay," I said cautiously.

"I know my dad comes to work on the farm. He really appreciates the work. He tells us Mr. Pop is always fair, and when he pays, he rounds up for Maliseet workers. Not all the farmers do that. I know I just said he'd probably cheat me today, but I didn't mean it. I've always heard Dad say that Paul Millar is always fair. Sorry, Mercy."

I had heard that from Mick. I remember telling Mr. Pop about the way some other farmers cheated the Maliseet, but Mr. Pop didn't even flinch. He said, "Mercy, what other people do isn't any of our business. We must do what we know to be right in God's eyes."

I had gotten so angry. I fumed and sputtered, "How can people do this?"

Mr. Pop had let me grumble on a bit until he said, "Mercy, we can only control the way we do things on our farm. As long as we know we are living right and doing right by others and before God, then we can sleep in peace each night."

I knew Mr. Pop was right, but it didn't take the burn in my belly away.

Now I tossed a few pods in the bushel and threw a shriveled one right at Joseph.

"This is what I mean," I said. "I've always known this about the other farmers. I see that life isn't fair just because you look different than we do. I know money is always an issue, and that sometimes it gets really tough for your family to make it through the winter. And it's horrible that other folks don't pay you what's fair."

Joseph shook his head and threw the shriveled pod back at me.

"You're not even on the right track," he said. "Everyone knows about that stuff and still does nothing about, but that's not what I'm talking about. I'm talking about things no one sees."

My palms began to sweat. I ran them against the stiff denim of my jeans before pulling a few more pods. Picking peas certainly causes a person to break a sweat. But today was a perfect July day with temperatures in the seventies and a downright coastal breeze. If I hadn't known Maine better, I could've closed my eyes and believed we were sitting on that pier in Bar Harbor where Mother and Mr. Pop once took me. I knew I couldn't blame the sweat that once again formed on my palms.

As Joseph began to talk, he quit picking peas altogether.

"Did you ever notice Mick's expression every morning when I begged to go with him to your father's farm? He knew I couldn't handle a whole day of farmwork, not with my asthma, but he also knew what would happen by leaving me in the Flats."

I was fascinated but almost didn't want to hear. "Merce, when you grow up with less than nothing, bad things start to happen. When you go through the deep kinds of losses like the Maliseet have experienced, the soul of a people starts to die. We lost our land and our dignity . . . and in a way we lost our identity. Common decency went out the window a long time ago. It's not only the way Whites treat us, but it's how we treat each other." Joe stared at me, but I was silent. I couldn't think of a thing to say.

"We don't get along with other redskins either. All the tribes in Maine are at odds with each other. Look at how the Maliseets hate the Micmacs. Lots of bad blood there and I can't even tell you why. Probably something that happened a long time ago. Anyway, this is why your father only brings Maliseet to work on his farm. He knows there'd be trouble if he brought workers from both tribes."

I still said nothing. Though I wanted to contest and offer the reasons I knew Mr. Pop invited the Maliseet, and though I wanted to tell Joseph it'd all be okay, I simply gave in to the sense that my tongue should stay still and kept my eyes and fingers trained on the peas.

Joseph was silent too, for a few moments, as he pulled another handful of pods off the plants and tossed them into the bushel basket. He ran his fingers along its weave and then asked, "Ever wonder why there aren't piles of baskets to sell when you see my mom and other Maliseet women weaving every day when you come? They don't weave all day. They put on a good show for you or Ellery or your father or whoever comes to pick up the men to work, but they don't spend much time weaving anything besides potato baskets that farmers order for harvest season. Why bother? Watsonville isn't that big. Who's gonna buy the baskets? We don't buy them from each other. Pretty much it's only your mother who buys the things anyway."

A smile escaped as I thought of her pantry, piled high with baskets, delicately balanced but ready to topple at the slightest push. My smile faded as I remembered the note, hidden in the baskets, delivered by a man said to be dying because of Mick. I closed my eyes tight. Not sure I could hear any more of what Joseph had to say, let alone face all that was to come with Mick.

Joseph took two quick breaths and started again.

"When you have nothing to live for, you change. When we heard that the Penobscot and Passamaquoddy were getting voting rights and the Maliseet weren't getting smack, it was another slap in the face of the Maliseet. It was one more time that we'd been passed over. Dad thinks it maybe was our last chance." He paused before going on. "It was like another part of us, of the whole tribe, died the day that Dad and Mr. Socoby heard that news. They kept on working, whenever someone came to get them, but I'm telling you, the anger grew and it keeps growing. I know I feel it. Something's gotta give. I keep wondering what the tipping point is."

I stifled a shudder. Mr. Pop had been right to notice Joseph's anger. But he had noticed it far too late. I'd read the stories in history class of violent clashes between Indian tribes and the settlers in the old days. I wondered if that could happen even here and now. My blood chilled within me, and I couldn't hide my shiver this time as the cold ran from my head down through my body.

"Honestly, I don't know why Mick even gets up in the morning," Joseph said. "Who cares if there's no food? We barely have shelter. I still don't understand why he doesn't drink his life away like half the other men. Dad fights it, you know. He tries hard to not to give in to the lures of whiskey, but he's only human. A human with a broken spirit. Some mornings he's passed out on the floor, and you can't raise him no matter how hard you yell or try to shake him awake. You know he's not just a heavy sleeper, right?"

I nodded.

"I hate that he drinks," Joseph said. "I hate that they all do.

But I don't blame them. Not if their lives have been like mine and Mick's. Not if they had to go through what we do."

I was reeling from the barrage of words, trying to escape the meaning accompanying the words Joseph was spewing. "What else do you endure?"

Joseph shook his head and closed his eyes tight. By the time he opened them and met mine, his tanned face had reddened. His shoulders heaved as he tried to get better breaths.

"Another day, Mercy. Another day. Maybe Mick should tell you."

Joseph and I continued picking in silence. At lunch, he told Bud and Ellery and Mr. Pop about his new job offer and apologized for not being able to come back for a while. Mr. Pop stood to shake Joseph's hand and pat his back and then insisted that we set down our forks and offer a thanks to God.

Joseph would later tell me that day was the first and second time he'd prayed. Certainly, the first time he'd ever been prayed for. Definitely the first time anyone had thanked a god for him and his God-given talents. It was the first time anyone's family made him feel worthy.

But Joseph didn't let on about this as we worked that afternoon in the farm stand, though he did manage a bit of goofing off, making me laugh with his dead-on mimicry of every last customer we had that day.

As we walked back toward Ellery's waiting truck—the truck that would drive Joseph back home to the Flats and whatever horror really awaited him there—Joseph apologized.

"For what?" I asked.

"For being harsh about your dad. He *is* a good man. It's just hard."

I looped my arm through his and stopped short of telling him I knew. Instead, I said, "I love Mick and Mr. Pop does too. 'Like a son,' Mr. Pop told me just before we saw him and Old Man Stringer, just before this whole mess."

Joseph's boyish bicep tightened under my grip. The anger rising once again.

"So you know what that means?" I asked.

"That you'll work hard to get him out of jail."

"Yes," I said. "Mr. Pop will, Uncle Roger will, we all will. But it means something else."

Joseph and I stopped on the gravel, just shy of where the rounded, white potato truck waited with its hood up. Ellery was clanging on something.

"It means I love you and Mr. Pop loves you. If Mick is like a son to Mr. Pop, then so is his brother."

Joseph smiled the tiniest bit.

"And I know that Mr. Pop is far from the perfect father. I mean, half the time he loves *me* like a son and forgets I'm his daughter!"

Joseph laughed.

"But when Mr. Pop loves someone, it means he's *for* them. Never against them. He's for you, on your side."

Joseph nodded. "And I'm sorry I was mean about your uncle," he said. "If he wasn't coming up, honest, I don't know what we'd do. Nobody has money to hire a lawyer. I mean, besides Glenn, maybe, and he's gone. So we all appreciate your uncle Roger, no matter what I said earlier. I want Mick out of jail. Whatever it takes. I want this mess over. And I don't want Old Man Stringer to die."

Joseph's eyes watered up a bit. "Old Man is my friend," he said. "He'd come take me out during the day. Did you know that? It was like he understood. Of course, he did. Mick would never have hurt him."

I hugged Joseph. "I know that. We all do. And when Uncle Roger gets here, he'll make sure the police and the judge do too."

"Ready to go there, Joe?" Ellery said, adding the slam of the hood for punctuation. "Turns out that rumble we heard this morning was nothing at all. Tightened a few screws and she's good to go. Like eating pie."

"I'm ready," Joseph said. "But now I'm in the mood for pie." He turned to me and put up a hand.

"'Bye, Joe. Thanks for your help today. Say hi to the chef for me tomorrow."

Joseph smiled, a smile I now recognized as being so like his brother's. Though I'd loved the pristine porcelain smile that so often emanated from Mick whenever I saw him, seeing it echoed in Joseph made me realize behind that smile was the reality that all was not quite right in Mick's world. Once I'd thought if he'd come with me to college, if we'd get married, and get him off the Flats, all would be okay. But in Joseph's same smile, I saw how wrong I'd been.

Chapter Twelve

I awoke to the cat, pouncing on something in the corner. That mice roamed our house at night was just part of farm life. I learned this long ago, probably the first time I squealed out in fright at the dash of the little bit of black in front of my playpen. Around that time, I'd also have learned that having a cat who insisted on skidding across floors, crashing into walls, and diving under beds or dressers or desks or wherever else the clumsy thing had tried to hide was also part of that life.

"Lickers," I said. "Let the poor thing be."

Mother, of course, encouraged Lickers's mouse-hunting skills. While many folks, even farmers pestered by the presence of mice, would balk at the weekly delivery of a dead mouse by a proud cat, Mother rewarded Lickers with a fresh bowl of cream whenever Lickers produced one.

"One less mouse in the house is always worth a treat," Mother would say before giving the cat a pat.

But I saw it differently. No matter how many mice Lickers caught, there were others waiting to take its place. Did it really make a difference? One less mouse? With all the troubles in the world?

I felt under my mattress for *The Catcher in the Rye*. Uncle Roger would ask what I was reading, and I realized I hadn't been reading much of anything this summer. At first, I'd taken to going to bed either dreaming of Mick and our magical future together, but now I'd taken to staring at the ceiling, replaying the events of the day, wondering what had gone so terribly wrong, and asking God to step in and rescue Mick and to heal Old Man Stringer. So far, God had done neither. Old Man stayed in his coma and Mick stayed in jail. Even my plan to send Tommy down for a visit, with an update on what was happening, had failed miserably. It nearly landed Tommy in jail himself.

When the deputy had asked Tommy to empty his pockets, Tommy had emptied his pockets, including the folded note I'd made for Mick. I'd redrawn the tiny fort and the woodchuck tunneling toward it. While I'd hoped to convey a secret message to Mick, about us once again being together, a message like the one he'd sent me, the deputy saw it as Tommy's message for Mick, one of more the jailbreak variety.

By the time Tommy got back to the farm to tell me the story, after Tommy had managed to convince the deputy that it was a joke from back when they were in grade school meant to cheer him up, Tommy was in stitches. Tommy had Ellery laughing; even Bud cracked a smile. Maybe one day I'd be able to look back on it and laugh, but then it only tore at my heart a bit. It only reminded me that Mick sat alone in that cell, feeling abandoned, and there was nothing, well, little, I could do about it.

I rolled over and looked at my closet door. Last night Mother had come up after supper, pulling out my few blouses and skirts and two of my dresses. Since we'd do no outdoor chores today—not even any work with the broccoli or peas—but would instead mill around the house while we waited for the sound of Uncle Roger's new Buick to crunch up the driveway, Mother said she wanted to see me in a skirt again. I had no idea why it mattered so much to Mother what I wore, but it did. Seemingly more lately. I'd catch her sighing and shaking her head each time my dungaree-clad legs would skip down the stairs. Though Mother had traded in her fancy life in town for a scruffier one on the farm, she was still more interested in seeing me become a lady in dresses than a farm girl in slacks.

Mother had hung two choices for me today. I could go with the starchy white blouse tucked deep into the wide-twirling, tan skirt or I could choose the baby blue dress, the one with the white collar and matching white cardigan that made me think of clouds in the sky. Neither looked as good as my blue jeans and checked blouse, but those weren't options for when Uncle Roger came. At least they weren't as ridiculous as the new cherry print dress with layers of scratchy crinoline Mother had bought me for the festival.

I chose the dress, slipping it on while once again chiding Lickers who had begun licking her paws on my bedspread. She'd already ruined one piece of furniture in my room. I didn't need her leaving marks on anything else now. Lickers eyed me. Sometimes her gaze was worse than Mother's.

"I look all right, Miss Kitty?" I gave the dress a twirl, which proved too much a lure for the cat. She pounced on my pleats before landing on all fours.

"None of that nonsense when Uncle Roger gets here, please. You'll find yourself sleeping in the potato house tonight. All right. Let's go, Lickers."

I grabbed my book, no longer caring if Mr. Pop saw what I was reading. I guessed he'd no longer care anyway. With a real friend in jail and a real girl run off and real grown-ups raging mad, my reading about Holden Caulfield's fictitious escapades in New York City surely couldn't matter much.

* * *

"The problem," Uncle Roger was saying as I stepped back into the dining room with the tray of lemonade Mother had sent me for, "is that he's Maliseet."

Mr. Pop laughed. "Baby brother, it took you all those years in school to tell us that?"

Uncle Roger thanked me for the glass I set in front of him and then shook his head. "I mean, of course, that the laws that protect you and me and Mercy here just don't always get applied equally.

The judge says he won't even get around to setting bail for a few weeks. 'Things I got to check out first,' he told me. It's baloney, of course. And unconstitutional as all get out. But up here, it's what goes. And who's going to challenge it?"

"You are," I said.

Uncle Roger looked at me and smiled. To see this man smile was to understand how he'd done so well in life, how he'd managed to make and keep friends on both sides of the political aisle, and how he would be able to defend a Maliseet boy and not make one enemy in town. There was just something about the way his white but slightly overlapping teeth shone on his otherwise plain face and how the smile lines from his bright blue eyes spread all the way to his graying temples that gave this man what Mother called *presence*.

"Roger may not be as handsome as my Paul," I'd once overheard Mother say, "but the man commands a room."

And he did. Though Uncle Roger only stood an inch or two taller than Mr. Pop, you'd have thought he had a foot on him.

"I am going to challenge it, Mercy," Uncle Roger was saying. "But the process takes weeks. Sometimes months."

I tried to calm my nerves by reminding myself that Uncle Roger had defended people in rough circumstances and taken on the most unlikely cases and had won. Many times. But it didn't work here. None of those other cases and causes had involved Mick.

"This just isn't right," I said. "He didn't do anything. How can they just keep him there?"

"Because, as I just said, Mick is Maliseet. And there's a man in the hospital, and people think Mick put him there."

"So what do we do?" Mother asked. "What can we do for Mick, at least, while he's there?"

"I'm going down to visit him this afternoon. They're still not allowing any outside visitors, especially after that Tommy boy tried to sneak in something. What was that, a jailbreak note?" Uncle

Roger raised an eyebrow at me. I simply cleared my throat.

"But," Uncle Roger continued, "they have to let him see his lawyer, Maliseet or no. They can throw up all sorts of other phony roadblocks for other people, but they have to let me in."

"Can you tell him anything from us?" Mother asked. "Or can I drive to the Flats and see if his mother has a message for him?"

Uncle Roger nodded.

"I'm happy to pass along any words of encouragement or hope or love that any of you have to offer," he said. "I'm sure he'll be desperate to hear it." This time Uncle Roger winked at me. I wondered what Mother had told him. And what she'd told Mr. Pop, for that matter.

"If you wouldn't mind," Uncle Roger said, "I'd love to see if I could take a thirty-minute nap, spend another thirty minutes to pull my head together, and then we'll be on our way."

"We?" Mr. Pop asked, motioning to himself.

"Well," Uncle Roger said. "I was hoping Miss Mercy would be willing to drive into town with me. She and I need to catch up."

I tugged at the ties of my scarf. I wanted to just let the thing go, let it fly right off into the wind that swirled around us as Uncle Roger and I headed toward town in his Roadmaster. Top down. Uncle Roger had honked at Old Bill Wilding as we passed his so-called golf course. While normally his place—full of broken down gas pumps and a plethora of lawn ornaments, not to mention five or six stray chickens scratching around—caused cars to slow and stare, this time it was Old Bill Wilding's turn. And who could blame him? When I had first seen the smooth mint green and the wave of white along the sides of this car, I couldn't peel my eyes away either. The Carmichaels' shiny red Riviera had nothing on Uncle Roger's beauty. But the width and curves of this car's outside couldn't even compare to the thrill of a ride inside. I'd grown too used to the lurching of the potato truck and even the dull bounces of my father's trusty Ford sedan, but this was luxury. In every sense of the word. Of course, a convertible in Maine—where a person could expect little more than a handful of top-down-perfect days—was extravagant enough. But the flashes of chrome, the shine of the dash, the smoothness of the leather seats made me feel like a movie star.

I tucked my scarf behind my ear to hear Uncle Roger.

"Did you want the radio on?" he asked.

I smiled and nodded. Of course I did. If he could get a station.

Uncle Roger took a quick look at the floor and moved his foot toward a button. He pressed a few times until we landed on WABI, out of Bangor. It fizzed in and out, but behind the static and amid the wind, I could hear music, faint and beautiful playing through.

"So I'd like you to tell me," Uncle Roger yelled over, "about Mick's constitution."

"I thought you said it didn't apply to him."

Uncle Roger laughed. "Right you are. I meant: What do you think sitting in jail will do to him? To his spirit?"

I thought about what Joseph had told me. "His brother told me this wasn't the worst thing that had ever happened to Mick."

"I suspect that's true," Uncle Roger said.

"So if that's true, I guess Mick'll be okay. His spirit, I mean."

"Glad to hear that. I'm still going to work as hard as I can to get him out. But you understand the complications, right?"

I pulled at my scarf and nodded.

"And you understand that there's a possibility I won't be able to get him out and that there could be a trial. For murder, or attempted at least."

I nodded again. But I hadn't actually understood that. I hadn't thought that far ahead. I never entertained the slightest possibility that Uncle Roger wouldn't be able to get the judge to understand that this was all some huge, horrible mistake and that Mick should be let go immediately.

"And if there's a trial, I might ask you to testify on Mick's behalf. Your father has already agreed to. As has your mother and Bud and Ellery. They will all be what's called character witnesses. But you would be especially important. Mr. Pop tells me you know Mick better than anyone."

"I suppose I do. At least outside the Flats. But you should ask his brother, Joseph. He really knows him best."

Uncle Roger shook his head. "Can't do that. Maliseet opinions don't matter much, do they? Truth be told, your father's word is going to be the most powerful. But as part of the esteemed Paul Millar's household, yours will carry lots of weight too."

Uncle Roger paused and breathed in deeply through his nose, as though he needed Maine's piney air to strengthen him. He glanced toward Mt. Katahdin's peak before returning his eyes to the road and continuing.

"The only thing," he said, "will be that I need you to keep very quiet about your relationship with Mick. You two have been friends since you were babies, practically. And everyone knows that, which is fine. But if anyone asks you about the true nature of your relationship at this point, well, of course tell the truth, but just state it factually, no romantic embellishments."

Now it was my turn to stare off at Mt. Katahdin. How I wished I was in the potato truck so I could drive toward it, park at its base and climb up its craggy trails. "Any bit closer we can get to heaven seems to help," Ellery had said when I confessed that the side of Katahdin was a better place to talk to God than church. But it wasn't so much praying I longed to do on the mountain as simply escaping.

I did my best to play the coy teenager Molly had tried to get me to practice being. "What do you mean, romantic embellishments?"

Uncle Roger laughed. "Your father said you'd deny this. Even to me."

I closed my eyes. Tight. "Mr. Pop said I'd deny *what*?"

"That you're sweet on Mick."

"Why on earth would Mr. Pop think that?"

"Oh, my dear. Do you really think love is so easy to hide? I'm no romantic, and I haven't seen you in what, six months? But if *I* can see the way your eyes lighten when his name is spoken or the way your body tenses when your concern for him kicks in, then surely Mr. Pop can too."

"No. I know it was Mother. I'm sure she told."

"So you knew that your mother knew about you and Mick, but not your father?"

"Mother and I talked about it. She promised she wouldn't tell my dad. Looks like she didn't keep that promise."

"I wouldn't be too sure about that, Mercy. Sometimes the things we take care to keep secret really aren't all that secret."

"But if Mr. Pop always knew, why would he have let me go pick them up in the morning? Wouldn't he think that would look bad?"

"I'm not saying he *always* knew—goodness, I'm pretty sure you didn't always realize you had a crush on Mick."

"It's not just a crush."

Uncle Roger laughed as he eased up on the gas. The farms and trees did their usual yielding to houses packed closer together. The steeples and rooflines were no longer on the horizon. I straightened my back and my head scarf, preparing myself for the stares that were certain to come.

Uncle Roger took his right hand off the wheel and leaned toward me.

"Sorry, Mercy. I know it's not just a crush. Just like I know your mother didn't tell. Your dad figured it out just like the rest of us. And if you'll notice, he stopped you from driving to get them just about the time he realized it. Because, as you said, he thought it would indeed be inappropriate. Now, as for you, when I go in there . . ."

I hadn't realized we were already at the courthouse. My nerves had taken over since we'd entered town, and, in an effort not to notice any stares from passersby, I suppose I'd stopped noticing buildings as well as people. But the courthouse, with its domed room and soldier-like rows of columns out front, should've been harder to miss. Though as I thought about it, I'd driven past this building so many times and never even given it a thought. Never thought much about what went on behind the stately facade. I certainly had never thought much about *who* sat in the basement jail cells, about who would've been nervously awaiting the arrival of their attorney, about who might've been anxious to have a visitor. Any visitor.

Uncle Roger turned off of Main Street onto Pine Ave, and pulled his car to a stop.

"You going to be okay?" he asked me.

"Of course."

"People may ask you questions."

"I know."

"And what will you tell them?"

"The truth. But no embellishments."

Uncle Roger smiled. "And if anyone asks if it's true that Mick is your boyfriend?"

"I'll spit on the ground and say I'd rather be dead than touch a filthy Maliseet."

Another smile from Uncle Roger. "How about we try something else?"

"How about I just say that my love life is of no concern to them."

"This isn't Hollywood, Mercy. Can we go with something less dramatic?"

"I could mention instead that Tommy and I have a date at the festival this weekend."

"And do you?"

"We do. Molly and I do."

"I see. That's fine. Changing direction would be just fine. Now I need about twenty minutes with Mick. You're running more heads of broccoli down to Joseph?"

I tightened my grip around the basket on my lap and nodded.

"Do you have anything you'd like Mick to know?"

"Tell him that the woodchuck is still tunneling."

"Jailbreak code again?"

"Just tell him I hope to see him soon and tell him . . . well, you know."

Chapter Thirteen

After Uncle Roger ducked into the courthouse using the side entrance, I headed up the two blocks toward Nelson's. Though I'd hoped to at least get a glance at Joseph as he chopped and stirred and smelled broccoli (or whatever he'd been hired to do) and maybe kill my ten minutes sampling Chef's specialties, the woman who met me at the door said Joseph and the chef were too busy with dinner and Potato Blossom Fest prep to be bothered. I left the broccoli with her and walked back onto the sidewalk.

Our normally bustling small town felt deserted. I wondered a moment where everyone could be. But then remembered. The same thing that kept Joseph and Chef tied to the kitchen kept the people of Watsonville tied to their homes. The Potato Blossom Festival started tomorrow. Though we wouldn't leave for the festival until the morning, and though we would only stay one night, many families spent more days, some even stretching their trip into one that spanned the festival and the next week's Northern Maine Fair. The idea of summer vacations to the Great Wild West or even Maine's coast or Vermont's Green Mountains were beyond the reach of most Northwoods families. So going to the festival and the fair became *the* summer travel destination of choice. Even Old Man Stringer usually managed to hitch a ride for the day.

Old Man.

At the thought of him rambling around Potato Blossom Festival, mooching food and drinks and cigarettes from festival-goers the way he'd mooched a ride up there, I turned tail on the sidewalk, double-timing my step once I realized how I needed to spend my remaining free minutes.

I was more than a little ashamed that I hadn't planned on this in the first place. And more than a little surprised that neither Mother nor Mr. Pop had suggested that a visit to Old Man might be in order. I wondered, actually, if anyone had been to see him.

But as I stepped into our town's tiny hospital, I was once again stopped by a woman at the front.

"I'm here to see Mr. Stringer, please," I said.

"I'm sorry, miss. Mr. Stringer cannot have any visitors. Only family."

"But he doesn't have any family," I said. "He lives near mine and takes most of his lunches with us. We're close as family."

The woman behind the front desk fixed the pin in her scarf and said, "If you're that close, then you would know that he does have family. His sister drove down from Caribou just yesterday."

"Old Man has a sister?"

The woman nodded.

"And she's here?"

The woman nodded again.

"Then, may I see her?"

The woman sighed and checked a clipboard. "Wait here a moment, please."

She returned with a woman who looked too young to be Old Man's sister.

"Miss?"

"Mercy. Mercy Millar."

"Miss Millar, meet Mrs. Calloway. This is Mr. Stringer's sister."

"Nice to meet you," I said as we shook hands.

Mrs. Calloway motioned to the pair of tapestry wing-back chairs by the window.

"I only have a minute," she said. "I don't want to leave Squeak in case he wakes up."

"Squeak?"

"Well, that's his nickname. Arthur's his real name. Don't folks here call him Squeak? They have everywhere else he's lived."

I shook my head. "We call him Old Man Stringer," I said, suddenly embarrassed as I looked into her face.

"Old Man!" she said. "Not sure how to take hearing my baby brother being referred to as an old man!"

"Ma'am? Your *baby* brother?"

"He's two years younger. But those two years made a lifetime of difference, as you can see. Mama died having him. At least I had two years with her. He never had much of a chance. Not being raised by our father—and that woman he married just to take care of us. You don't grow up well without anyone to love you right. *That* was Squeak's trouble."

Mrs. Calloway was a woman of slight frame, so in that way she looked like Old Man Stringer, but that's where the resemblance stopped. She had reddish, shoulder-length hair, Old Man was almost bald with a few stray strands of brown hair. She looked to be around fifty, so Old Man had to be in his late forties even though he looked like he could be at least sixty. Mrs. Calloway was clearly a productive citizen and Old Man, well, he was a drunk.

I had no idea what to say to her. So I did what Mother had taught me to do when no words came. I leaned a bit closer and listened. "Sometimes people just need an ear," Mother would say. "So just be that ear."

"Of course," Mrs. Calloway said, "I loved him. But sister-love isn't the same as mama-love. Or even love from your daddy. And I was only a little girl myself when our father married that woman. I tried to protect him, but I had to fend off the meanness from our stepmother myself. She just seemed to be worse on the boys than she was on the girls. Even her own she had from her first marriage."

"How horrible," I managed. I wasn't used to people I *knew* airing their dirty laundry, let alone strangers.

"I suppose I cannot even imagine what folks in this town must think of him."

"People like him plenty," I said. "He works for my dad nearly every day."

"But does your father understand why he drinks?"

I shrugged. "We've never talked about it. My dad calls drinking like this 'wrestling demons.'"

Mrs. Calloway nodded before letting her eyes stare out the window beyond where we sat. "Maybe your dad *does* understand, then," she said. "When our older stepsister, Penny, got married, she actually sent for us kids to live with her. Penny knew how bad it was for me and Squeak. After all, she'd heard all the squeakin' Squeak did when our stepmother would be chasing him with that belt of hers. So Penny sent for kids she barely even knew, who weren't even blood. Can you imagine? *That* was love. But by then Squeak was maybe just seven but already so broken. He first ran off by the time he was ten or so. The Maliseet took him in. You know that?"

I shook my head. I realized I knew nothing about this man. Apparently Joseph was right. I didn't know anything about anything.

"The Maliseet were good to him. They gave him a place to live, food to eat, friends to talk to. Of course, they also gave him whiskey. He's been hitting the bottle since he was twelve. At least, that's what he says."

"Old Man—I mean, Mr. Squeak—lived *here* with the Maliseet?"

"Yes."

"In the Flats?"

"What?"

"The Flats. What we call where the Maliseet live. Over at the dump."

"They live at the *dump*?"

I nodded.

"When Squeak lived with them, it was in a little group of houses, down country near the base of Katahdin. Some of them lived here in town, however. I seem to remember his friend, um . . . Anton? Ashley?"

"Ansley?" I asked.

"Yes, Ansley. I seem to remember Ansley lived in an attic apartment with his family. Nice enough that Squeak was quite jealous. The stairs to that apartment had a fancy railing that led right up from the second story of the house."

"Ansley lived here in town? In a house? With white people living downstairs?"

"Yes. That's how they live in Caribou as well. This bit of living at the dump sounds peculiar. Most definitely un-Christian, don't you think?"

"I do think," I said, just as I noticed the clock on the wall. My remaining ten minutes were more than up.

"Mrs. Calloway, I'm sorry, but my uncle is going to be waiting for me. I just wanted to know how Old—how your brother was doing."

Mrs. Calloway sighed. "Still the same. The doctors aren't hopeful. They say the years of drinking have taken a bigger toll on him than cracking his head on the cement. But Squeak's survived so much. Hard to believe a punch from a scoundrel would do him in."

"You know, that 'scoundrel' is Mr. Squeak's friend, Ansley's boy. Hard to believe he would punch him at all."

Mrs. Calloway knit her eyebrows. "That *Mick* boy is Ansley's son?" she asked. "Squeak knows him?"

"Of course."

"No one told me. I assumed it was an attempted robbery."

"Lots of people have assumed lots of things in this." I stood up and reached out my hand. "Very nice to have met you, Mrs. Calloway. I hope Mr. Squeak gets better soon."

Mrs. Calloway smiled and thanked me for coming. "You can come back any time. I hadn't heard from Squeak in a few years. I'd love to know more about what he's been up to down here."

I smiled and nodded, then left to head back toward the jail.

Uncle Roger had been waiting next to his car for me. I thought he'd be annoyed. Though Uncle Roger was bighearted, his years of deferential treatment as one of Maine's top lawyers had turned him into the sort of man who didn't believe he should lean against a car waiting for others. Certainly not for a girl who should have been the one leaning against the car waiting for him. But as Uncle Roger walked around and reached his tweed-jacketed arm toward my door handle, he offered no reprimand. I was desperate to ask about his visit and to tell him about mine. Yet somehow I sensed that it was a time for quiet. Uncle Roger was lost in his thoughts. He didn't speak until the road wound and curved us out of town. I was too terrified to interrupt.

"Mick wants you to know that he's doing okay. Pastor Buell from Second Baptist has been by and so has Father McMahon from St. Mary's. Clergy get visiting rights like lawyers do."

"How did he look?" I asked.

Uncle Roger laughed. "Handsome as ever? Is that what you want to hear?"

"No. I mean, was he, I don't know. Did he look *peaceful*?"

"Ah, well, no. I've visited plenty of men in jail before, and I've not yet seen one of them full of peace. But he looked *well*. He looks like he's been able to get rest and that his anxiety over being charged with attempted murder isn't getting the best of him."

"*Attempted murder?*" I asked. "So it's official then?"

Uncle Roger nodded. "Yes, bail's been set. Too high for his family to pay, of course. So he's got to stay put. But Mick swore he was okay. He said he's been 'getting out' by going someplace in his mind. To a fort in the woods, he said? Is that a place where he played as a boy?"

I fought my own anxiety and smiled before fibbing: "Must be."

"And he's eating well. He says the jailhouse food is better than he's ever had. On top of that, somehow the new chef at Nelson's heard about Mick and brought over a plate of spaghetti Bolognese and freshly baked bread."

"The chef was allowed to visit?"

"No. But the main guard, Fritz Herbert, is a decent man. He allowed the delivery and is letting Nelson's bring Mick supper every day. Wonder why he's doing that."

"Mick's brother works for the chef, Chef Barone. We met him at the farm stand two days ago."

"And the chef just hired the boy?"

"After he heard that Joseph smelled the broccoli, he did."

Uncle Roger scrunched his nose and shook his head. "I'll be. Interesting turn of events there."

To keep my mind off of the charge against Mick and my worries for him, I started talking. I told Uncle Roger about the other interesting turn of events, about Old Man not being old and having a sister and that the Maliseet took him in when he ran away.

Uncle Roger listened and at the end simply said, "I remember."

"You remember?"

"Surely your father has told you that Ansley and Squeak and Frankie Carmichael and us were boys together? Running around fields with baseballs and bats? Splashing in the Meduxnekeag, hunting rabbits and beavers in the woods by the water?"

Mr. Pop hadn't told me any of this. Well, he'd told me plenty of stories from his boyhood and referred to his buddies and their wild romps, but I'd never imagined that Ansley and Old Man were among them.

"So why then does Mr. Carmichael hate Ansley and all of them so much? Is it just because of Marjorie running off with Glenn?"

Uncle Roger shook his head. "Not sure what I can tell you about this. Not sure I understand it all myself. Well, I understand some of it. Let's just say Marjorie isn't the first woman in that family to want to run off with a Maliseet boy."

My mouth gaped open. "What?"

"This is all I'll say: Mrs. Carmichael, back when she was Muriel Fulton, I guess, had quite the thing for Ansley. Of course, it couldn't happen. So she married Frankie. With him fully knowing that he was the also-ran. And Frankie Carmichael has spent his married life trying to convince her and himself and everyone in town what filth the Maliseet are."

"So all this because Mr. Carmichael wasn't Mrs. Carmichael's first love? This is all about jealousy?"

"Well, it started out that way. But it's bloomed into something much more. What does the Good Book say about envy? It rots the bones. His bones are rotten with the stuff."

"But Mr. Carmichael is a Christian man. How could this happen?"

"Only God can judge his heart, Mercy. So I'm going to step carefully here. But I'm comfortable saying that Frankie Carmichael is a churchgoing man, but I'm not sure he's all that great a Christian one. There's a difference. Your Mr. Pop would have my hide for repeating this, but not long after Frankie and Muriel married, Mr. Pop remarked on what a mistake Mr. Fulton had made, thinking he was preventing his daughter from marrying a pagan."

"A pagan! But Mr. Carmichael has been baptized and confirmed. He professes Jesus and takes communion like the rest of us."

"And again I quote from the Good Book. I'm on a roll! Your father would be impressed. Jesus Himself said, 'Not everyone that saith unto me, Lord, Lord, shall enter into the kingdom of heaven.' But who will, Mercy? Finish the verse."

"'He that doeth the will of my Father which is in heaven,'" I said.

"That's right. Just before this, Jesus talks about the false prophets who are ravening wolves underneath. How do we know people's hearts?"

"By their fruits," I said, hiding a smirk.

Uncle Roger raised an eyebrow as we turned into our drive. "It's funny?" I wasn't sure how he knew.

"Well, Ellery says if Jesus were in Maine, He'd've told us we'd know them by their potatoes. That's all."

"Glad you're able to laugh a bit through this, Mercy. It's going to be a tough stretch. School starts in, what? Two or three weeks?"

"Yes, sir. Two weeks. Just after the state fair. It'll feel different this year."

Uncle Roger stopped the car and nodded.

"When will you be back?" I asked. I already knew that he'd stay for supper that night, get to bed early, and then head out first thing in the morning.

"It'll depend on the judge And on if I can get any pressure from the state. But it could be a few weeks. A month even."

"A month! Mick might be in jail that long?"

"Might be. I hope not. But he might be."

We both looked up at the squeal of the front door. Mother waved hello and then shook her head. I realized only then that I'd not put my scarf on for the ride back.

"My hair," I said to Uncle Roger. "You should've reminded me about the scarf."

He laughed. "It's lovely. You could be a real contender for Miss Potato Blossom."

I pulled the scarf from under his front seat and swatted him with it. It was nice to have something to laugh about. If even for a little while.

Chapter Fourteen

U naware that Mr. Pop had been working to convince Frankie Carmichael that attending the Potato Blossom Festival, even if for a day, would be the best thing for his family, Molly believed she had succeeded in talking her father into letting her drive up with us to the Potato Blossom Festival. But who convinced who ultimately didn't matter. What mattered was that Molly was going with us. As disappointed as she was about not being able to compete in the Miss Potato Blossom Queen Pageant, at that point Molly just wanted to get away from Watsonville, from all the pain and sadness foisted on her by Glenn and Marjorie. And Mick.

Barely one year earlier the festival was full of promise and excitement when Marjorie won the pageant. Molly was the proudest little sister I'd ever seen, and the Carmichaels the proudest parents. They boasted about their daughter's accomplishments everywhere they went. What a difference a year made.

"Molly, I waited forever for Mrs. Garritson to get off the line," I said into the phone. "I know she was annoyed at me picking up every five minutes, but really, she should have just driven over to Mrs. Burt's for a visit and not tied up the phone for so long! I'm just calling to say that we are leaving at 8:00 a.m. sharp on Saturday for the festival. You're still coming, right?"

"You know I am. Every minute I'm at home, I spend holed up in my room. I'm so mad at my father, I can hardly breathe when I think about it."

I had heard the click of the hall closet behind her, the favored talking place of the Carmichael girls. I wondered how long it'd be before I heard Mr. Carmichael's knock on the door. But at least he let her talk on the phone. Lately, when I'd called their house, he'd tell me Molly was busy with her chores and not available to speak. He never offered to take a message or invited me to call her back.

"So things at home still haven't gotten better?" I asked.

"Nope. Well, maybe a little. I don't know. They're letting me go to Potato Blossom—the surprise of my life!"

"I'm so glad! I can't wait to catch up. We'll have two whole days of it! You know Mr. Pop. He can't be away from the farm for more than two days at a time during growing season, or any season for that matter. I tried talking him into letting Mother and me stay a couple extra days, but no deal. See you Saturday morning?"

"I'll be there. Can't wait!"

The wonder of the Potato Blossom Festival was its timing, of course. It was held at the height of the blossoming fields. No better time to drive around Aroostook County than when the blossoms were at their peak. It was this sight that made me never understand how anyone could move away. As we drove up The North Road toward Fort Fairfield, the vast fields spread out before us like a gently rolling sea of lilac and green. Pinkish purple in some fields and creamy yellow in others, potato fields in bloom are truly a sight to behold. My parents had told stories of the POWs who once farmed these fields during the War. I didn't remember ever seeing them, but I'd heard the story of the German prisoner who had fallen in love with a local farmer's daughter and caused the biggest romantic scandal Aroostook County had ever seen. Until now, I supposed.

But I didn't let my mind linger there long. Riding in the car for this long was too much of a treat. So different from the bouncing along in the old potato truck I was used to. I thought Molly and I were riding in style in our Ford sedan. Of course, Molly was used to more style than I was with her father's new Buick Riviera, but to me the Ford meant luxury and a ride that didn't scramble your insides with every bump like our truck. I can still feel the cloth seats. I loved the gray cloth interior in contrast to the black exterior. I thought it looked high class, but Mr. Pop bought it because he didn't think it drew attention, not like Frankie Carmichael's bright red Buick. Molly and I kept our windows down, at least for part of the trip to Presque Isle. It was a beautiful day as long as we were on paved roads. As soon as the gravel started, the dust was unbearable and we had to roll up the windows quickly.

The view mostly consisted of rolling hills and potato fields. The potato itself is so mundane, utilitarian really. Used in so many dishes to bind things together instead of being the star attraction, at least that's how most people think. But being from Aroostook County, I think different. There's nothing like new potatoes and freshly shelled peas with sweet cream. Add Mother's homemade rolls and that's always our first potato meal of the season. Eating what the sweat of your brow has nurtured and worked hard to produce is something only those who work a farm can fully understand.

Sure, the coast has its lighthouses and lobster boats. But even those can't top the wide-open sky full of billowy cumulonimbus clouds with the flowing rows of potato blossoms, sun kissing every field in bloom.

With all the bad things that have happened in the past few days, Molly and I, not to mention Mr. Pop and Mother, needed the full orbed beauty of this drive north. A little more than an hour, the drive was the perfect length to leave behind the cares of Watsonville. I was thankful for a bright, sunny day to enjoy the vistas. We also got a peek at what the parade would have in store for us. The town floats for Mars Hill and Easton were both out on the main road in full view.

We kept our eyes peeled for moose and bear. Didn't want that kind of encounter to end our trip early. Mr. Pop reminded us of when Pastor Murphy's daughter Sharon drove home from church on a Wednesday night, she crested a hill on Foster Road and ran right into a young bull moose. It's not hard to imagine who got the worse end of that.

"Poor Sharon," Mother said. "It's been two years, and she's still finding pieces of glass working their way out of her."

Mr. Pop glanced back at us in the rearview mirror. As soon as our eyes met, I giggled. Mr. Pop did too. Well, at least, he smiled. Ellery had a whole routine about poor Sharon picking the glass and "moose fur" out of her.

"She's just lucky to be alive," Mother said, unaware of the image of Ellery that was running through my and Mr. Pop's minds. "Too bad her car wasn't as lucky."

"You two girls are unusually quiet," Mother noticed with distinct curiosity in her voice. "Aside from your giggling, that is."

"Oh, nothing to say really," Molly said. "Just enjoying the sights. Been awhile since I've been up country. Certainly awhile since I've seen the fields in bloom like this."

"We're really glad you could come with us," Mother said. "I know Mercy is awfully happy to have a friend along. It's been hard for you two to have time together lately, so I hope this little trip will make up for that."

"Thank you, Mrs. Millar. It was nice of you to invite me along."

"Nonsense! You're like a sister to Mercy."

"Mr. Pop, we're almost there, right?" I asked. He had surprised us even more by booking a room at the Aroostook Inn. My mother loved nothing more than the privacy and elegance of a hotel room.

"Yep. Probably just ten more minutes," Mr. Pop said, "and we should be there, fair and square."

"Just what I thought," I said. "Molly and I want to get a good spot on the main route where we can watch the parade."

"Just so long as you help your mother and me take the bags to the room. Then you two can make hay while the sun shines!"

It was good to see a smile in Mr. Pop's delivery of that line. His tone gave me a bit of hope. I knew while Molly and I watched the parade, he would be off to the Indian Rights Council meeting, something I couldn't allow myself to think about.

Staying in a hotel, even for one night, felt so luxurious. We hauled our overnight cases up to the hotel room, since the room was ready, but didn't have time to linger and enjoy it. We had to find a good spot on the parade route. Molly and I found a great place next to the local ice cream joint. Brilliant! Mr. Pop had given each of us money for lunch and an afternoon treat. As soon as we saw the ice cream shop, I elbowed Molly.

"I think we found our treat."

She nodded back, before scanning the crowd that had gathered. I wondered when Tommy Birger and his family would arrive as well.

"So Mol', what's your favorite part of the parade?" I chimed in with my own. "Mine is seeing all the old farming equipment, even those horse-drawn plows and diggers."

Every year Mr. Pop would point out the equipment to me, talk me through their functions and how they'd been so innovative at the time. All I could do was thank God I didn't live back then. Farming was hard enough work today.

"I like the town floats," Molly said. "Definitely. Watsonville always has a good one. I'm looking forward to seeing our entry this year. Of course, the float with all the Potato Blossom Queen contestants used to be my favorite." Her voice trailed off with a measure of sadness.

I wrapped my arm around her shoulder.

"Let's not think about that today," I said. "Not Glenn and Marjorie, not Mick, not the Indian Rights Council."

I waved my arm, widened my eyes, and let my best ringmaster voice ring out. "We need some good ole fashioned fun. Let's take in the sights, the smells, the sounds, the people, everything but what coulda' been. Deal?"

"It's a deal, as long as you stop talking like you're in some silly movie."

I laughed. Of course, Molly and I had no idea what people in silly movies talked like. Going to movies was off-limits for good Baptist girls, though we knew all about the glamorous stars.

Not long after we'd found our spot, the old-fashioned cars starting coming down the boulevard. The parade's grand marshal was a boy about nine or ten years old. I remembered hearing about him a couple months ago when I was in town. Bud told me about an article in the *Watsonville Chronicle* about him too.

"Molly, hey! Remember me telling you about this kid?" I asked. "He had to have some big operation down in Portland and the whole community was doing a fund-raiser to help pay for it? Looks like he's on the mend. I don't remember what kind of operation, though."

"It wasn't an operation," Molly said. "He got polio, a bad case, and needed some special device to help him walk better. The whole town rallied."

Our parade neighbor, evidently a local, overheard our conversation and filled us in on the details of his illness and the town's help. Polio was bad business. Mother took part in at least two walks for polio with a bunch of Watsonville mothers. We filled up a few of those March of Dimes cards and turned them in at the hardware store.

After the grand marshal car came the politicians. First came an old Model T for the mayor of Fort Fairfield, followed by all the surrounding communities' mayors, including Watsonville's, riding in a variety of antique cars.

"I suppose most of them are heading over to the Indian Rights Council as soon as they're done with the parade," Molly said. "Wouldn't want to be in that room today."

"Me neither. But we're not supposed to be thinking about that. Remember our deal?"

Molly rolled her eyes.

"Hey, there's Governor Cross," I said. "I bet he's nervous about the election in September. Mr. Pop says he wouldn't be surprised to see Mr. Muskie win. Wonder if Governor Cross is going to the Indian Rights Council. I've heard Uncle Roger talk about being in meetings in Augusta with him."

"Look who's breaking our deal now!" Molly said, with a laugh. "Oh, look! Here come the Clydesdales. I love them."

I loved them too. So beautiful and yet cloddy, with their fur fluffing around their ankles as they pulled the old-time fire engine.

Although I hadn't been able to keep my end of the deal—not only talking about the Indian Rights Council but by thinking non-stop about how I wish Mick could be here with us—the parade was all kinds of fun, from the Clydesdales and old farm equipment to the men dressed up in Civil War uniforms from the Battle of Gettysburg.

By the time the parade ended, Molly and I were tired of standing and glad to find a nice spot to sit and eat our lunch. We started roaming the festival grounds for the best eats and across the yard I spotted Chef Barone.

"Molly, there's the chef from Nelson's!" I said, pointing to a white-tented table across the street. "He's the guy I told you about, the one who hired Joseph."

I took Molly's arm and dragged her across the street. The closer we got, the aromas began to intermingle. The divine smell of all things fried from the Elm Tree Diner booth captured me. They had the best fresh-cut, deep-fried french fries. Add a basket of fried clams with some freshly mixed tartar sauce and Chef Barone had serious competition. I smelled, before I spotted, the annual Rotary Club booth with the buttery goodness of fresh corn on the cob served alongside lobster rolls. We'd already made eye contact with Chef, so that's where we were eating whether or not we were tempted to go elsewhere. Besides, I'd eaten Elm Tree food and festival food my whole life. Italian food was a real treat, something new in the county.

"It's the broccoli lady, hello!" Chef Barone said. "Welcome to Nelson's at the festival! I'm sorry; I can't remember your name, although Joseph talks about you all the time."

"Mercy, it's Mercy," I said, putting out my hand. "And this is my friend Molly. It's wonderful to see you, Chef. How's Joseph doing at the restaurant?"

"You can ask him yourself. He just went back to the car to grab another tablecloth and a couple of aprons. This is my first time at the festival, so I'm learning how everything is done. I hope you girls are hungry. My lasagna is delicious, and so is my eggplant parmesan." He brought his curled fingers to his lips and gave them a rapturous kiss. "I have some delectable greens for a salad, or you can get wilted spinach as a side dish. What's your pleasure?"

"I don't know about Molly, but I'm going for some lasagna."

"You've had lasagna before?" Chef asked.

"Only once. But I loved it!" I said, my eyes grazing the choices in front of me. "And I'll take the spinach with it, please. I may not *smell* broccoli, but I do love spinach. It's one of my favorites. If I can't have fiddleheads, that is."

"Ah, yes, fiddleheads," Chef said. "I keep hearing about this mysterious vegetable. Only in season in the springtime, right?"

I nodded.

"Joseph has already promised to take me into the woods and show me what it looks like and how to harvest it. A fern, they say, just a curled-up green fern? Curious!"

"Yes, it is," I said. "But it's the best-tasting fern in the world."

"And for you, young lady?" Chef turned to Molly. "What would you like to have today?"

"The same for me, minus the spinach. I'll go with a salad please."

"Good choice, good choice! There are picnic tables right over there and sodas for sale at the booth across the way. Then come back and say hello to Joe. Although, you might want to wait till the crowds die down."

We paid Chef and thanked him. Quite a line had formed behind us. For Chef's sake, I hoped Joseph got back soon to help. I also needed to find Mother and tell her to try Nelson's for lunch as well. She'd been anxious to meet the man who hired a boy because he smelled her broccoli.

"Molly, I'll take our lunches to the table and you grab drinks, okay?

"Sure; what do you want?"

"I'll take a Grape Nehi. Thanks!"

It felt great to sit down after standing for over an hour watching the parade. Mr. Pop always said how standing around made people more tired than actual hard work. And he was right. As I bent over to rub my calf muscle, I broke my own promise once again and thought of Mick sitting in a cell. That active boy, so used to spending days foraging in the woods and working in the fields, so used to walking and running miles and miles, now confined to a ten-by-five cell. I shuddered and wondered how exhausting just sitting would be for him. *Jesus, be with him,* I prayed silently while smiling at Molly's triumphant return with the two Grape Nehis.

As soon as she sat, I began pointing out the people I pretended to have noticed while she was gone. But it wasn't hard to do. Watching the people at the festival while we ate lunch was great entertainment. As I pushed worried thoughts about Mick out of my mind, we spotted a guy with an enormous handlebar mustache.

"If only the festival had a mustache contest," Molly said. "He'd be a shoo-in. Oh, there's your mother."

Molly pointed across the yard from where we ate lunch. Sure enough, there was Mother talking to her friend Mrs. Brown and another woman I didn't recognize. But each of them looked crisp and fresh, beautiful in their best summer dresses and polished shoes. I tried to get Mother's attention with a wave, but she didn't notice. Her skirt swished as she turned back into the crowd. As good a farm wife as my mother was, never did she seem more in her element than when she was dressed up and being sociable. Mother may have spent the past twenty-five years on a farm, but at heart she would always be a town girl, where shops and restaurants and festivals and friends kept life more vibrant than growing broccoli and providing flowers for the communion table.

Molly and I had just started to plot out the rest of our day just as I noticed Joseph was back at the Nelson's booth.

"Hey Joe," I yelled over to him, unwilling to get up from the picnic table yet. "How's it going?" The lunch crowd had died down, so Joseph came over to our table and sat for a minute.

"I didn't expect to see you here."

"I didn't expect to be here," Joseph said. "Heck, three days ago I didn't expect to be anywhere. I definitely never expected to be spending my days cutting broccoli. I've cut so much, I'm not sure if I can ever eat broccoli salad again."

"So it's working out okay, then?"

"Yeah. I like it. Chef doesn't seem to care if my skin is red or brown or purple. I figure it's 'cause he's from New York. No wonder Glenn likes it there."

"Heard anything from Mick or Uncle Roger?"

"Since I got this job, I haven't had time to do anything else. I heard Roger stopped by to talk to my folks, but I was at the restaurant. It's good not to be around for all that. I'm so glad I've got this job."

I smiled at him. "I'm glad you've got it too. We're all so proud of you."

"Not sure what there's to be proud of," Joseph said. "Pretty sure Chef Barone had no idea what he was doing, hiring someone like me. Most people are just waiting for me to punch a hole through something, but Chef says he sees something in me. And it almost seems like it's something special he sees."

"Almost seems like Someone was looking out for you," I said.

"Right. I was thinking maybe it was you. Or your dad or mother. I mean, she did take the phone order for those broccoli. Did she put him up to this?"

I laughed. "I meant Someone with a capital S. You know, God."

"Oh, right," Joseph said. "I don't know about that. But Chef does have two expectations for me as his *sous chef*. That's what he calls me. It means *assistant*, but it sounds better. It's French."

I didn't know, but I nodded as though I did.

"I'm supposed to ask any question that pops into my head, and he says I've got to go with him to church this Sunday. He wants me to go to church to learn about Jesus, I guess," Joseph said.

I wondered what our minister would think about that. I was sure it wasn't a Baptist church Chef Barone attended. But as I watched Joseph's face, I noticed he never grimaced or hardened as he spoke about church. This was the first time I'd ever heard him say the name *Jesus*. I realized I'd never heard Mick say it either.

Joseph noticed my smile and shrugged. "But anyway, either it was God or your mother. Sometimes it's hard to tell the difference, I guess."

"Joseph, I promise you: my mother is not God, and she never talked to Chef Barone about hiring you. Goodness, she'd never even heard of him before that phone call. But definitely, it sounds like Someone is looking out for you."

Joseph turned back to Nelson's tent. Chef Barone pointed to his wristwatch and waved him over.

"I gotta get back," Joseph said. "Gotta do some cleanup and then prep for our supper service. Maybe I'll see ya later."

"Sounds good, Joe."

Molly had been unusually quiet, but I figured it was a bit awkward for her. Her being seen with a Maliseet could be very bad news for her, if that news reached back home to her dad, at least. I could tell Joe was sensitive to that too, something he wouldn't have been just three days ago. Perhaps being invited to ask questions and go to church was doing something to him.

Molly and I ate the rest of our lunches in silence, a silence broken only by the noise of the chatter at tables around us and the sounds of kids laughing and crying and the little boy behind us begging his parents to get him ice cream.

"Mol', let's get an ice cream and head over to the baseball game," I said. "We've got to cheer on our Watsonville Sluggers. Ellery says they're really good this year. Even beat the Mattawamkeags."

"Yeah," Molly said, "and their pitcher is really cute too."

Mercy raised her eyebrows. Molly having eyes for another could be good news for Tommy Birger.

Chapter Fifteen

The game was as lively as the crowd was loud. I hadn't been to a game since the previous summer. Of all the things that bothered me about being the "son" my father never had, baseball was not one of them. I knew all about the sport and loved it—playing it, watching it, sprawled out on the living room rug listening to it on the radio with Mr. Pop and Bud and Ellery. So much so that my comments bored Molly, who only had eyes for the pitcher and other cute boys in the crowd.

But for once during the festival, my eyes and mind were focused on nothing but this game. And it was a good one, a hitter's game. Neither pitcher had good stuff, and the ball was flying out of the park. Unfortunately when the ninth inning ended, Brewer had beaten out Watsonville by one run, twelve to eleven. With lengthy innings due to all that offense, by the time the game ended, it was late afternoon and time to regroup and find Mother and Mr. Pop. After managing to finally put the Indian Rights Council out of my mind, I resented the fact that it had just taken up residence again.

Molly and I headed toward the front entrance to the festival grounds and found Mother sitting on a bench waiting. She spotted us almost at the exact time we spotted her.

"Hi there, you two. How was your day?"

"Good," I said. "Some people-watching, good food, ice cream, and the baseball game. We saw Joseph too."

"Joseph?" Mother asked.

"Yeah. He was helping Chef Barone at the Nelson's booth. We ate some lasagna and got to talk with him a little."

"How's he doing?"

"A lot better than three days ago at the farm," I said. "It seems this job has transformed him. It's a clean slate for Joe."

"Wow. That clean slate talk makes you sound like Pastor Murphy," Mother said. "What's that he always says? God's in the business of offering clean slates and new mercies? Sounds like Chef Barone might be in the same line of work!"

"That's funny," Molly said. "Joseph was just equating *you* with God, Mrs. Millar."

"Me? Goodness. Apparently Joseph hasn't heard that I'm a confrontational shrew who humiliates her husband and drives him out to sit in the car."

"Who says that?"

Mother smiled and shrugged one shoulder. "Well, that's what some of the talk is around here, I guess. Martha Brown introduced me to a woman who nearly fainted dead when she learned who I was. Her husband is bringing a very different view to the Indian Rights Council than your father. Certainly a different view than I'd have brought. But then again, I've gotten quite a reputation as a lover of Indians."

"Mother!"

"I'm sorry. But I've just had enough. Enough of all this baloney. Enough of good, white Christian folks acting like Jesus died for us alone."

"So have you heard anything from Mr. Pop?" I asked. "It's felt good not thinking about it this afternoon. Now I kind of dread hearing news."

"There won't be much news today, honey. They're just starting to raise these issues about Indian affairs."

"I meant news about Mick. Or Marjorie and Glenn even."

"Well, I'm hoping they didn't talk much about any of that. Would most likely just be gossip and not helping the situation at all."

Molly stared at her shoes. When she'd first gotten the shoes last fall, something about the smooth of the white overlaid with the black stitched saddles brought out an envy I didn't normally feel. As I looked at them, I noticed how the scuffs overtook the whiteness, making the shoes less black-and-white and more shades of gray.

And within that gray area was where we'd all moved. Once life seemed so cut-and-dried, so right and wrong. Now it had gray areas, some rights seeming muddled and some wrongs seeming not so bad after all.

Mother had been talking while I stood lost in my thoughts. Something about not seeing Mr. Pop and not holding out much hope either.

"But," Mother said, "he did say he'd meet us for dinner. Maybe we ought to walk back over to the hotel and get ready."

* * *

"Governor Cross was there," Mr. Pop said. "Roger guessed he might be. The town council president of Presque Isle, mayor of Caribou, and mayor of Watsonville, along with a handful of other town council representatives from other small towns around the county."

"Okay, okay. Never mind who was there! Don't keep us guessing. What happened?"

"These are delicate issues, Mercy," Mr. Pop said. "And one meeting doesn't solve or fix everything. We began by talking about some of the broader issues related to Indians in Maine, like land rights and the recent passing of the law that allowed Passamaquoddy and Penobscot to vote in federal elections."

"Like president?" I asked, making sure I understood.

"Right. Some people wondered why the Maliseet and Micmac weren't included in this too. Of course, what they don't understand is that each tribe has its own government that interacts with the state government," Mr. Pop added. "There is the Wabanaki Confederation, with all four Maine tribes, but that only goes so far. The four

different tribes don't always agree on how things should happen
or even on what needs to happen. Truth is, some tribes have better
leadership than others. Some are better at knowing how to navigate politics than others."

"But what about Mick?" I asked. My leg bounced under the
table. I wasn't interested in the grand scheme of things or in one
of Mr. Pop's lectures. I wanted to know about Mick. "Is he going to
have to sit in the county jail forever?"

"Hold on, Little Miss Mercy. You haven't hardly given me a
chance to say anything."

"I know, I'm sorry. I'm just worried for Mick."

"We all are," Mr. Pop said. "There were good people around the
table in this meeting today. We all don't see eye to eye on everything, but we all want resolution. Even if resolution is wanted for
the wrong reasons by some, I'll still take that. God works in all
kinds of ways to accomplish His business in this world. Everyone
around the table agreed that things have to change. The way I see
it, it's the attitude of Whites that has to change.

"Look at what's happening in the South with the ruling that
came down in May on *Brown vs. Board of Education*. Schools there
are going to be integrated. Now we already have that here, but the
attitude toward Maliseet students in our schools certainly needs
improving. And look how many Maliseet children don't even go
to school. Their parents keep them at home to help out, or they
don't want them going to school with white children. Certainly,
not many white folks are complaining when the Maliseet children
don't show up. There are issues on both sides of the fence, but it's
easy to see who the major perpetrators of injustice are."

"Yes, it is," I said. "Mr. Carmichael!"

Molly's mouth fell open, and she slapped her hands on her
armrests. While I knew she was angry at her father for how he
treated her in the wake of her sister's scandal, Molly and I had managed never to talk about all this. When my eyes met her alarmed

glare, I realized I had assumed too much. I had no idea whether she believed her father about Mick or how much she blamed the Maliseet for Marjorie's disgrace.

I thought Molly would bound out of the restaurant. I immediately and rather dramatically pictured us spending the night not at the pageant but wandering through the streets, calling Molly's name. But all that was thwarted when Mother placed a hand on Molly's shoulder, offering a gentle invitation to stay seated.

"No," Mr. Pop said. "Actually the injustice I'm talking about falls squarely at all our feet—at the feet of all white people, I mean. We were the ones who came in and took away Maliseet land."

"I didn't take anything," Molly said. She had accepted the invitation to stay but now leaned back in her chair, arms crossed against her chest.

"No," Mother said. "But your grandparents' land and your home and Fulton's and your schools are all built on land that was taken, even if it was ages ago."

"So you think we should just give it all back then?" Molly asked. "Let the Maliseet move into the house my grandparents built, let them take over the hardware store my father gives his life for? Are you going to turn *your* farm over to Ansley when we get back?"

If I spoke to Mr. Pop this way, I might expect my mouth getting a nice visit from a bar of Ivory. Certainly, I'd have been sent away from the table with no promise of food till morning. But Mr. Pop only smiled at Molly. All the questions I had about how Molly felt about her father and Mick and Marjorie and Glenn were answered in her body language.

"Well now, Molly. You're getting right to the heart of it," Mr. Pop said. "How *do* you make right that problem? Now that's complicated."

"So was Mick's situation even talked about?" I asked. "Were Glenn and Marjorie mentioned at all?"

"Well, the conversation regarding Mick started with the status of Old Man Stringer. His outcome is central to how we proceed with Mick. We also went around the table and asked for honesty about what members of the council had heard regarding the incident with Mick and Old Man Stringer. The good news is, there is confusion about what happened, and at least two versions of the story are being told. The bad news is that news travels fast. Who knew there were so many people wondering about what went on in our little neck of the woods? I suppose I should've gathered that an Indian 'attacking' an old white man would still be news."

Mr. Pop sighed and looked down.

"But I'm sure none of these busybodies bothered to ask about Mick's version of the story."

"Now Mercy, they did ask what the police version was. And since they took down his statement, it included that."

"Yeah, I know, but does anyone on your council believe Mick's story? When it's up against someone like—sorry, Molly—Mr. Carmichael? He's a prominent businessman in town. What good is Mick's statement against all that, Mr. Pop? It feels so hopeless."

"Mercy," Mr. Pop said, "I'll remind you that it seemed quite hopeless when Jesus was headed to the cross, but we know there was resurrection. Hold out a little faith. Uncle Roger is still at work on the case. Governor Cross mentioned that today at our meeting."

"So was there any progress at the meeting? It feels like a bunch of talk and no action."

"With these delicate issues, there is always a lot of talk before there is ever any action. We had to be brought up to speed, get the issues on the table, and make sure we were all on the same page, at the same starting point, before we could move forward." He looked gently at his daughter. "But Mercy, action will come. Mark my words: action will come. The next meeting is set for a week from today, the first weekend of the Northern Maine State Fair. We'll meet in Presque Isle again. The land grant for the Maliseet is at the top of the agenda. But I've asked that we speak about more urgent issues: like how we as Christians are doing at loving our Maliseet neighbors. Uncle Roger will come again if he's able."

Action couldn't come soon enough as far as I was concerned. And I still believed that if the tables had been turned, and it had been one of the council members' teenaged sons accused of assaulting a Maliseet man, he wouldn't have even spent one night in that cell. A lawyer would have easily managed to see the judge, and the boy would have been sprung before day's end.

"Ah, look," Mother said, "our dinner."

After the waitress set our plates in front of us, Mr. Pop led us in prayer. We ate the rest of the meal in relative silence. Molly asked for salt and butter to be passed, but otherwise stayed quiet throughout the rest of dinner. I knew she wondered what was said about her family. As I watched her cut her steak with her face fixed squarely on her plate, shame filled me. I was her friend, just as I was Mick's, and yet I had showed her no sympathy.

I breathed deep and put my hand on Molly's arm, seeing if Mother's technique would work for me too.

"I'm sorry I talked about your dad like that," I said. "I know this is hard for you."

Molly just nodded and returned to her steak.

"I mean, I can't believe your father's doing this to Mick but—"

"Mercy," Mother said. "That's enough. No more."

I huffed out a short breath and shook my head. "I'm sorry, Mol'. Really."

This time she looked up from her plate and spoke. "I know my dad is wrong. I know he's lying or at least mistaken about this. And I know that Mick didn't hurt anyone. But he's still my father, and we're all going through a lot. You saying the same awful things as everyone else, it just hurts a lot worse."

It was my turn to stare at my plate.

"We've all said and done a lot of hurtful things during this," Mr. Pop said. "That's for certain. There's going to be a whole lot of forgiveness that needs to go around before all this is settled. It's during times like this that we can discover that the mercy God offers us, and expects us to offer others, comes in many shades."

We left dinner having offered and accepted apologies and forgiveness, but Molly and I were still cool toward one another. I figured we'd walk toward the pageant stage in silence and that the silence would continue throughout the night. But I also hadn't figured the Birger family stepping out from the ice cream shop as we passed.

"Mercy! Molly!" Tommy said. "Been looking for you guys all day."

"Hey Tommy," I said. Molly just smiled.

"Did you see Joseph at Nelson's booth?" Tommy asked. "It was funny seeing him decked out in that white outfit. Can you believe Joseph suggested that my mom try some eggplant dish? She said it was the best thing she ever ate. She's making us all eat it for lunch tomorrow. You should join us."

Tommy looked straight at Molly when he said this. Molly was standing in a building's shadow, and he couldn't see the red rise in her face.

"We'd love to," I said. "Well, I hope. I'm not sure when we're heading back. You on your way to the pageant now?"

"I wasn't going to," Tommy said. "But I will. If you're heading that way."

Again, Tommy's eyes were fixed on Molly. As I followed his eyes, I realized why. I hadn't noticed it during dinner; I'd been too preoccupied with her anger at me. But something about her very countenance, her face, had changed, just since arriving at the festival. While Molly had been pretty all her life, now her loveliness had deepened. No longer was it her perfectly proportioned and symmetrical features, her sky-blue eyes, and bouncy brown hair that radiated, it was her very essence. The strain of the past weeks had worn down the veneer of bubbly Molly and let her truer self show through. And though her eyes were still blue and her smile still kind, the hint of hurt and anger and frustration now glowing from beneath had an allure all its own. This Molly was no longer a cute little girl living in her even more attractive sister's shadow but a stunning young woman unafraid to push back and defend her place in the world and the people she loved in it.

Mother and Mr. Pop led the way to the pavilion where the little girls were being primped and primed for their pageant. Mother wove her arm through Mr. Pop's and they leaned close as they talked. They'd never been the sort of married couple to show physical affection in public. But the festival had a romantic effect on people. As the sun set behind the buildings, casting long shadows across the street, and as the music from the band shell rose above the din of the crowds, the mood was set.

I was glad to see them like this. I'd been worried after the incident at the Hendersons'. But they'd had disagreements through the years, some of which I'd seen resolved, some I hadn't, and they always pressed on. Mother had told me this was the blessing of being married to a man who loved her for her mind as much as anything else. A marriage in which thoughts mattered, Mother said, meant that there would be disagreements. But love would prevail. That's what she said. And that's what I held to.

I turned to look at Molly and Tommy behind me. We had started off walking together, but they'd fallen behind. The festival's air of romance caught them too. I'd seen other "couples" pair off with lightning speed like this before and normally it left me rolling my eyes. But Molly had liked Tommy for so long, that Tommy finally noticed her for the amazing girl she was and that they could enjoy this easiness with each other filled me with a jealous kind of joy. Though their fingers weren't intertwined, their hands swung close enough together and their eyes shone as they talked. I wondered when their hands would subconsciously reach for each other's, the way Mick's and mine did when we were alone.

As I walked between my parents with their decades' long tried-and-true love and Tommy and Molly and their fresh sparks, something like envy rose within me. I wondered if this experience would ever be mine.

* * *

"Aren't the little girls adorable?" Molly asked. Tommy nodded and turned to smile at her. As they whispered, their faces met close enough that Mr. Pop, sitting behind us on the folding chairs, cleared his throat.

I was trying to block out their conversation. The flirting that had commenced was starting to turn my stomach. I knew it was jealousy, but I also knew that even *if* Mick and I could be out like that, we'd never act like this. Although, maybe once upon a time we might have.

Suddenly Molly stiffened. She breathed deep and her eyes widened. All sense of coyness evaporated as her dark mood and earlier allure reappeared.

"I just realized," she said. "Marjorie should be at the Potato Blossom Queen Pageant tomorrow night to pass along her crown." Molly turned around to Mr. Pop. "You haven't heard, have you? Mother hasn't said a word. Is she coming back up?"

Mr. Pop shook his head.

"The Little Miss Potato Blossoms are so sweet," Tommy said trying to distract her. "I didn't ever notice before."

"I've always had a soft spot for the little ones," Mother said, helping Tommy. "Look at Little Miss Van Buren. She's adorable."

Accepting the gesture, Molly nodded. "She is. But there's Little Miss Monticello and that huge mass of curls on her little head. I wonder if it's natural or if her mother puts her hair up in curlers. I wish I'd brought my camera!"

Tommy patted his pockets as though maybe he had a tiny camera hidden in them. Molly giggled. I rolled my eyes once again but turned them back to the stage. We could hardly keep up with the Little Misses from all the small towns in the county. Although Molly was right. Curly-haired Little Miss Monticello was the one who brought the most applause from the crowd. Evidently Little Miss Monticello caught the eye of the judges too, as she was named Little Miss Potato Blossom. Mother declared her "cute as a bug's ear," claiming one of Ellery's favorite sayings as her own.

We said our goodbyes to Tommy outside the gym, Tommy promising to call on Molly when we were all back in Watsonville. And Mr. Pop, Mother, Molly, and I returned to the Aroostook Inn for a good night's rest. We'd brought our Sunday clothes with us. Mr. Pop wouldn't think of missing church. It didn't matter where we were or who we knew on a Sunday, we didn't miss church. Especially not here. Mr. Pop had several farmer friends who attended First Baptist in Fort Fairfield, so I went to bed knowing our time here at the Potato Blossom Festival would be over before it started. We'd miss the crowning of Marjorie's successor, which now I realized was probably intentional. We'd check out the following morning and head to Sunday services at Fort Fairfield Baptist before heading home, which now included wonderful promise for Molly and more of the same great unknown for me.

Chapter Sixteen

*F*or all the odd happenings of the last week, Monday brought routine again and brought us right back to the grind of harvesting vegetables. On the trip home from Fort Fairfield, Mr. Pop told me the green beans and cucumbers would need tending to. Bud took the truck down to the Flats while Mr. Pop, Mother, and I finished breakfast. I was thankful for the gospel reading at the breakfast table. If it weren't for that, no one would've uttered a word. The air hung heavy with the hard work that lay ahead: getting the vegetables out of the ground and getting Mick out of jail.

"Our reading for this morning is from the gospel of Luke, chapter 4, verses 14 through 21," Mr. Pop said. He read to us about Jesus in the synagogue and finished with the Lord's words: "'The Spirit of the Lord is upon me, because he hath anointed me to preach the gospel to the poor; he hath sent me to heal the brokenhearted, to preach deliverance to the captives, and recovering of sight to the blind, to set at liberty them that are bruised, to preach the acceptable year of the Lord.'"

We all said "Amen" simultaneously. I wanted to thank Mr. Pop for picking that appropriate passage, considering Mick's circumstances, but realized he was just reading what came next in the devotional book. Instead, I had God to thank for planning that perfect passage for this morning. I hoped somehow God would work this passage into Mick's cell and his mind. I wondered if Mick had any idea, any small grasp on the fact that God wanted to "set at liberty them that are bruised." From the little I'd gleaned from Joseph about the kind of upbringing he and Mick had had, there was a significant amount of bruising to be set free from. *Please God, help me keep the faith. Protect Mick in that cold cell. Bring someone to him who can heal his broken heart.*

"Mercy," Mr. Pop was saying. "Mercy, you're daydreaming."

"What? Oh, sorry. What were you saying?"

"Would you pray for us before our workday begins?"

"Sure." I bowed my head and folded my hands, the same way I'd been taught in Sunday school and reminded of four times a day growing up. "Dear God, help us today to accomplish all we need to get done. Be with Mr. Pop, Bud, and Ellery in the field along with the other workers. Help Mother as she gets our dinner ready, and Lord, please be with Mick today. Please. Amen."

"Thank you," Mr. Pop said. He rested his hands on his thighs, ready to push himself up. This change of posture always indicated the switch from godly reverence to ready-to-get-to-work-ed-ness.

"I've sent Bud to the Flats to pick up the men. I'd like you to grab some bushel baskets to pass out to them in the bean field. Then I'll send you and Ellery over to the cucumbers to harvest a bunch of those for the stand. If we get enough bushels of green beans today, I'll make a trip down to Bangor to sell them to the IGA stores there."

"To Bangor?" I asked.

"To Bangor," Mr. Pop said. "If I go, I'll spend the night with Roger and see what progress he's making."

I was thrilled at the prospect of Mr. Pop making a trip to Bangor. Though his bringing produce to IGA wasn't unheard of, it was uncommon enough an occurrence to make me hope that talking to Uncle Roger was the real reason for the drive. I hoped and prayed that there'd be big news as I flew to the shed for the bushel baskets and skipped all the way to the field. I beat Bud and the men to the field by at least ten minutes and just sat and waited, indulging myself with some daydreaming about Mick, about what it'd be like when he was released. I had to shake my head clear when I heard the rumble of the truck approaching. I passed out the bushels, then took one with me to meet Ellery in the cucumber field.

I saw Ellery coming on the run toward the field.

"I'm busier than a one-armed paperhanger with hives, Miss Mercy!" Ellery said. "Your father had me fixing some shingles on the shed before runnin' over here. Did he say how many cucumbers he wanted us to harvest?"

"No, but he wants them for the stand, so I figure a half to three quarters of a bushel should do it for today. Take a look around for the ones that are fully ripe, and we'll grab them first. These cukes are beauties this year. Mr. Pop must have sprayed for the cucumber beetle. I don't see any. They were terrible last year, remember?"

"Ayuh, they sure were! The cukes weren't worth a plug nickel last year. This year it's the yellow crookneck squash. Some kinda squash beetle got at 'em, and they ain't worth a hilla beans. Makes me mighty sad, it's my favorite of all the vegetable crops yer father grows."

"One of my favorites too," I said. "When Mother boils them fork tender and then slices them in half and slathers them with butter, I'm in heaven."

"Enough of this, Miss Mercy," Ellery said. "We gotta stop talkin' 'bout food if we're gonna make it to dinnertime."

I laughed. Standing in rows of cucumbers and squash, peas and beans, surrounded by hundreds of acres of nothing but potatoes, it was impossible *not* to think about food, though the snorts coming from the pigs and the smell rising from the chicken coop near the garden did help curb the appetite.

I knelt and began cutting the cucumbers free from their vines. Ellery joined me, gently wiping off the bristles before placing them into the baskets.

"What happened up country, Mercy? Anything good come out of that council meetin'?"

I shook my head and handed Ellery two cucumbers.

"It was a start, but sounds like they barely got anywhere. I don't always understand things like that. I surely thought Mr. Pop would come back with good news about Mick. I guess I should know by now that there's not going to be much good news when it comes to Mick, or the Maliseet either."

"Well, I wouldn't go so far as to say there won't be *any* good news. Gotta hold out *some* hope. But this ole world can be mighty cruel at times. And I'm sorry that you've had to wake up to this fact so young. When you and Mick played together as kids, no one cared. Somethin' about kids that can cross all kinds of barriers. But now you're of age, you're a young woman and people start to wonder, to ask questions about whether it's okay for you and Mick to even be friends, let alone more than friends."

"We're not more than friends. Why does everyone say that?"

"Mercy me! There's a sucker born every minute, but I'm not one of 'em. You don't 'spect me to believe you two are just friends. I didn't just crawl out from under a rock, ya know."

"Sometimes I wish I could crawl under a rock, you know?"

"I know. But you can't. None of us can."

"Ellery?"

"Yup?"

"Did you know Old Man Stringer had a sister?"

Ellery wiped down a cucumber with the edge of his sleeve before crunching right into it. "This one was no good to sell at the stand," he said. "Yup, I knew. So tell me, Mercy, how did *you* know he had a sister? He tell you about her?"

I shook my head and cut through another vine. "I met her in the hospital."

"The hospital?"

"Trying to visit Old Man. Squeak, I guess."

"Lord have mercy! I haven't heard him called Squeak in a coon's age. But you mean you met Elizabeth?"

"Elizabeth?"

"Stringer. Squeak's sister."

"Oh, Mrs. Calloway. Yes, I met her. When I went into town with Uncle Roger, I had some time to use up. Thought I'd pay a visit. But they wouldn't let me see him. Nice of them to send out his sister though."

"I'm sure she was happy for the company. Makes me feel terrible for not visiting him myself."

"Well, don't. He's out cold still, I guess. But is it true what his sister says? That Old Man isn't so old after all? And that he and Mr. Pop and Ansley and Mr. Carmichael were friends as boys? Like Mick and me?"

"Well, certainly not like you and Mick. I don't think they ever snuck any kisses behind the chicken coop."

I rolled my eyes. "You know what I mean."

"Surely, I do. Yes, it's true. They were friends. Shoot, we all were. Roger too. All of us playing and hunting and fishing. Like nothing. Those were good times."

"So what happened?"

"What'd'ya mean?"

"Well, why did Mr. Pop turn out so okay, and the other men so messed up?"

Ellery took another bite and looked back toward the house.

"You mean why doesn't your Mr. Pop have to be shaken awake out of his drunken stupor and why doesn't he hate men enough to make up a crime against them?"

"I guess."

"Well, your Mr. Pop would say it's God's grace alone. And I suppose he's right. Though I hate making it sound like God's grace doesn't reach Ansley and Squeak and even Frankie Carmichael. Because certainly it does."

"But why were they all friends and now they aren't?"

"Hard to say exactly."

"Uncle Roger says it's because Mrs. Carmichael wanted to run off with Ansley."

Ellery nearly choked on the cucumber. He wiped the seeds from the corner of his mouth and asked, "He told you that?"

I nodded. "Is it true?"

Ellery paused, then said, "Yes, it's true. But she didn't. Story goes that Old Mr. Fulton promised Frankie Carmichael his store if he'd marry Muriel, Mrs. Carmichael, but I don't know if I believe that. Pretty sure just common sense got hold of Muriel. Or fear did. Running off, leaving your family behind, and marrying a Maliseet would take guts."

"Her daughter did it."

"She did."

"So do you think this is why Mr. Carmichael is so angry? Even more so than he was before?"

"I can't say exactly. And I don't like to speculate or try and get inside another man's head. But it'd be hard to think that his daughter's running off didn't remind him that the woman he loves might've rather made that same choice." He was quiet for a moment. Then, "But it's these choices we need to learn to live with, Mercy. Where your Mr. Pop sees God's grace as the reason he's the man he is today, I see choices. Maybe it's the same thing. Frankie Carmichael could've chose to let bygones be bygones and chose to believe his beautiful wife loved him, but instead, he let bitterness fester and set out to seek vengeance on the Maliseet. Starting with when he convinced folks in town to stop renting spaces to Maliseet and got the town council to push them out to the Flats."

"Mr. Carmichael did that?"

"Well, he didn't do it alone, mind you. But he was a champion."

"But how could Mr. Pop stay friends with him?"

"Because your Mr. Pop also made choices. Choices to love his neighbors as himself. Look how he treats Squeak and Ansley. Lots of good Christian men would've stopped associating with folks who drown their sorrows with a bottle instead of taking them to Jesus, but not your dad. He made the choice to love them and look out for them. And to hope and pray God would let a little of His graces seep out on to them."

I scooted toward the cucumber bushel and stared down our load. My worry had worked its way up from my stomach, through my throat, and up into my face. It was a long speech for Ellery. I didn't want him to see my lip quiver or my eyes water. In my fifteen years, he'd only seen me cry once—when I was seven and I fell out of the maple Mick and I had chased Lickers into. She wouldn't come down, but I sure did. And hit the ground hard. Mick had grabbed Lickers and jumped down after me. He must've landed as hard as I did, but he never said a word about it.

Ellery put his hand on my shoulder, his callouses scratching against my shirt.

"But here's why your Mr. Pop likes to talk about God's grace more than our choices. Because we all make terrible choices at times, and God still manages to do all kinds of good and work all kinds of wonder. And nobody has seen evidence of that more than your father. It's why your name is what it is, after all."

"I thought it was because they'd been married so long before I came along. God showed them a great mercy in giving them me, and so on."

Ellery laughed. "Well, maybe that too. But your father will be the first to tell anyone that he and your saint of a mother, even, haven't always made the best choices. But they've tried to live as Jesus asks and they've sought forgiveness when they've messed up. That's where the grace—where all those shades of mercy show up in life. When you realize that." Ellery wasn't done sermonizing. He went on. "And because I know you need to hear it, I want to tell you: I'm not the saintliest man, and I've made my share of mistakes, and I've been too afraid my whole life to take on a wife or anything more than working for your dad. But I'm a churchgoing and

Bible-believing, baptized man, and I think I can recognize God on the move when I see Him out shaking and stomping and working up something mighty. And I think it's going to happen."

I was still blinking away tears while Ellery continued.

"You and I both know if it's up to your Pop, it will turn out okay. Your uncle Roger is on the case too and if there's anyone who can clean up this mess, it's him. Since Hector was a pup, Roger could argue his way out of anything. When we were in school together, everyone always wanted Roger on their side. I think we all could see his lawyerin' skills way back. So don't you worry your pretty little head, Miss Mercy. Before you know it, Mick will be free and this mess will be behind us. I think God Himself wants you to know that. But since Mr. Pop himself wants these vegetables, I think we better get back to work."

I hadn't hugged Ellery in a couple years. But as I tightened my arms around his neck and felt his tighten around me, I felt a peace I hadn't felt in a long time. It was like he squeezed the worry and the fears right out of me. At least in that moment.

Ellery's words weren't quite the same as Mr. Pop's, but almost as good. And I hoped they were true. We needed God to move in a way that it would leave no doubt about His will for all of us.

Ellery patted me on the back, stood, and headed over to the bean field, leaving me to finish the cucumber bushel. But I felt better than I had in a long time. My strength returned and my cucumber-cutting pace picked up. When my bushel was three-quarters full, I took it out to the stand where Mother thanked a customer and turned to greet me.

Mother held her hands on my shoulders, keeping me at arms' length while looking into my face with her eyebrows squinched.

"Have you gotten another message-in-a-basket or something?"

"No, ma'am."

"Then why do you look so happy?"

"Just happy to be done in the cucumber field, I guess."

Mother laughed and turned to count the money in her cash box.

"I can help with dinner if you need it," I said.

"Actually, can you tend the fryer? I've got molasses doughnuts all ready to lower into the oil. I want to close up out here, but then I'll head back to the house."

"I'll be glad to help you test them when they're done," I said with a soft chuckle before I turned to run back to the house. Molasses doughnuts were my favorite. I picked a good time to help out in the kitchen.

"Of course, you will," Mother said. "You let me know when the first one is done. By the time I get in and get the table set, it will be cooled enough to test." Our long kitchen counter made it easy for both Mother and me to work side by side. We had placed the electric fryer next to the porcelain sink, then put a small bowl of sugar for dipping some, as well as a sugar shaker to dust others with powdered sugar. I could never decide if I had a taste for sweet or savory when I smelled oil heating up. My taste buds and my nose didn't work in concert until I spotted the powdered-sugar shaker, then I was all about the sweets.

Before long, Mother and I were arranging the cooled dough-nuts on a platter, dusting some with powdered sugar. Mother pointed to the last two doughnuts left behind on the cooling tray.

"Going to wrap these up and drive them into town," she said. "I heard Mr. Herbert sneaks treats to Mick. I thought he'd like one."

I smiled and looked down. Amazed at the things my mother could communicate through a doughnut.

"I'm also dropping one off at the hospital for Mrs. Calloway. If she's anything like her brother, she'll love these."

My eyes widened and my mouth readied to ask.

"But no," she said. "You may not come with. I'd like a private conversation with her. It sounds like she already told you plenty."

"Did Uncle Roger tell you?"

"He didn't tell me any details; you know he's not like that. Well, not mostly like that. But he did tell me she was in town, and that you and her had a most interesting conversation. As did you and your uncle, I gather. We will talk about that later."

With that Mother carried the platter into the dining room. The way her skirt swished behind her as she turned to push the door with her hip always made her look like a movie star. "Like Grace Kelly," Bud would say.

And it was true.

Chapter Seventeen

*M*ercy, time to get up!" Mother's voice sounded faint and far away, almost like a dream. I couldn't get up. I was too tired to think, let alone get dressed and go work.

"Mercy, breakfast in twenty minutes!" This time Mother's words were much louder, sharper. It definitely wasn't a dream.

I continued to lie there in a kind of twilight sleep. I must have been half dreaming about Chef Barone or New York and Glenn and Marjorie because I woke up with a taste for lasagna.

As I blinked my eyes open and tried to kick-start my mind and body, I imagined Marjorie and Glenn in their Brooklyn walk-up. Thanks to a library book about New York, I could picture beautiful brownstones all along a block. I imagined Marjorie and Glenn sitting at their breakfast table, set in a bay window, chatting over coffee and toast while admiring the oaks and elms that lined the street.

Though I pictured them smiling, I wondered if Marjorie had any regrets, if she looked out her fifth-story window and squinted, wishing to see Mt. Katahdin's peak, if she ever longed for home when she saw man-made buildings instead. I wondered what she'd tell her children someday about where she came from and who her family was.

For Glenn, with Marjorie and a good job in New York, life could only get better. But Marjorie, I began to see, had taken a big risk. She was the one with more to lose. Or so it seemed. Moving to New York sounded fun and adventurous, but moving away and being unable to come home, not nearly so. But Molly said Marjorie wrote letters that were filled with excitement and joy. We couldn't know if it were for show or for real. But then again, I wasn't sure it mattered.

I hopped up and out of bed, finally, and started to get dressed. Mr. Pop decided to wait for today's harvest before taking the load to Bangor, so it was another day of hard work to fill as many bushels with beans as we could.

It was getting harder and harder to wait on news about Mick. Mr. Pop didn't want me picking up the men in the Flats, so I couldn't get anywhere near town let alone the jail. I could hear Ellery's words in my head, "What doesn't kill ya makes ya stronger, Mercy." Based on that, I figured I must be pretty strong on account of I was still breathing. I hoped Chef was still bringing supper to Mick. I could handle the thought of him in jail if I knew he wasn't going hungry. Maybe I could volunteer to go to the IGA for Mother and at least stop in to see Joseph at Nelson's. Surely he'd know something.

"Mercy, breakfast's ready," Mother said. "Come on downstairs."

I jumped on the bannister and slid to the bottom. Something in this day had to be fun. I was desperate for some. And I knew it wasn't going to be bean picking.

Breakfast was predictable. In the midst of so much chaos, that was something I really appreciated. I could count on good biscuits and bacon and eggs, thanks to "the girls" as my father said. I could count on Mr. Pop to quiet us and read Scripture. Starting the day with the sense that God was with us helped me keep putting one foot in front of the other when there were so many unknowns.

I looked up from my half-eaten plate and asked, "Mother, maybe after I help you clean up the dinner dishes at noon, I could head into town to the grocery store for you. I saw the list you started."

"Well, I could use more lard sooner than later," Mother said. "I seem to be baking more than usual these days. Guess it's helped me keep my mind off things. I'll look over the list this morning while you're out gathering eggs from the girls, and I'll take you up on your offer to go after dinner."

I wanted to leap out of my skin. I glanced at Mr. Pop to make sure he didn't put a stop to it. When he patted me on the back and walked toward the kitchen door, I knew I was home free. Just the prospect of getting an hour to be near Mick, to find out some little tidbit from Joseph, gave me hope. It gave me the boost I needed for tending the animals and picking beans all morning. Maybe I could stop in and see Molly too. I hadn't been able to reach her in two days thanks to Mrs. Garritson's big mouth, tying up the phone lines day and night. *Lord, forgive me, but it's true!*

I gathered a bucket of feed and a basket for egg gathering and headed out to the coop. Chickens were great companions that didn't talk back, or at least not much. Their low-level clucking and chattering was a nice mask for my voice calling out to God in prayer in a more personal way than I dared at the breakfast table. The girls' volume ebbed and flowed with my own, and their voices felt like a cloud of witnesses surrounding me and agreeing with my prayer. All creatures were loved by the Creator, and though I felt nearest to Him in the shadow of Mt. Katahdin, the chicken coop was a close second.

I scattered the feed after I'd gathered the eggs, and I headed back to the farmhouse secretly hoping Mother would ask me to head into town now instead of waiting, but no such luck. Grabbing a couple of bushel baskets from the shed, I headed back down to the bean field. About two-thirds of the field had been picked already, so at least the end was in sight. If we could finish up this field, then Mr. Pop ought to have enough beans to make it worth his while to head to Bangor.

The morning passed quickly and I headed toward the farm for dinner along with the other workers. I would soon be one step closer to Mick, or at least information about him. I picked at my food.

"Young lady, you're gonna wither away to nothin," Bud said.

"Not that hungry. Been around beans all morning. Feel like I've already eaten."

"Ha! Well I have too and it's created a voracious appetite," Bud said. "Women! Can't quite figure 'em out. Guess that's why I'm not married. What's your excuse, Ellery?"

"I couldn't marry, not when I have to look out for the both of us, Bud." Ellery had a smirk on his face, for Bud's sake, and he winked at me. I knew the real story even if Ellery didn't want to admit it to Bud.

"Mercy, if you'll clear the table, I'll do the dishes, and you can go ahead and head into town."

"Yes, Mother," I said with as much calm as I could manage. I could hardly wait to get in that car and point it toward town. Mother walked into the kitchen awaiting my delivery of the dishes.

"My grocery list is on the kitchen table," she called from the kitchen. "Pick up anything you think I missed. Oh, and I promised to give a dozen eggs to Mrs. Garritson. Would you drop those off on your way?"

"Sure, if she can get off the phone long enough to walk out to the car and get them," I mumbled.

"What was that, Mercy?"

Grateful that she was still in the kitchen and unable to catch my tone, I just said, "Nothing, Mother. I'll head to town in a couple minutes."

Since I wasn't heading to the Flats and I didn't need to hide my presence or my purpose, I drove the main route into town. Everything appeared a little greener today, the sun a little brighter. Just the prospect of learning something about Mick made me smile from ear to ear. I drove straight to Nelson's before going for groceries. Joseph was in the dining room, waiting on tables, but had time to talk. The after-lunch crowd was in no hurry. Joseph was in good spirits, though I couldn't tell if that was because of

Mick, or because he finally felt valuable, useful. Either way, seeing him felt like coming home. Joseph had become family, whether he knew it or not.

"Hey Joseph, how's it going? Looks like Nelson's is the place to be in Watsonville. It never used to be this crowded when Mrs. Nelson was cooking."

Joseph laughed as we looked around the dining room, both suddenly worried that Mr. Nelson would make one of his surprise appearances. I'd always loved the way this restaurant looked. It wasn't fancy, not in the way some think of fancy, at least. When I was little, the red and white checked tablecloths made it feel like a picnic inside. And yet, the stamped-tin ceiling and sconces on the papered walls reminded me to use my manners. Once upon a time, the place had smelled like onions and pot roast. But since Chef arrived, the basil and garlic wafted through. Years ago, no one might have guessed Italian food would go over so well here. But Chef was making a huge success of his second chance. Whatever he had meant by that.

"You should have seen it an hour and a half ago. I could have used help! We really need to hire someone part-time just to wait tables around the noon hour."

"If I could get away from the farm and if school wasn't starting so soon, I'd do it in a heartbeat."

"Oh, right," Joseph said. "School. Chef says I gotta go back, but I don't want to."

"Of course, you've got to go back! What a silly thing to say."

"What's the point? I'm learning everything I need to learn here. But Mick says I need to go back too."

"Mick! Have you talked to him?"

Joseph shook his head. "I haven't talked to him. Not directly. But I get to take supper over to the jail almost every night. I don't see Mick, but when Mr. Herbert is on duty, he usually tells me about Mick's frame of mind that day. He says that he tells Mick

I'm the one bringing his meal. He says Mick smiles every time he hears that."

"So how'd Mick know about school?"

"Oh, Mr. Herbert asked me if I was excited to go back. When I said no, that I wanted to stay working at the restaurant, he told Mick. Next night when I dropped off dinner, I had Mick's opinion waiting for me. Mr. Herbert agreed with him, though, so who knows if Mick really said that."

"Well, of course, Mick would think you should stay in school. Will Chef let you stay on? Can you work weekends and after school?"

"So long as I keep going to church with him on Sunday mornings, yes. Chef even arranged it with my ma. I'll stay over at his place above the restaurant on Saturday nights when we work late. It's nice up there. Chef's got a wife and a little girl, Giana. She calls me JoeJoe. I help her learn her colors and shapes while Mrs. Barone cleans. They're a real nice family. Like yours. Mick'll get a kick out of them."

"Soon, I hope."

Joseph shrugged and looked behind him. Chef had popped out of the kitchen to wave at me and hold up a finger for Joe. "Take one more minute, son," Chef said. "Then we've got to finish these vegetables."

Joseph nodded. "Anything you want me to tell Mr. Herbert to tell Mick? I'll be there in a couple hours."

I wanted Mick to know I loved him and that I never stopped thinking about him. Or worrying about him. Or wishing we could be back, snug and secret, in our little lean-to in the woods. But I couldn't pass that on. Not through this route.

So I said, "I want him to know that we are headed to the Northern Maine Fair Saturday morning, and the Indian Rights Council is going to have their second meeting. Mr. Pop will be there and maybe even Uncle Roger. Tomorrow Mr. Pop is taking a load of beans down to Bangor, and he's going to see my uncle and find out what's going on to get him out of jail. Old Man Stringer is still in a coma." And I decided to tell him, "But Bud says he's been hearing a whole mess of stories going around about the incident that day in front of Fulton's. Not everyone is standing by Frankie Carmichael's story."

"You want me to tell Mr. Herbert all that?"

"I want Mick to know. So he can hold out hope. I guess I want *you* to know too. For the same reason."

"Hope. Sheesh! That's all I hear about from everybody. I want to have hope—I really do—and Chef and Father McMahon keep telling me God still works miracles and that Jesus was born to bring hope and all that. And maybe that's true. But maybe it's just true for white folks. Because, at the end of the day, Mick is still Maliseet, and I'm not sure God's too busy working miracles for the Maliseet."

"Pretty sure the Bible is full of stories of God working miracles for all kinds of folk. But I know it's hard," I admitted. "I can barely hang on either. But at least hold out some hope for the meeting in Presque Isle, for Uncle Roger, for God to do a miracle. Listen, I'd better get going. I'm supposed to be picking up groceries. But I'll see you soon. I promise!"

I gave Joseph a quick wave just as Chef reappeared to wave him back to the kitchen. I was grateful Joe didn't have a chance to respond to my hold-out-hope speech. I couldn't hear any more negative talk. I was struggling with everything in me to hold out my own hope for Mick.

Driving through the square heading to the IGA, I caught myself daydreaming again. I pictured Mick and me walking hand in hand on the square just like normal folk. There was that word again. *Normal.* What is normal anyway? For the first time I realized it was time to decide what normal might look like. And to do that, Mick had to be released from jail.

* * *

Mrs. Garritson finally got off the phone long enough for me to call Molly and arrange for her to go with us to the state fair. Of course, she jumped at the chance to once again get away from the gloom of her home life, especially since her father had put a stop to her seeing Tommy right after the festival. The last thing he needed, Mr. Carmichael told her, was to have another lovesick daughter mooning around. Mr. Pop said we should see this as a positive sign that Mr. Carmichael's fury was spreading more equally. That he put white-as-white Tommy Birger in the same category as black-haired, tan-skinned Glenn was "progress in an odd way" as Mr. Pop said.

Maybe because the fair didn't hold the same kind of memories of Marjorie and her family for Molly as the festival did, I had a feeling this trip would be a relaxing time for both of us. Fewer memories and less stress. Even though the Indian Rights Council was meeting again, I had more hope than dread. I kept replaying Ellery's words. "I think I can recognize God on the move when I see Him out shaking and stomping and working up something mighty. And I think it's going to happen." Those words of hope, along with the knowledge that Uncle Roger would be attending the meeting, kept me moving forward. One step at a time. One step at a time. Maybe Uncle Roger could make the same kind of difference as Mr. Brown had with the Board of Education.

Chapter Eighteen

I feel like we were just driving this road," I said.

"We were," Mother said. "I don't know why they have these two big events so close together. One at the beginning and one at the end of the summer would make more sense, but then when did they ever ask my opinion?"

"Well, it does make a nice last hurrah of summer before we have to head back to school."

"So Molly," Mr. Pop said. "I heard the Birgers were coming up to the fair today too."

Molly blushed.

"Oh yeah?"

"Well, I thought that might be of interest to you." Mother swatted Mr. Pop's leg and shot him her best "stop it" glare before revealing a smirk.

Molly had to work to keep a straight face. Her nonchalance was noted but not believed by me or anyone else in the car. I could see Mother's profile from the backseat; she had a big grin on her face. Even Mr. Pop cracked a smile. Poor Molly couldn't cover her true feelings for long. We decided to let it go rather than embarrass her any more than we already had.

"So do you think the Henderson kids will win more Future Farmers of America ribbons this year?" I asked Mr. Pop.

Mother responded first. "I think they'd be devastated if they didn't. They spend the whole year grooming their cattle just for the state fair."

"Mr. Pop, what do you think?"

"I think it's likely, but I've been hearing in town that the two

Brown boys are finally at the age where they will be serious competition for someone. It should be fun to watch it all unfold."

"You know what I want to watch? The Indian Rights Council unfold in a way that lets Mick out of jail. That's what I've been praying for. That everyone will see that Mick being locked up is nonsense and wrong. Please tell me you think that's what will happen after this meeting."

Mr. Pop sighed. Though I knew this was foremost on his mind every bit as it was on mine, Mr. Pop had urged me before we left not to let it consume my every thought and every bit of conversation. I had tried, but I could hold back no longer.

"Mercy, I wish I could say I know what the outcome will be," Mr. Pop said. "But I can't. And these meetings are not about Mick and his situation. At least, not explicitly. I can tell you that there will be more forward progress just because your uncle Roger will be there. He's used to working with politicians and knows how to push a meeting forward. He knows how to ask the right questions and raise the most necessary issues, and as you know, they have a number of things to discuss."

He smiled kindly at me then said, "Try to enjoy your day. Take in all you can, and we'll meet up at supper time and decide exactly what time we'll head back. Since we're almost there, Geneva, would you lead us in a prayer for this day? I know we all sense the importance of the next few hours."

Mother turned around, making sure we'd closed our eyes and bowed our heads before she began.

"Almighty God, ruler of all, You know the end from the beginning, and we desperately need Thy help today. We need Thy presence in the meeting this morning. Give Paul and Roger Thy wisdom as they speak up for the least of these. Oh God, may Thy ways prevail, may You sway the hearts and opinions of men who would wish harm on any Maliseet. Remove the scales from their eyes. Do whatever it takes, holy Lord. Work a miracle, God! Lead them to see the truth this very day. Amen."

A round of amens followed.

Mr. Pop reached a hand over to grab Mother's and smiled. "Thanks, dear," he said. "A real courage booster."

Mother nodded. I never doubted Mr. Pop's courage, but I suspected that Mother knew his weaknesses and fears better than anyone.

"That was beautiful, Mrs. Millar. Thank you." Molly had confided to me that she'd given up on praying. She felt that either God wasn't listening or He wasn't even there.

"Oh, Molly," Mother said. "You are welcome. I just took the words that were pent up in my heart and spilled them out into the ear of God. You know any of us can do that. He is always waiting for us to be with Him."

"Doesn't always feel like it," Molly said in a small voice.

"No, it does not," Mr. Pop agreed, slowing as we pulled into town and traffic began to build around us. "But if we always *felt* like this, I don't think we'd need faith. Certainly, our faith would not grow. Well, look at this. Here we are already."

I didn't know what, if anything, Molly heard of Mr. Pop or Mother's little sermons. As soon as we pulled into town, the crowds and passing cars had pulled Molly's attention toward the windows. I scooted toward Molly and leaned to look out her same window. People bustled past carrying ice cream cones and pastries, pushing baby carriages, and pulling wagons. As Mr. Pop pulled into a parking spot, a familiar family stopped in front of our car, pointing and smiling: the Birgers.

Molly blushed once again and straightened up to see herself in the rearview mirror.

"You look beautiful," would be just about the last thing I said to her all day before she and Tommy wandered off into the throngs of people in their own little fog.

"Really, Mercy. Why don't you come with us?" Tommy had

urged, turning around as they walked three steps ahead of me. I assured them I was fine and slowed my steps so they could carry on without me.

"See you at the entrance at 4:30!" Molly had yelled back. That was the time Mr. Pop had said we'd all meet up.

I turned away from the crowds of the fair and wandered back toward the Presque Isle Free Library where I figured I'd sit and finally finish *The Catcher in the Rye,* after I found where its Beulah Akeley Boardroom was, where the Indian Affairs Council meeting would commence, just after lunch.

* * *

I found the room without much trouble, that is, without having to ask the librarian. I was glad this librarian did not know me, so she wouldn't be inclined to wonder why I was asking the location of a conference room.

But now that I knew where their room was, knew the place where Mr. Pop and Uncle Roger would gather with politicians from across the state—I needed to find a perch, a place comfortable enough that it would make sense for me to be sitting and reading there; a place where I could hear when the meeting started and, more important, when it ended but not be seen by anyone coming from or going to the room.

I selected a musty old wing back set in front of a window two stacks over from the boardroom. But no sooner had I settled in and started reading than did my stomach growl. Though a "No Eating. No Drinking" sign hung in a gilded frame not far from where I sat, the chair I'd selected and my deep bag that concealed my tightly wrapped sandwich and polished apple, offered protection from those who might want to catch me eating. So with one hand on my book and another dipping back and forth into the bag nestled up against me as I ate my lunch, I waited for the Indian Affairs Council men to assemble and start their meeting.

I read all of three pages in the next hour. My ears had been trained to the coming and going of folks behind me. I became accustomed enough to the regular library folks passing through the stacks, that it was easy enough to pick up a change when the politicians began arriving. They didn't seem to care about staying hushed or walking gently through the library. Their steps hit hard on the wooden floors, creaking and clacking as they went. Their voices rang out above the whispers and the otherwise stillness of the library. I froze in my chair as they began filing in behind me. I kept my head bowed toward the pages as I tried to count the number of times the door opened and closed, letting new people in. I slunk a little farther down in my chair when I heard Uncle Roger's quiet tone.

"Could be interesting, brother," he said. "Lord have mercy, indeed."

And with that, Uncle Roger and Mr. Pop walked into the Indian Rights Council and the door clicked closed for the last time.

*   *   *

For the next half hour I was able to roam the streets of New York with Holden Caufield, but I became quickly as restless as Holden was and I could sit no longer. Unwilling to leave the library or risk being seen, I roamed through the stacks beyond the door, where I could still hear any loud rumblings or when the meeting ended, but wouldn't be seen should Uncle Roger or Mr. Pop leave for any other reason.

My eyes wandered over the spines of the burgundy and black and brown leather-bound volumes of poetry that lined the shelves, seeing nothing really. But I stopped when DICKINSON appeared on a yellow-bound volume. We'd talked about Emily Dickinson in English class. "The best poet this country has ever known!" our teacher had declared. I pulled the volume from the shelf and opened it to "Grief."

I measure every grief I meet
With analytic eyes;
I wonder if it weighs like mine,
Or has an easier size.

I wonder if they bore it long,
Or did it just begin?
I could not tell the date of mine,
It feels so old a pain.

I wonder if it hurts to live,
And if they have to try,
And whether, could they choose between,
They would not rather die.

I wonder if when years have piled
Some thousands on the cause
Of early hurt, if such a lapse
Could give them any pause;

Or would they go on aching still
Through centuries above,
Enlightened to a larger pain
By contrast with the love.

The grieved are many, I am told
The reason deeper lies—
Death is but one and comes but once,
And only nails the eyes.

There's grief of want, and grief of cold—
A sort they call "despair";

There's banishment from native eyes,
In sight of native air.

And though I may not guess the kind
Correctly, yet to me
A piercing comfort it affords
In passing Calvary,

To note the fashions of the cross
Of those that stand alone,
Still fascinated to presume
That some are like my own.

I hadn't yet read enough American poets to form an opinion on who was the best. As I fought back tears reading this poem, I realized my teacher must be right. Because somehow, this woman who grew up in a broad white house in the best part of town, educated and well-fed and not without love interests, recognized grief in all its forms, and spoke words that even desperate boys from the worst parts of town in the worst sorts of shelter would recognize.

Trying to shake getting lost in my own grief and my despair over the conversation that I imagined taking place in the room not twenty feet behind me, I flipped through the pages, closer to the front and stumbled upon Miss Dickinson's "Hope."

I'd just begun to read,

Hope is the thing with feathers
That perches in the soul

when I heard a sharp shuffling of feet and the librarian's voice. "Sir, please just allow me to knock first. You'll disturb the patrons."

I turned to see two deputies flanking who I'd later learn was Sheriff Dolling. He ignored the librarian's request and flung the door open without so much as knocking.

With my volume still in hand, I slid along the shelves until just outside the door. I no longer cared who could see me.

"Gentlemen," Sheriff Dolling said, "sorry to disturb you. But Mr. Millar—"

I heard two chairs push back and two men, both Mr. Pop and Uncle Roger, answer, "Yes?"

My heart pounded in my chest.

"Mr. *Roger* Millar. Judge Dodd is requesting your presence in his courtroom immediately."

Now more chairs backed up, and the hubbub overwhelmed the room. It took two seconds for both Uncle Roger and Mr. Pop to exit the room. Both looked at me immediately but said nothing. Mr. Pop pulled the door closed behind him as Uncle Roger spoke to the sheriff.

"What's this about?"

"It seems," Sheriff Dolling said, checking his notebook, "one Arthur Stringer has woken up."

PART 3

"I am with you."

Chapter Nineteen

The return to Watsonville was a blur. Mr. Pop had sent me to find Mother, to have her meet us at the car immediately. I found Molly with the Birgers and told them. Mrs. Birger offered to have Molly stay with them, and they'd bring her home the next day. Mother was harder to find, but after some searching, I found her admiring the stitching and creativity of some of our state's finest quilters. Though she'd been ready to purchase one of the blue-ribbon winners, instead Mother settled with getting the quilters' address, with promises to write with an order.

I don't remember racing back to the car. But when we arrived, Mr. Pop had it already running. Uncle Roger had left twenty minutes before. Supper would wait until we got to Watsonville. But none of us were really thinking about supper, only about what Old Man Stringer might have to say.

Once again, I was barred from visiting Old Man Stringer. Instead, I was sent to Nelson's to rest and eat. Chef and Joseph had already heard. Joseph shook as he sat down at my table, putting a plate of cannoli in front of me. "What do you think he's going to say?" Joseph asked.

"I don't know. The truth, I hope."

"Do you think he'll remember?"

"I don't know."

"You want to know what's weird?"

I looked up from my plate. Though Joseph still shook, I noticed a serenity I'd never seen before.

"What?"

"Last night, I went to visit Father McMahon to ask him about what you said, you know, about God working miracles for all kinds of folk. Plus, I figured if I had to go to church, I might as well try to understand."

I nodded.

"So I told him about Gluskap."

"Gluskap?"

Joseph smiled. "Never heard of him? Really?"

I shook my head.

"He's the one Maliseet—all the Indians here, all us Wabanaki—believe in. He's like a creator and a hero because of how he said we should live."

"So how does he say we should live?"

"He taught us that we should live together with respect—people and animals and everything and respect the earth. We don't do a great job of it always. Actually, a lot of us—of them—do a pretty lousy job of it. But living together *with respect* is the thing we believe. It's what we hear from the time we're born. Whether we live it or not is a different story."

"So what did Father McMahon say about that?"

"Well, maybe Mr. Pop wouldn't like this, so don't tell him, but he said Gluskap sounds something like Jesus."

I raised an eyebrow. "Like Jesus?" I was glad Mr. Pop wasn't around to hear this.

"Well, Father McMahon said Jesus taught about how we're supposed to live too, like loving each other, even our enemies. And how we should treat one another in the way we want to be treated. And that *does* sound like Gluskap. Finally, *something* about Jesus made sense to me."

I took another bite and waited for Joseph to say more.

"Then Father McMahon asked if I wanted to hear more about what Jesus had to say. And about who Jesus is."

"What did he say about that?" I'd never gone to a church like Father McMahon's, and I wondered. Joseph continued. "And he said how Jesus is God's only Son and he started to talk about how if I confessed my sins, Jesus would forgive me because He loves me. I told him Jesus didn't even *know* me, and if He did, He wouldn't love me. Because nobody really did. Besides Mick, maybe."

"A lot of people love you—" I started to interrupt, but Joseph was still talking.

"But he said Jesus *does* know me, and loves me no matter what I've done. And if I truly believe, Jesus will make me like I'm brand-new. A fresh start and all that." Joseph looked down.

"Like the fresh start Chef gave you?" I said.

"Sort of. At least that's what Father McMahon said. That Chef was acting on behalf of Jesus, maybe. Chef says he was just giving a boy who loved food an opportunity. But Father McMahon thinks how I got hooked up with Chef is more than that."

"So what do you think?" I asked.

Joseph shrugged.

"I don't know what to think," Joseph said. "But if it's true, if this Jesus does love me and offers fresh starts, then—"

Tears filled Joseph's eyes as his chest heaved with struggled breaths. All those years in Sunday school should have prepared me for this moment. I should've known the right words to say that would lead him to the next steps to true faith in Jesus Christ. I should have been ready to recite, "If any man be in Christ, he is a new creature: old things are passed away; behold, all things become new."

But words failed me. And maybe they weren't needed. It was clear God was reaching out to this boy—this young man— and could bring him where he needed to be without words from me. Instead, I nodded and stood up to hug Joseph. As his body shook in my arms, I felt the fluttering Miss Dickinson had written about—that feathered thing of hope in my soul.

* * *

Old Man first reported that he didn't remember anything at all about the incident that landed him in the hospital. That is, he didn't remember until someone told him that Mick had been sitting in a jail cell for two weeks because Frankie Carmichael said Mick tried to kill him.

Only then did Old Man break down and come clean. Mr. Pop told me all about it and soon everyone knew.

"I'd been so horribly drunk," he admitted. "Worse than normal. And it was still morning. I'd stayed up all night, drinking. Just outside the Flats. Mick found me as he walked into town. He helped me, I think. But by the time we reached town, when we stood in front of Fulton's, I told him to go on, to leave me. I wanted to go back to McGillicuddy's Tavern, but Mick said no. He wanted to take me to the hospital. He said that I wasn't looking too good. On a stack of Bibles, that's all I remember. How did that cockamamy story get around that Mick tried to kill me? The Maliseet are my family. If I'm not at McGillicuddy's or at the Millars', I'm with them."

And with that, and well, with the reporter from the *Bangor Daily,* who Uncle Roger had called up, waiting to run the story of the small town bent on tromping on an innocent boy's civil rights by forbidding visitors, Judge Dodd ordered Mick released from jail.

I was picking at the cannoli Chef had brought to my table when Mr. Pop burst in the door.

"Joseph," Mr. Pop called. Joseph appeared at the kitchen door. "He's out, son. Your brother's going home." My father finished that statement with a clap of his hands.

* * *

The rest of the time in the restaurant moved like a dream.

Chef had popped a bottle of champagne, which of course Mr.

Pop refused, though it appeared harder for him to pass up than I would've thought. We were headed home ourselves, Mr. Pop said. Would Chef be willing to let Joseph off for the night? Mr. Pop would send Bud or Ellery down to substitute, if that helped.

Chef had laughed. "No substitutes! Tonight," he said, raising a glass of champagne toward the ceiling, "we celebrate. God is good. He heard our prayers. We'll close up early tonight, but free lasagna to anyone who walks through those doors first!"

Joseph and I had hugged. As I walked out the door, Chef lifted him into a bear hug. "Do you see? Do you see what I've been telling you?" Chef was saying.

Mr. Pop told me it was time to go. I wanted to see Mick, I said. Tomorrow, Mr. Pop told me. Tomorrow.

And together me and Mr. Pop rode back to the farm. Mother had stayed in town, to sit with Mrs. Carmichael after hearing Mr. Carmichael had been taken to the police station for questioning. Turns out, reporting a crime that didn't happen is a crime unto itself.

I sat in bed with my copy of Emily Dickinson's poems on my lap. I'd taken the library's copy by accident in the rush. But I'd left my *The Catcher in the Rye* behind.

"Even swap," Mr. Pop said when he sat on the edge of my bed and I confessed. "I think we'll be able to work it out with them."

When Mr. Pop and I were this close to each other, it usually meant we were riding in the potato truck or out in the field together, or sitting at the dinner table. Now I had the perfect vantage point to see the crow's feet at the corner of his eyes and the graying around his temples and above his ears.

For the first time ever, I didn't feel as much like the son he never had but truly like Mr. Pop's daughter. The one he trusted to shuttle farmhands from one field to another, to run the roadside farm stand, or take care of the livestock. Or, maybe more importantly, the one who had fallen in love with the boy who walked into jail and stayed in love with the one who walked out.

"Is Uncle Roger still with Mick?"

"Yes. He was going to drive him to the Flats, then head back to Bangor."

"So is this over then?"

Mr. Pop nodded. "The Mick in jail part is. Not sure how much of the rest of it."

"Well, that Mick is out is enough for me."

"Yes. But not enough for the Maliseet. Not even enough for Mick. I can't stop thanking God that he's out, but this really is only the beginning."

"Of what?"

"Of changes that have been a long time coming. That Mick sat in jail that long was un-American. That the home he heads back to sits on our dump is inhumane. That his family has neither the resources nor the will to help him become the man God obviously gifted him to be, is just wrong." He paused, shaking his head. "For generations now, the Maliseet have had so much injustice heaped on them. All of them. I don't know how Mick, or any other Maliseet, for that matter, can keep getting back up after continually being knocked down, then putting one foot in front of the other again and again and again. It's time somebody stopped all the knocking down. Beginning with giving back some of their land."

I looked at Mr. Pop. "Their land? I thought they used to live in apartments in town."

"Mercy, you know better than that. You know that once all this land belonged to the Maliseet."

I nodded. "But they sold it, right? A million years ago? That's what Grandpa Millar always told me."

"Yes," Mr. Pop said. "They sold it. But most of us or most of our grandparents or great-greats or whoever lived here all those years ago paid very little for it. When the land was taken, the Maliseet were promised new land, which never came. Living in shacks down at the dump is not the land they imagined, not the life they wanted for their families. So now the Maliseet leaders—Mr. Polchies, Mr. Tomah, and Mr. Sabattis—are pressing for a land settlement claim like the Passamaquoddy and the Penobscot are working toward. And I think they're right. But if they get their land, a lot of us, me, and all of our neighbors, may lose our farms."

That had never occurred to me. "Can't we just share?" I asked.

"It's not that easy, Mercy."

"But it can't be that hard, either."

"I imagine it shouldn't be. But people are still fighting this very hard. Frankie Carmichael and his posse will have lost plenty of credibility, but they're still going to fight this. And things could turn uglier for the Maliseet for a time. I love Frankie like a brother, but I don't trust that he's going to let this go. Let's just pray that God intervenes. That God squashes the revenge that burns in his soul."

A chill ran through me. I pulled my comforter up tighter around me.

"But for now, my dear Mercy, I wanted you to know how happy I am about Mick." Mr. Pop patted my shoulder. "You must be eager to see him."

"I am," I said, with a gulp. "But I don't suppose he'll be up for working on the farm for a while."

"I don't know. He might be up for it. Roger said it was school Mick wasn't too keen on going back to. I can't blame him, actually."

Yet another blow to the old predictable way of things. I couldn't imagine a year at school without Mick.

"But," Mr. Pop said, "I'd like to see if you could convince him otherwise."

"Convince him otherwise what?"

"To go back to school. Even if he wants to wait a month. Or two. He's too bright to drop out. He should be thinking about his future, even about college. I hoped you'd be willing to drive out there tomorrow, actually, and talk to him."

Mr. Pop smiled at me while I lunged toward him, nearly knocking him off my bed as I hugged him.

"Really? Tomorrow? I can drive out to see him?"

"After church," Mr. Pop said. "You take Mother into town. She wanted to drop off some bread and flowers for Old Man at the hospital. He said he woke up craving some of your mother's homemade bread, you know, those rolls she makes that go with our Saturday night bean suppers, and can't think of anything else. Then you both can head to the Flats."

"But what will people think?"

Mr. Pop laughed and shook his head. "That my wife is delivering bread on a Sunday? Or that I let my daughter visit her Maliseet beau? People will talk about both. We know that. Just like people have talked about me hiring Maliseet and drunks and me leaving a party while your mother voiced her opinion. Some of these things I regret. But most I do not. And I can't help what people say. We answer to God, Mercy."

I nodded and tucked my legs back below the comforter, pulling it up closer to my face this time.

"You know Mick was my beau?" I smiled at the word. So old-fashioned, but so elegant to say. "Did Mother tell you?"

"Only after I asked. I confess to being slow about these things. Of course, looking back it seems obvious. I don't know how I could've missed it. One day you and Mick were punching each other's shoulders and hurrying up with your chores so you get back to work building your forts and then next day, or so it seemed, you were walking slowly together at the end of the day. Or disappearing altogether."

I felt the red rise into my face.

"I don't know how I didn't piece it together earlier. But I confess to not having taken the time to stop and notice you and who and what you've become. You are strong and smart and beautiful. It's the reason poor Tommy Birger couldn't keep away. And it's what Mick sees in you. Of course, I loved you even when you were gangly and scrappy."

We laughed and I leaned forward to hug my dad once again.

"So you're okay with this? With Mick and me?"

Mr. Pop breathed in deep, then exhaled for a while. The lines on his face looked deeper than I'd ever noticed. "I've told you: I love Mick like a son. He's one of the best young men I know. But to say I'm fully okay with this would be untrue. I'll be okay when Mick acknowledges Jesus as Savior and Lord. And when you both grow a little older. I'm going to keep praying for his salvation, and I expect you are too."

I looked down and nodded. I wanted to tell him about my conversation with Joseph, as if his steps toward salvation counted toward Mick's. Instead I asked what burned deeper on my heart: "But I can see Mick? I can go to the Flats? And he can sit on the porch here with me?"

"Yes, you can. Though I don't want to hear any talk about getting married someday. Not for a long time. Or about running off. And I'm tempted to put the same conditions that Chef put on Joseph."

"You want Mick to go to Chef Barone's church?"

Mr. Pop smiled. "I was thinking Second Baptist, actually."

"Not First? Not with us?"

"Just trying to give Pastor Buell the benefit of the doubt. He seems to have finally noticed that Father McMahon was the only clergy concerned with Maliseet souls. And their living conditions, for that matter. He's asked to join the Indian Affairs Council."

"Pastor Buell?"

Mr. Pop nodded. "So we'll see. But for now, young lady, get back to your reading and then sleep. A big day tomorrow."

Mr. Pop leaned in to kiss me good night. It'd been a long time since the scruff of his face offered such comfort. After he closed my door, I got back to my reading. But sleep had a hard time coming.

Chapter Twenty

Where getting out of bed had been such a chore when Mick was in jail, the next morning, I leapt out of bed with joy overflowing. I could barely contain myself. I knew we had to go to church before I could see Mick, and while I felt impatient on one hand, I also knew I needed to be at church, to spend time in praise to God for what He had done.

It had felt good to be more out in the open about my feelings for Mick, at least with Mr. Pop and Mother. I had to remember there were still plenty in the community who wouldn't be happy with the outcome of Mick being released. Mr. Pop warned me over breakfast not to gloat and reminded me that my praise might have to be a bit muted. But it didn't matter. Everyone knew where Mr. Pop stood on the issue, and I couldn't wait to see who spoke to him and who might not this morning.

"Meet us in the car!" I could hear Mr. Pop bellowing up the stairs. I fairly flew down the stairs. I felt like sliding down the bannister but it never worked as well with a dress on.

"So a great day to go to church, huh?"

Mr. Pop raised an eyebrow at me, then reached a hand out to feel my forehead.

I laughed. "I mean it," I said. "Really."

"Well, you don't seem to be feverish, so yes, it *is* a great day to go to church," Mr. Pop said. "Of course, I think it's always a great day to worship God."

Mr. Pop wrapped his arm around me as we closed the front door behind us.

"Though it seems to me," he said, "how you feel about going

to church and what you have to say to God this morning probably depends on your opinion of the Maliseet and whether you believe we really all are made in God's image. Seems cut-and-dried to me."

"To me too. But why can't some people see this?"

Mr. Pop shrugged and held the car door open for me.

"If there were no mystery in this universe of ours," he said, "it would be a boring place to live. And if everyone lined up perfectly with our opinions and beliefs, there'd be no need for grace, either. The good Lord knows we need a lot of grace around here."

Church was uneventful. There couldn't have been more than three or four people who spoke to Mr. Pop or Mother about what had happened. It could've been that the word of Mick's release hadn't reached everyone and Pastor Murphy certainly didn't mention it. Or maybe it just wasn't as earth-shattering for other people like it was for me and my family. It was like any other Sunday. Like nothing at all had changed. Maybe it hadn't. After all, when we got back home, I assumed that the aroma of dinner would greet us, as always. What I didn't know was that Mother had gotten a picnic basket ready, filled with pot roast, creamed corn, green beans, along with bread ready for me to deliver a fully cooked, nice and hot, Sunday dinner down to the Flats for the Polchies family. She'd packed all this alongside the specially made rolls to drop off for Old Man Stringer at the hospital.

I helped gather up everything needed for a proper meal for the Polchies, from napkins to a big knife to slice the meat, as well as serving spoons for the corn and beans. Mother wasn't sure what they had along this vein, and she was right to wonder. After we loaded up the car, Mother slid into the passenger seat and Mr. Pop walked me around.

"Mercy, temper your excitement a bit. Lower your expectations. And don't be hurt if Mick isn't as excited to see you as you are to see him."

I bristled at Mr. Pop's words. "What do you mean? He's free, he's been waiting to see me. I've sure been waiting to see him."

"I understand that," Mr. Pop said. "But he's been through a lot. Mick's not the same boy he was when he went to jail, that's all."

I wanted to push back, tell Mr. Pop he had nothing to worry about. But instead I straightened up in my seat and smiled.

"It'll be great."

"Okay. Don't forget Old Man's bread," Mr. Pop said, handing me the rolls before closing my door.

I smiled tightly as I said goodbye to Mr. Pop. I didn't want him or Mother to see my frustration at his words. I didn't want to invite any more comments or any more warnings from either of them. I hated that Mr. Pop's warning had matched my greatest fear. But I pushed that fear out of my mind as I drove Mother first into town, where she ran into the hospital while I waited in the car. Then we drove on to the Flats, where I learned that Mr. Pop and my fears had been right.

✳ ✳ ✳

It was as though Mick knew I was coming. He stood at the base of the Flats, just off the road and stepped aside, two steps closer to the woods, when we pulled up.

Despite what Mr. Pop had said, I expected a huge grin from Mick when he saw me. Instead, I was crushed at his subdued manner. I would never admit it, but I had imagined Mick seeing me, rushing toward me, and holding me so tightly that I'd have trouble breathing. I was looking forward to being kissed.

But none of that happened. Not that it would have, with Mother right there. But it might have been nice to at least sense he wanted to catch up on all our summer apart had cost us.

But as soon as we got out of the car, Mick stood still. Though he returned my smile, Mick said nothing. At least, not to me.

"Mrs. Millar," he said.

Mother rushed toward him and wrapped her arms right

217

around him. She stepped back and held his arms wide apart, taking in every bit of him as though he were her boy, simply gone away for the summer.

"You look terrific, Mick," she said. "What a sight it is to see you! Oh, here . . ."

Mother turned back to the car, surprised that I hadn't gotten out.

"Mercy! Come say hello to Mick!" She shook her head at me, the way she did when I was little and too shy to hug my grandparents.

Mother motioned toward the car.

"We brought you some pot roast," I said. "For you and your family."

"Thanks," he said with a nod. "Wow. Want a hand carrying it up?"

Up. That wasn't the direction I'd wanted him to take me. But it was the one we'd take.

"Sure. Thanks."

Mick walked to the car and opened the back door, pulling the basket out. I couldn't resist his being so near. I reached out a hand and rubbed it across his back. He shivered.

"It's good to see you," I said.

"You too." The two words got caught in his throat and choked him a bit. I thought I noticed the shine of tears in his eyes. But then he coughed and smiled again. "This goes to my parents, then?"

I nodded and we walked up the hill toward the shacks. His mother and the other women sat in their circle, weaving and talking. When they saw us, they stopped.

"Ma, Mrs. Millar sent some food for us."

Mrs. Polchies muttered a thank-you and went back to talking to the women. One of them motioned to Mother. She excused herself from us and sat down on a stump in the circle of women.

"She doesn't mean to be rude," Mick said. "Ma's had a hard time. First with me being gone, now Joseph."

"Has Joseph been at Chef's a lot?" I asked, my eyes on Mother as she watched the women weave. She asked a question of one of the women I didn't know.

"Yes. He's been working lots. It's good, but he stays with Chef more often than not. He even told Ma he wanted to stay with Chef when school starts. She says it's like she's lost two sons at once."

"But you're back," I said, taking a step closer, desperate to grab his hand but aware of eyes all around us.

"For now," he said. "You wanna go for a walk?"

My heart pounded. "Sure," I said.

He led me down the path toward the woods. Once we'd moved beyond far enough, beyond all the spying eyes, Mick stopped and reached for me. Finally. He held me tight around the waist and put a hand on the back of my head, running his hand down my hair. I wanted nothing more than for him to lean down and draw me into a kiss, but he let go, stepped back, and simply grabbed my hand. Either way, it felt good to be this near to him again, to feel our fingers intertwine the way our lives once had.

I had wanted to tell him a million things, but as we walked, I could think of nothing to say, except finally, "I can't believe we're here. It's so good to see you."

"Good to see you too," he said.

"I've been thinking about this, dreaming about this."

"Have you?" Mick asked.

"Pretty much nonstop."

"I've been doing a lot of thinking myself," Mick said. "I mean, what else could I do, stuck in that cell? It was rough, not the conditions so much but the lack of contact with anyone. Mr. Herbert was nice enough, letting Joseph drop off supper for me. When I found out Joe was delivering it . . . well, I knew at least one person cared. I didn't know other people besides Tommy had tried to come visit me. No one told me. Except for Father McMahon and your uncle, I was so alone."

My heart sank. I had understood that Mick wasn't as excited to see me as I would have liked, but not even Mr. Pop would've thought that Mick would be disappointed in me, maybe even a little mad.

"But Mick, I wanted to come. I asked if I could, and Mr. Pop said no. He said I wouldn't be let in to see you. He said if I came to visit, it could make things worse for you somehow and that you'd be fine, and that Uncle Roger was able to come in and see you. I was going crazy, Mick. I didn't know how long it would take, or what was happening to you in there. Uncle Roger assured me you were okay and you were in good spirits. Was that all an act?"

Mick ran his thumb along mine, a small act of affection amid some hard words.

"I'm not saying I wasn't all right," Mick said. "No one hurt me; it's just the reality of being Maliseet slapped me in the face every morning when I woke up to realize I was still alone in a jail cell. I thought a lot about it and knew that if I looked different, if my last name was Millar or Carmichael, I wouldn't've been in that cell waiting for something to happen. I'd be free, walking the streets like anyone else. Anyone White, that is."

"We talked about that too, me and Mr. Pop, me and Mother."

"Mercy, I also thought more about who I am and who you are and—this is hard to say—but I'm not sure it's a good idea for us to continue to dream of 'someday.'"

My heart felt like it was falling to my feet. I spoke quickly. "Mick, a lot changed on the outside while you were in jail too. Mr. Pop and Mother both know about us, and it's all right with them; well mostly. But we don't have to hide it anymore. We don't have to sneak around."

"It's not just that," Mick said. "There's a lot about me you don't know."

"But you can tell me. Joseph said you should, in fact."

Mick sighed. We walked past the path where we would've

turned off to go to our little lean-to in the woods. Instead we wove among the pines and birches, stepping over fallen branches until we came upon a fallen ash tree. Mick sat on it, then patted the place next to him. An invitation to sit next to him, even as the invitation to his life was being revoked.

"Merce, you know how much I like your father and appreciate all he's done for me. I still can't believe he got your uncle Roger to come up from Bangor and attack this whole situation head-on. I'll be forever grateful to your family. And you know how much I care about you, how much I always have and always will. It's just, I'm not sure us moving forward is a good idea. For you or for me. There's just too much."

For the whole of the walk, I had successfully fought back tears, fearing what was coming. Now it was a losing battle. The tears streamed steadily from my eyes down my cheeks. Mick reached forward to brush them off my face.

"Mercy, you've got to believe it hurts. It hurts a lot to say all this."

"Then don't! Just stop! Let's go back to the way things were," I almost begged. "You and me in our fort before we loaded up workers to pick. Maybe you did too much thinking in that cell, Mick."

"Mercy, you mean you didn't think twice about us while I was in jail? You didn't wonder if maybe somebody like Tommy Birger was a safer choice than some Maliseet boy who might be locked up for a long time?"

"No! Not once did I think that. You know why I invited Tommy over."

"Yes, but that was before all this. When we thought we were just keeping a distance until the Glenn and Marjorie thing blew over. But this stuff going on is bigger than Glenn and Marjorie. It's not going to blow over. Or go anywhere."

"But things will still get better. I know it. The Maliseet will get the land settlement and all this will change . . ."

221

"The land settlement," Mick said, his voice drifting off into the woods. "Yes, that would be nice. But that's not everything, either, Mercy. Let me try to explain something that happened to me when I was locked up. Every morning I woke up and I felt really rested, like I'd slept better than I had in years. The truth was, I did sleep better. Mercy, living in the Flats means always having to watch your back, always watching out for Joseph and my mom. When my dad is passed out drunk, or drinking too much to function or even care, I'm it. I'm all they've got. If I don't protect those two, no one else will. There are some men who aren't always the safest to be around, not if you're a woman. There are women who aren't too safe either. I've seen my mother do some horrible things and have some horrible things done to her. Things no kid should ever see. Although it doesn't happen much now, truth is: I've never been able to fall asleep in the Flats without fear. It's the reality of my world. I'm sorry I've never told you—or anyone—this. It's been a way of life in the Flats, and frankly, being alone in a cell for three weeks was a relief. For the first time in years, I wasn't afraid for myself or my family when I fell asleep."

I thought about my own mother, sitting in the circle of women. Were they talking about this too? Did my mother know this? Did Mr. Pop? Did Mr. Carmichael?

"So, as much as I hate Frankie Carmichael for what he did to me," Mick said, "what I hate most about him calling the Maliseet 'filth' is that he's got a point. Not all of us, but the stories he's heard would make me afraid for my daughter to marry one of us too. It makes me afraid to think about marrying someone someday. I can't bring anyone into our mess."

I looked deep into Mick's face. Tears brimmed but didn't fall. He held his jaw tight, his cheek muscle flexing. When I reached out to hug him, I thought he might push me away but instead his body softened and engulfed me.

"Please don't let this be it," I said. "We don't have to talk much about the future. We don't have to talk about it at all. I don't even have to be in your mess. I just want to be in your life."

"More and more," Mick said, "I'm realizing my mess and my life are the same thing."

We both looked back. My mother was calling me from somewhere not far behind.

"Better go," Mick said. "I'll walk you back."

We walked through the woods and Mick waved up the hill to Mother where she waited with Mrs. Polchies for us. "Meet you at the car," he yelled up to them.

"Will I see you in school?" I asked. "First day's Wednesday already." I had heard that other schools didn't start until late August or even September. But schools in Northern Maine got started the second week in August to leave room for our long Harvest Break.

Mick shook his head. "Nah."

"Didn't think so. Could you come in October after Harvest Break, maybe?"

"I don't know. Maybe. Not sure high school's going to teach me what I need to be learning right now."

"Well, stuff for college, at least."

Mick's laugh had a brittle edge. "College. Right. That's another one of those dreams I'm not sure can come true. But I don't know. I'm sorry, Mercy. Maybe. Okay? Maybe. But I'll be around for harvest. Mr. Pop already made sure I was planning on it. So I'll see you then."

"But that's nearly five weeks away! Not before then?"

We had reached the car. Mother was working her way down the hill, sidestepping the bits of trash, discarded toilet seats, scraps of sharp-edged aluminum, splintered bits of lumber, as she came down.

"How wonderful to watch your mother at work, Mick!" Mother said. "She's amazing. Her fingers must be magic."

"Something like that," Mick said.

"Well, I hope we see you around soon," Mother said. "It's been too long. We've missed you. All right, Mercy. Time we got back."

I nodded toward Mick and he smiled back.

"I'll see you soon, Mercy. Promise."

"Okay," I said, nearly choking out the word. "Soon, then."

Chapter Twenty-One

*I*t had been three and a half weeks since I'd seen Mick. But "soon" could've meant months for all I knew. Everything was different, even as it was the same. School was school. Same classes, only harder. Same people, only older. Same bus ride, only longer. Or so it felt. But as Mr. Pop always told me, my job at fifteen was to work hard on my chores at the farm and work hard in school. So I did.

Molly and Tommy tried to cheer me up, inviting me with them when they went to Woolworth's for sodas after school or to join them at Tommy's house to see if we could sneak a listen to that "Shake, Rattle and Roll" song Marjorie had written Molly about. Although I was curious to hear what this rock-and-roll was all about, I didn't want to risk getting in trouble from my parents who worried like everyone else about the lyrics and the dancing it might bring out. So I simply went to school and came back home.

The first weather report broke through while Mr. Pop was listening to the Red Sox game on the radio. Weather reports first indicated a hurricane moving up the southeast coast. Hurricane Edna was battering the Carolinas, Myrtle Beach, then the Outer Banks, and would probably be headed out over the Atlantic before it reached the Northeast. But we needed to be on guard anyway.

Mr. Pop kept the radio on even after the Red Sox trounced the Tigers. The second report had changed. Forecasters now predicted Edna would keep moving up the coast. And no longer were they calling for it to cut east across the ocean; instead, they warned, it would move inland. Hurricane Edna, it seemed, was headed our way in just two days.

* * *

We made sure we had enough wood stacked in the shed for the duration of the storm before we hunkered down. It wasn't often that a hurricane made its way this far north. The cold and dampness that served as a prelude for the storm meant Mr. Pop would have to get up a couple times in the night to keep the fire in the wood-burning stove stoked. As soon as the spring thaw occurred each year, Mr. Pop would spend any spare moments starting to chop wood for the next winter. It took all of late spring and summer to cut and haul enough wood to last through the tough Maine winter. On cold damp nights Mr. Pop started the wood-burning stove—our only heating source in the house—off to a roaring blaze, then in the wee morning hours he'd get up and build another nice smudge that would take the edge off the morning cold. There was something about the dampness of hard-driving rain that soaked right into you even though you were indoors. Dampness needed a lot of heat to dry it out.

"Mercy, I need you to run into town and grab a few things for me before Edna hits," Mother said. "The list is on the end of the counter."

At least this bit of normal had returned: me being sent on a mission some parents might have regarded as too dangerous. But being trusted felt great. Watsonville was buzzing. At the IGA people were stocking up on perishables, for items that weren't already canned and on their shelves at home. It looked more like preparation for a wartime siege, not a couple of days of high winds and rain. For a town used to big winter storms, this certainly wasn't the first time we'd ever had to get prepared to be shut inside for more than a couple of days. But something about the oddity of a hurricane in our Northwoods threw us all off, especially with harvest just one week away. Still, when I saw Mrs. Williams, who lived just a block down from the market and was known to brag about her basement shelves lined with canned goods lest those "dang Communists" decide to invade Maine pushing a shopping cart loaded with supplies, I had to turn my head to keep from giggling.

Mother's list had milk and some baking soda, plus a package of Rice's red hot dogs and some split top buns on it. I loved the snap of those red dogs, especially one loaded with mustard and relish and a few leftover baked beans. The casing and bright red color made them unlike any other hot dog in the world. Mother's list was relatively short; of course Mother kept her pantry and refrigerator well stocked, so we were okay even if Mrs. Williams's Communists did invade.

Time would tell who was right, I guessed. But just then, I needed to get my items and get back to the farm. Cars jammed the streets as farmers left their chores to head into town and stock up. The traffic volume made me feel like I was in Bangor. I wanted to drive over to the Flats but didn't dare. What would a hurricane look like on Hungry Hill? I didn't want to think about it. I already knew that Chef Barone asked Joseph to stay with his family on the square to help keep an eye on Nelson's. At least I didn't have to worry about him.

Heading home on the main road didn't afford the usual opportunity to think and dream, especially not today. The North Road was loaded with cars, filled with others trying to get home before the storm hit full blast. The dark sky was starting to spit rain. I could see the trees waving with small gusts of wind. It felt like a good nor'easter just winding up. The difference was that this one was a hurricane and she had a name. Edna. I suppose I should've been scared, but somehow the wildness of it all thrilled me. Although the wind whipped dirt and leaves into the truck, I kept the windows down, enjoying the rush and hearing the booms and creaks as the wind picked up.

I pulled into the farm to see Ellery and Bud scurrying around helping Mr. Pop finish last minute storm preparations. The chicken coop received needed fortification, and Bud was busy moving the pigs into the shed closest to the house. Mr. Pop was still up on a ladder closing the shutters on the second story windows. Ellery nailed boards across the first floor windows for good measure. I got out of the car just in time to hear Ellery holler over the howling wind, "Mercy, you're a day late and a dollar short! I nailed down everything but the kitchen sink and you weren't here to help one lick."

With the final nail pounded into the porch window, Bud and Ellery took off to manage their own households. I knew Bud well enough to know he'd do nothing but bring in some firewood into his one-room cabin. As a bachelor, Bud didn't really fuss much about himself. He didn't have electricity or running water, so less could go wrong for him, was the way he figured it. But still, Bud ran toward his cabin to do what he could to shore it up.

Ellery's place was bigger than Bud's and with more that could be damaged if he didn't protect it, so Ellery hammered in new nails and covered windows with spare planks. After that, I was sure he'd gather some firewood also and then hunker down for the duration. Those two were loyal as they come. They loved us like family and we loved them back.

Mr. Pop's real concerns about the hurricane had to do with harvest, just a week away. Potato fields couldn't handle the amount of rain predicted. By the time the soil dried out, it would push harvest back later than the school break would allow and then there'd be fewer workers to accomplish the task. If there was high standing water and the weather took a turn, like it might that time of year, crops could be ruined. Weather like this could potentially cripple some of the smaller farmers, but this wasn't just an issue for them. As Mr. Pop reminded me, if finances went south for farmers, some of the Maliseet—those who depended on work from the farmers, even throughout the winter—could starve this winter. And a suf-

fering community might mean there'd be even fewer in Watsonville to lift a finger to keep it from happening.

As I pulled into the driveway, I lifted a hand over our farm, much like I'd seen Mr. Pop do at the beginning of planting season and just before harvest. "I know this is all Yours, God," I prayed aloud, "but I ask for Your protection on our community. I ask for Your mercy in the midst of whatever's to come. And please, please, please, keep Mick safe."

"Mercy, dear, get inside quick," Mother called from the porch. "Your father will grab the groceries. It's starting to blow pretty hard!"

Even though Mother was shouting, I could hardly hear her. The drizzle had just shifted into a steady downpour, and the wind had picked up. Once I got inside I headed for the phone to give Molly a quick call, but once again Mrs. Garritson was monopolizing the line. I kept picking up hoping she'd get the hint. I guess everyone needed to check on someone before the hurricane got going, even Mrs. Garritson. I suppose I could afford her some grace this time around. I slumped into the chair in the foyer and picked up Lickers. She's been weaving between my ankles while I tried the phone.

"Bet you're glad you're not an *outside* cat now, aren't you, scaredy-cat?"

"How about you put down the cat, come into the kitchen, and help me roll out the molasses cookies?" Mother said when she saw me in the chair. "After you wash those hands, of course."

I scooted Lickers off my lap and stood, brushing her tiny hairs off my skirt. The thought of having a batch of molasses cookies, my favorite, to snack on with a cup of tea or cold milk sounded divine. And with nothing else to do but be inside, I had all the time in the world to help out.

"Be right there. Just trying to get Molly on the phone, but you-know-who is on the line."

I heard Mother chuckle from the kitchen. I set the receiver back down and followed the laugh. I could wait to talk to Molly.

"What can I do first?" I said, pulling an apron off the hook.

"Grab the flour and sprinkle a good handful on the counter, then start rolling out the lump of dough. I'll find the cookie cutter and get the baking sheet ready."

I picked up the recipe card, bent at the edges, dots of brown stain on the back, and filled with Mr. Pop's block lettering. Mother never put away her recipe cards until the recipe was completed. It was a "quirk," Mr. Pop said, but one of his favorite things about my mother.

One of my favorite things about Mr. Pop was how handy he was in the kitchen. Not only was he a good farmer but a good baker as well. This molasses cookie recipe was his, or had been his mother's actually. She'd never written it down, but as a boy, he'd baked beside her and memorized it. After she died, he wrote it down, afraid to lose yet another piece of her.

This recipe was not only my favorite, but it was often requested when we had potluck suppers at church. Mr. Pop said it was the love everyone could taste in them. But love wasn't the only thing I felt when making them; sore arms certainly played a role. It took a little elbow grease to get the refrigerated dough rolled into a big round circle a half inch thick before using the cookie cutter. Then I had to pull the scraps together and reroll it a couple of times to use all the dough up. I wasn't about to waste one bit. I couldn't wait to smell them in the oven.

"What was that?" I asked after Mother and I jumped.

"Paul, did you hear that?" Mother was shouting through the kitchen door toward the living room. Mr. Pop came at a run.

"Sounded like a big branch off the oak tree in the side yard."

We didn't have a clear view of outside as the upstairs shutters were closed and the first floor windows obscured by the boards Ellery had nailed over the windows. Mr. Pop, however, was able to see out the living room window enough to verify what he thought to be true. Mother and I got the cookies in the oven then retired to the living room with Mr. Pop.

"This is looking just as bad as the weatherman predicted," Mr. Pop said.

"I'm scared for Mick," I said. "And Ansley and Mr. Socoby and . . ."

"You have reason to be scared," Mr. Pop said. "All we can do at this point is watch and pray. For all of us. To be honest, everyone is at risk with the way the wind is gusting, not just those on Hungry Hill. We'll know more in a couple of days."

Outside we heard more sharp cracks and dull thuds. The wind was snapping and throwing whatever got in its way. Our shutters rattled, the roof creaked and moaned, and the very walls of our home worked to resist the push of the wind. The rain continued to pulse down. We heard its persistent tap on the roof and the porch; we hoped when we couldn't hear it against the ground that it meant the soil was keeping up with the downpour, sucking in every drop that fell. But we wondered how long that would last.

The timer in the kitchen rang, though we didn't need it to tell us the cookies were done. Mr. Pop rose from his chair and went into the kitchen. The sound of the trays sliding across the racks and clacking on the counter was a nice bit of familiar for my ears, now accustomed to trying to discern the troubling sounds coming from outside.

Mr. Pop returned with a plateful of warm cookies next to three glasses of cold milk on a tray. As he passed out the milk, Mr. Pop raised his own. Toast-prayers were his speciality. "To our mighty Creator," Mr. Pop said, "the One who controls the wind and the rain and who holds us all in His hands. We thank Him for this blessing of a dry home and warm cookies and one another. We pray for those who need His hand more than ever and that He will use this for His glory."

"Hear, hear and amen," said Mother and we all took a sip and reached for a cookie and waited as Edna roared. As she would for the next two days.

*   *   *

The nice thing about living on a knoll was the view it offered. And while normally this view meant we could sit on the porch and look north and south and survey the beauty, after a storm or blizzard, our knoll gave us quite the vantage point to assess the damage.

After Edna had finished her brutal beating, we stood on our porch and gasped. Though our home had been rather miraculously spared, our trees had taken a beating. We could see up the road to Widow Nason's house, where great punches of roof were missing. In fact, the shingles were blown clear off and her clothesline and the now-splintered poles were leveled below it. Down the road where Silas Engalls lived, we could see *most* of his house. Where two days before, it sat on dry ground, this day it sat in the middle of a small lake. He drove a truck for Dead River Company and was gone much of the time. But we could see him home that day trudging through the water in hip waders. Mr. Pop said we'd take him our canoe later. Who only knew what was floating in that water, especially since it appeared that his outhouse didn't survive the storm.

Mr. Pop did a quick walk around the farmhouse, the shed, and the barn. But we could see the swampy mess that was the fields. My father only shook his head and said we wouldn't know more until he saw the full extent.

"But," he said, "if everyone's fields are as bad as ours, there's no way we can start harvesting potatoes next week. We'll be lucky to be able to harvest in two."

"But we'll be out of school next week for harvest," I said. "We'll all be."

"That's good," Mr. Pop said. "We'll need everyone to help clean up. Starting now. Let's get some gloves and start pulling the big branches out of the driveway, so we can take a trip into town and check on some folks. When we come back we'll start sawing and stacking the branches that blew down."

I did a quick check of the pigs, and they were all right though a little spooked. The girls were happy to see me. I fed them and let them out of their coop to stretch their legs a bit and so I could muck the coop.

I pulled and hauled branches for forty-five minutes and finally had the driveway cleared of debris. Mother brought out a basket of cookies and set them in the truck.

"Goodness knows someone is going to need just a little love," Mother said. "Even if only in cookie form."

Mr. Pop nodded and smiled. "Actually," he said, "why don't you come along too? We need to check on several people and your woman's heart might be just what's needed in town."

I wondered a moment why Mr. Pop wouldn't have thought my woman's heart would be enough, and felt the familiar sting of being seen as the son he'd never had. But when I saw Mr. Pop wrap his arms around Mother and kiss her long enough to make her pull away and swat him, I realized he was merely flirting. Suddenly, I wanted to be alone.

Making an excuse, I ran inside to call Molly real quick and make sure she was all right.

I had tried calling her several times during our days holed up at home, to no avail. We'd only gotten reports on the radio that Watsonville and Presque Isle were hit hard, and that neither town had seen damage like this in more than a hundred years.

But as I stood in the hall, tapping my foot as I held the phone, I got nothing. Not even Mrs. Garritson. The phone lines were still down. I was still in the dark about how Molly and her parents, along with Mick and Joseph, and everyone I'd fretted about fared in the hurricane.

* * *

Our eyes could hardly take in the damage. I'd never seen a hurricane hit Watsonville in my lifetime, at least not more than with heavy rain. Mr. Pop and Mother had been through them before, but nothing like this.

Though debris was strewn everywhere, most of the houses we saw were intact. But many outbuildings were flattened; sheds and outhouses listed or lay on their sides in tatters. Coops and pens stood without livestock. Indeed, most fields were far worse than ours. While our fields could pass for swamps, now lakes and ponds puddled the landscape.

What wasn't nailed down was blown everywhere. Branches snapped off trees and dropped like a game of pick-up sticks. The high-standing water compounded the problem. While we didn't lose electricity, plenty others had, and it looked like phone lines were down everywhere.

As we rounded the big bend to get into the heart of Watsonville, we saw that the town had been hit harder than where we were in the country.

"Oh my heavens!" Mother said. "Look at the IGA!"

My mother's exclamation turned my head in a hurry to see the roof of our local grocery store rolled right up like a sardine can. It was good that people had stocked up before the storm, for surely water and roof debris now filled the store.

Mr. Pop drove slowly as we all gasped and pointed at the wreckage that lay ahead of us. A crack ran from top to bottom down the middle of the plate glass window of the bank, most likely caused by a large branch being hurtled toward it at high velocity. My father stopped the car completely when we saw Second Baptist's steeple bent and dangling like a broken elbow.

"Lord have mercy," Mr. Pop said, starting to drive slowly once again. "We've got to check on people."

"Are we going to the Flats?" I asked. "Can we, I mean?"

Mr. Pop nodded. "Yes, but I thought we ought to drive through the town square first. See what the damage is there before heading toward the dump."

"Okay," I said. "I want to check on Molly."

Chapter Twenty-Two

*W*atsonville looked like the pictures that had filled the newspapers during the War. Except unlike back then, when I was real small, Mr. Pop and Mother didn't try to shield my eyes from it, and we saw this wreckage in living color.

Few people ventured out yet, though plenty mingled and commiserated on their front sidewalks. Mr. Pop had to turn after the first block of the square because glass, shingles, and roofing tin, as well as branches, littered the road. The scene was overwhelming to take in, as was the thought of cleanup. Mr. Pop was right, that if we didn't harvest next week, we'd be available to help, but where would we even start when everyone needed so much? But before I could get too far into this thought, Mr. Pop turned another corner and I saw Fulton's. We all did and were startled into stillness. The back end had completely collapsed.

"Oh, goodness!" Mother said. "The entire storage area is gone! After all the Carmichaels have been through, they'll have this mess now. But Nelson's looks like it weathered the storm okay. I'm sure Joseph is fine."

We all shifted our eyes from the disaster at Fulton's to Nelson's, right across the street. It looked like it had more than simply weathered the storm. It looked bright and cheerful and welcoming as always. I breathed a sigh of relief.

"Can we head to Molly's now?"

We'd barely gone four blocks when Molly shot across the street ahead of us.

"Wait!" I said. "There's Molly!"

Mr. Pop slowed as I rolled my window down with lightning speed to shout to Molly.

"Molly! Molly, wait!" She turned her head to see who was yelling. As soon as she realized it was us, she made a U-turn and continued at a gallop toward us.

"Mr. and Mrs. Millar, Mercy!" Molly said. "My dad never came home last night. I mean, he was home when things were really sounding bad, but during the eye, when things settled, he thought he should go check on the store. He said he could make it back before it got bad again, but he never came back. Mom and I have been worried sick, but we promised him we would stay put."

"She sent you alone?" Mother asked. "Where is she?"

"Back home. She's a wreck. She's been praying nonstop. But she won't leave because she's worried what Dad will do if he finds out she didn't listen to him."

"But she let you go?" Mother asked.

"No, she doesn't know I left. But I couldn't stand not knowing. We'd been sitting there for hours, just wondering."

"Hop in, Molly," Mr. Pop said. "We'll turn and head back."

Molly scooted in next to me, and I wrapped an arm around her. Her body quaked next to me.

"I tried calling you so many times," I said. "But the phone lines have been down."

"Yeah, I know. We tried calling the store so many times I lost count."

We drove back toward the square, at an angle that highlighted the collapsed warehouse portion of the store perfectly. Molly reacted just as we had.

"Oh, oh no! Stop!"

"Hang on, Molly," Mr. Pop said. "We're almost there. I'm going with you."

He slowed the car along the street, looking for the safest place to pull over. Just as Mr. Pop and Molly jumped out of the car, the door to Fulton's opened and we could see someone backing out the door, lugging something behind him.

"What's he doing?" Molly's shaking voice betrayed her nervousness.

Then we saw. It was Joseph. As he stepped backward onto the sidewalk, we saw he had a hold of Mr. Carmichael. As soon as they were both outside, Joseph started hollering for help. As though we'd rehearsed this, our car doors flew open, and we all shoved out of the car. Mr. Pop took off at a run with Molly right on his heels. My stomach knotted up. All I could think of was those weeks ago when Mick and Old Man Stringer were on that same sidewalk.

Mr. Pop knelt beside Frankie and put his head to his chest. Molly heaved great sobs at his side.

And once again, Mr. Pop looked up at me and told me to go. "Hospital," he said. "And Geneva, take Molly home to get her mother."

We all took off. Behind me I could hear Molly crying and Mother's soothing words—straight from her woman's heart.

✳ ✳ ✳

"Mr. Stringer went home before Edna struck," the receptionist said as soon as she saw me.

"No! Not that. There's a man hurt!" I could barely get a word out for breathing so hard. "Frankie Carmichael. At Fulton's. We need help." I had run as fast as I could, but navigating around or hurdling over downed trees and debris made the few blocks run from Fulton's to the hospital treacherous and exhausting.

The woman pushed back from the desk and raced into the back. She returned moments later with a doctor who double-checked his black satchel for supplies and then told me to lead the way.

When we had reached Fulton's, two police officers and a few bystanders now surrounded Mr. Carmichael. Chef Barone stood to the side comforting Mrs. Carmichael.

Molly rushed to me when she saw me.

"Father woke up," Molly said. "For a moment, I mean. He looked right at Joseph and nodded. Looked like he was trying to *thank* him."

I looked at Joseph. He stood with the officer, explaining the situation. For a moment, my heart sank and a chill settled in. No matter what it looked like Mr. Carmichael was saying, what good could ever come of Mr. Carmichael, a Maliseet, and a couple of police officers?

But then the officer patted Joseph. "You did good, son," I heard him say.

Molly and I walked forward. Joseph's eyes met mine and he headed toward me.

"Joe," I said as I pulled him toward me. "So glad you're okay. What on earth happened?"

"Chef and I were out checking on folks," Joseph said. "Not sure how I missed it when we left Nelson's, but on our way back, I noticed Fulton's front door opened. Chef said to leave it. Probably the wind blew it open, but I don't know. Something kept telling me to go in and see. So I did. I found Mr. Carmichael in the back. Would've missed him except for his shoes sticking out from under some shelves. The one was bent all wrong."

Molly pushed past me to hug him. "You saved his life, Joseph. You're a hero."

"I don't know that I saved his life." Joseph shrugged. "Somebody else would've found him."

"But that somebody else could've been too late," Mr. Pop said, coming up behind Joseph to pat him on the shoulders. "Dr. Sahmby says he should be okay. But Frankie lost a lot of blood from a cut on his head. By wrapping that wound, you most likely saved his life."

Joseph pointed to Chef. "He gave me his jacket and helped. Chef saved his life too, wasn't just me."

"'Course it was you!" Chef said as he walked up behind us. "This boy not only has the finest culinary instincts of anyone I've ever worked with, he's a hero too!"

Chef stuck his hand toward Mr. Pop.

"Wonderful to see you again," Mr. Pop said. "Wish it were under better circumstances."

"It's always the way," Chef said. "But right now, this boy needs to head home to see how his family is. I told him I'd drive him."

"No need," Mr. Pop said. "As soon as Frankie and Muriel and Molly get settled at the hospital, we're heading to the Flats ourselves. We can take him."

"That'd be wonderful. Just let me prepare a basket of food. And a note that tells them there's more where this came from. You'll be okay, Joseph?"

Joseph nodded. Although he looked less okay than he had since we'd seen him. The look on his face suggested somehow the idea of rushing into a toppling building to save a man was less frightening than heading home.

As we drove out of town and rounded the bend toward the Flats, I knew Joseph was right to worry.

* * *

Though once shacks and shanties of various shapes, sizes, and materials topped off the crest of the dump that was home to the people of the Maliseet tribe, not one structure had survived Edna's wrath. Water ran down the sides of the dump in steady, filthy streams, carrying with it bits of waste. As Mr. Pop pulled up and shut off the engine, a basket rolled down toward our car.

"Lord on high," Mother whispered.

None of us was eager to step out of the car. The damage was too great, the sight too overwhelming.

Mr. Pop turned to look at us. "You all should wait here," he said. "I'll go check on everything and see what needs to be done. It might not be safe with all this debris. And there's no telling what this will do to Joe's lungs."

Joseph sniffled and breathed deep, as though the car contained the last good breaths he could take. As I watched him breathe in and out, suddenly struggling for air, I chided myself for not noticing how easily he breathed on the farm and also when he was with Chef. I wondered if it was the air quality of the dump or the stress of home that brought this on.

"No," Joseph said. "I've got to go up. I've got to see."

"I'm coming too," Mother and I said in unison.

Mr. Pop didn't object. In fact, I assumed he never thought we'd actually listen to him. He was warning us to assuage his own sense of duty.

But coming with proved easier said than done. While climbing the side of the dump had always been a challenge even for the sure-footed, that day, reaching the Flats needed more of an upward crawl than a walk. With each step forward, we slid back when our feet didn't sink altogether. We grabbed on to anything to help steady ourselves, including one another. And somehow, we made it to the top, covered in mud and who-knew-what else.

Louise Polchies was the first to see us. She ran toward Joseph and rocked him in her arms. "My baby, my baby," she said again and again.

"I'm all right, Ma," Joseph said. "It's okay."

Ansley joined us, patting his son on the back before reaching out to shake Mr. Pop's hand.

"Good of you to come," Ansley said. "Hadn't gotten a chance to thank you proper for your help with Mick."

"You sent a letter," Mr. Pop said. "And the basket. Was more than proper. All I did was call my brother. But for all this . . . tell me what you think you need and we'll see what we can do."

Ansley's jaw tightened.

"I assume *your* house is still standing," Ansley said.

Mr. Pop nodded.

"And the folks in town? Frankie's home, still okay?"

"Well," Joseph started to say before Mr. Pop hushed him with a look.

"You all have homes or at least a place to go if you don't," Ansley said. "You all have food stocked up and stored. Your kids all accounted for; your babies not crying, not running around without their pants on, screaming because they haven't eaten in days."

Mr. Pop nodded and looked straight at his former playmate as he spoke.

"You all put us out here," Ansley said. "You left us exposed where we could have died. And now along comes Edna and you ask what you can do? You're a good man, Paul. Always have been. Nice of you to put us to work when no one else would. Good of you to call your brother and to sit on that council to discuss the what'd you call it? Indian trouble? Did even one Indian get asked to have any say in what you talked about? But I'm not going to tell you what I think needs to be done. I'm not going to tell you how you can help us. Because you, along with the rest of them, wanted us here, like this."

Ansley waved his arm across the destruction, the mess of garbage and tin roofs and toilet seats and soiled and soaked mattresses laid bare, a stain on the beauty of the Maine woods.

"Frankie'll say we had this coming," Ansley said. "That this is God's wrath. His judgment on our wicked ways. Maybe he's right. Maybe this is how your great God does feel about us. But then we've never needed your God, and we don't need Him now. Roger says things are changing. Negroes in the South are changing things. They're going to change for us up here too, Roger tells us. We've been too passive for too long. But things change now, Paul. It's time for things to change now."

Ansley turned to walk away. Joseph stepped toward him.

"But Dad," Joseph said. Ansley stopped. "What if this isn't God's wrath? What if it's something else?"

Ansley laughed. "And what'd that be, son?"

"What if it's His mercy?"

Ansley looked at me questioningly.

"Not *that* Mercy," Joseph said. "God's mercy. Like, His love."

Ansley shook his head. "That's right. I heard you'd been going to church. So now you got religion? Found Jesus now, have you? Well, if this is God's mercy, I'll take His wrath, I guess."

And Ansley walked away.

"Don't mind him," said a voice.

We all turned. Mick. Mr. Pop thrust his hand forward, and when Joseph rushed toward him the brothers clasped hands tightly. Mother squealed delight in seeing him safe and sound. I felt dizzy. All during the climb to the Flats and during Ansley's speech, my eyes had scanned Hungry Hill in vain for a sign of Mick. I was trying to listen carefully as Ansley spoke, but all I wanted to know was if Mick was okay.

Throughout the greetings, Mick's eyes stayed on me. Even as he held his brother, Mick looked at me like I was the only person in the world.

"Mercy," Mick said as he stepped forward toward me. He held his arms out, just as I'd longed for them to be those weeks before. And in front of Mr. Pop, Mother, Joseph, and the throng of Maliseet that were now aware of our presence, Mick brushed my hair away from my face and kissed me.

Around us, the world faded—the people, the mess, the destruction, the confusion melted away, becoming nothing that mattered in light of us together.

"Can I show you something?" Mick whispered in my ear.

I nodded, and he grabbed my hand.

"We'll be back in a minute," Mick said. I thought Mr. Pop would send Joseph with us as a chaperone. But he let us go, let us head down toward the backside of the Flats unaccompanied.

Chapter Twenty-Three

The trail toward the woods was still in decent shape. Edna had sent water and debris toward the road instead of the woods. Though branches and limbs and even whole uprooted trees criss-crossed the path, one might have guessed it was merely a rough thunderstorm that passed through. The vast forest protected this side of the dump.

"You need to see this," Mick said as he pulled me closer to where our little lean-to stood. I was sure Edna would have blown it away. But I was wrong. Through the trees, I could see the charred side of the yellow doors of the place we'd hoped to sneak away and plan our future and near the place where not long ago Mick had told me we had no future after all.

"It withstood," Mick said. "Everything else—my house, the Socobys', the outhouses, the sheds—those are all gone. But this stood."

"You came down and found this?" I asked.

"No, I stayed here throughout the storm."

"You stayed here? In our fort?"

"Dad was stomping around raging about white folks having nice places to weather the storm. Ma was rampaging about Joseph not being here. I just needed to get away. To find some quiet. And to feel near you."

"But I didn't think you wanted to be near me."

"I'm sorry, Mercy," Mick said. "Come here."

Together we bent and crawled back into the space below the trees. Immediately Mick pulled me toward him and kissed me again.

"It's not that I didn't want to be near you," Mick said. "It's that I thought we couldn't. I thought that we had no foundation for a future. But somehow, when I was sitting in here as Edna roared all around me, as I heard the shacks blowing around the Flats, and I heard people yelling and kids crying as they huddled between trees in the woods, I was shaking harder than the walls of the fort. But I wasn't just terrified for myself. I worried about you, about Joseph, about those kids I could hear crying up in their shacks, afraid of the sound of the wind. I was angry, even angrier than my dad is now. I called out to Gluskap, asked him what we'd done to upset nature so. I cursed the white folks for messing up this forest with your garbage and making us live on it. And for bringing on Edna and her winds. But after yelling all this, I felt nothing. Except more terror."

Mick ran his index finger along my hand, tracing my fingers with his. He took a deep breath and looked straight at me.

"And then I called out to your God," Mick said. "I said the same thing again—cursing white folks, asking what we'd done to upset nature, to bring this on. But I couldn't stop there. I asked why, if He's as good as your Mr. Pop says, why He allowed me to be thrown in jail, why we gotta live out here, why my dad has to drink so much, why my mother never kept us safe, why the kids had it so hard here, why I just couldn't be with you. I raged to your God until I could barely breathe from crying so hard. But I just kept talking."

I nodded.

"And then the strangest thing happened. I felt completely safe. Like someone was here, with arms around me. You're going to think I'm crazy, Mercy, but I heard a voice saying: *I am with you*. I heard whispering even through the noise of the storm. *I am with you, I am with you*. And even though the fort and the trees blew and shook so hard and even though I thought I would die out there, somehow, I felt comforted. I fell asleep.

"When I woke up, the storm had passed, and I could see that the Flats were leveled, but I was safe. *Our* little fort made it. Someone was with me, protecting me, this place, and somehow giving me a new view of the future. Of someday. I realized for the first time, this mess, this garbage I tried to push you away from isn't permanent. Or it doesn't have to be. I don't have to grow up and be the same kind of man as my dad. My kids don't have to grow up like this. And, in the strangest way, I felt like the Flats being taken out like that was, I don't know, like us being given a fresh start, like what Joseph said up there. Like—what was that?"

"A mercy."

Mick stared ahead into the forest. I wondered if he'd heard me. But then he turned back toward me and nodded. "Exactly," Mick said. "A mercy."

Branches crackled and snapped behind us.

"So here's where they hide," Mr. Pop said.

"Or *think* they hide," Joseph said. "We all know about their fort."

The knock on the roof set us both crawling out of our lean-to. But not before I stole one last kiss.

"Mick, Mercy," Mr. Pop said, "we will talk about *this* and other places you may and may *not* go with each other later. But we've got to head back. We've got to round up shelter. Plus, Joseph wants to check on his patient."

"His patient?" Mick asked.

"Not my patient," Joseph said, visibly nervous for Mick to hear what he'd done. "Just some guy I helped in town."

"Newell's riding to town with us," Mr. Pop said. "Want to come too, Mick?"

"Let's go," Mick said. And he grabbed my hand and led the way.

* * *

This time the receptionist let all of us in, albeit with a warning that the patient had just woken up and needed rest. However, she said, he had told her that when we came by, he wanted us to stop in. So Mr. Pop opened the door slowly.

"Frankie," he said, peering in.

Mick stopped and grabbed my arm.

"Wait," he said. "Who are we seeing? I thought this was Old Man."

"It's Mr. Carmichael, Mick," I said. "He's Joseph's patient."

"What do you mean?"

"Just come in."

Mick followed me into the room where Mr. Carmichael lay bandaged and sleeping on a bed. Molly rushed up from her chair toward me, past where Mrs. Carmichael already stood shaking Joseph's hand so hard I thought his arm might come off.

"You saved his life. Thank you. Thank you," she repeated as she swayed with an uncomfortable Joseph.

Molly gave me a quick hug and Mick a surprised glance.

"Dr. Sahmby says he should be okay," Molly said. "I don't know what I would've done if I'd found him like that. But I couldn't have gotten him out. Not like Joseph did."

I turned to Mick, thinking he'd be ready to hear the rest of the story, of just how his brother came to save the life of Mick's enemy. But Mick just stared at the bed. I realized that the last time he'd seen Frankie Carmichael, Mick had been at the accused end of Mr. Carmichael's long, pointing finger.

"Visiting time is up, everyone," the nurse said too soon. "Mr. Carmichael can't rest with everyone in here."

"He seems to be sleeping just fine with all of us," Mr. Pop said. I smiled. Mr. Pop was getting good at questioning authority.

"Goodness' sake, Paul," Mother said. "She's looking out for your friend, and you come in with a sass mouth? All right everyone, let's scoot. The man needs to rest. Molly, Muriel, we'll be praying. And I'll send someone back with some supper for you. If you want to come stay at the farm, just let me know. We'll make up a room right away."

Mr. Pop walked over to the bed, mouthed a quick prayer, and then followed Mother out of the room. Mrs. Carmichael walked them out, her arm still around Joseph's shoulders. She was promising him gifts and her famous butter cookies as a reward for his kindness.

"You don't know what this means to our family, Joseph."

Mick approached the bed. For a moment, my heart froze as I wondered what he'd do. Alone here, except for me, next to the man who tried to destroy him. But Mick reached out and touched his head first, just below where the bandage left off, and then touched his hand.

Mr. Carmichael flinched, his eyes fluttered and his fingers circled around Mick's hand and squeezed.

I gasped. But Mick stood still, just staring into his face.

"He's just a broken man," Mick said. "Just like the rest of them. Weak and sad and broken. But I don't have to end up like this. Do I?"

I shook my head. "Of course not," I said.

Mick nodded and pulled his hand away from Mr. Carmichael's.

"Let's go," he said. "Let the man find some peace."

Mick put his arm around me and we walked out of the room and back into life.

✳ ✳ ✳

Mr. Carmichael woke up completely two days later. He had no memory of the accident or of being saved. Publicly he rejected the story of Joseph having much role in saving his life, preferring the version where Chef was the hero and Joseph more of a sidekick.

But when at the next Wednesday's prayer meeting, Pastor Murphy said we'd be joining Second Baptist in holding a special offering to build new housing for the Maliseet, my ears perked up. Fulton's, Pastor Murphy said, had offered to donate the nails and provide the rest of the building materials at cost. The Maliseet wouldn't be sleeping under blanket lean-tos for much longer.

Mr. Pop laughed out loud when he heard this news. "I'll be—" was all he said.

"What's this mean?" I asked Mr. Pop.

"It means the rumors I've heard that Mrs. Carmichael wrote Marjorie and Glenn, asking them to come home for a visit once the baby comes might be true after all. Or sooner if they can make it."

I stepped through the crowd who'd gathered at our home to pray and eat and gossip and walked out onto the porch.

I looked across the fields, toward the other farms. The flood-waters had receded enough that harvest would only be pushed back another week, though no one expected much from the crops. Predictions were that as much as half of the potatoes would have rotted before we could get to them. Even still, we gathered that night to thank God for His past abundance and His protection from the storm and to pray for His provision. One thing farmers knew for sure: we did what we could, but ultimately, growing po-tatoes was God's business, not ours.

The potato truck pulled into the driveway as I sat on the front steps. Ellery stepped out first, followed by Mick.

"I didn't think you were coming back here," I said.

"If you think I'm going to let this boy sleep in that horrible beamy Widow Nason's place one more night, you don't know beans," Ellery said.

"Ellery invited me to stay at his cabin tonight," Mick said. "And he's right. I'd had enough of that big feather bed and Widow Nason's claw-foot tub and hot water. Her stacks of hot cakes with butter and bacon, her hot coffee and cold milk in the morning was getting *real* old."

Mick winked at me and I giggled.

"Sounds horrible, Ellery," I said. "Thanks for rescuing him."

"Well, it's only for one night. That woman says she wants him back tomorrow. Her roof won't fix itself, she says."

Mick said, "That's not all she wants. Mrs. Nason said I could stay here with you so long as you joined us for dinner and a game of Scrabble tomorrow."

"Ayuh. She did say something to that effect. Well, tomorrow then. The door'll be open for you, Mick. 'Night, Miss Mercy."

I'd never seen Ellery blush before and because it was twilight I couldn't even be certain that he did. But he certainly turned away fast enough, and his slight smile and shuffled walk back toward the direction of his cabin betrayed what I imagined was a blush.

Mick stepped closer toward me. I reached up to wrap my arms around his neck and to let him kiss me. Which he did, though quickly and with his eyes on our front door at all times. He grabbed my hand and led me toward the chicken coop.

"Let's go check on the girls," he said. I knew, with a houseful of Baptists asking for help with the harvest, the front porch wasn't a place he'd want to sit with me. Even if Mr. Pop had given us a blessing, of sorts.

"Uncle Roger called today," I said.

"Yeah?"

"Looks like Edna whipped up some roaring in Augusta. Seems like the governor wants to see to it that the Maliseet have some *real* land to build some permanent homes on. News of the Flats reached New York papers, I guess. Caused a real embarrassment for him. Embarrassed politicians are the best kind, Uncle Roger says. They're usually the ones you can work with."

"Well, that's good to hear, I guess. Though, who knows? Think any farmers are going to be willing to give up their land?"

"Mr. Pop says it might be forest land. State-owned."

"Ah."

Mick grabbed a handful of feed and tossed it toward the hens. They crawled over themselves trying to reach it.

"Think you'll come back to school after harvest break, Mick?"

"I don't want to. But Mrs. Nason says if I'm to stay with her, I'm to go to school. So unless Ellery's cabin proves to be much comfier than I'm picturing, I guess I'll be back."

"Has it been okay with Mrs. Nason?"

"She's okay. Kind of a funny one. I guess she's taking guff from the women at her church for housing me. They think it looks bad," he said with a shake of his head.

"Oh, so I've got some competition, do I? What do you think, girls? Am I going to have to fight Mrs. Nason for Mick?"

"Stop it," Mick said, leaning down to kiss me, just as the front door creaked open and a crowd of pray-ers stepped onto the porch. He pulled me farther behind the coop, out of the line of sight. "No competition. Pretty sure she's only got eyes for Ellery."

We both laughed.

"So how will things be at school?" I asked. "I mean, just because Mr. Pop and Mother are okay with us doesn't mean the other kids will be."

"I'm not too worried about that," Mick said. "But I am worried about—"

"What?"

"Well, college."

"College?"

"Mrs. Nason said somebody's agreed to pay my way or at least put money in a college fund for me."

"What? Who?"

"I dunno. A mystery, she said. I'd just like to know who to thank. But she says sometimes it's better not to know as it makes things more complicated than it need be. I just don't get why all this stuff is happening, Mercy."

"Just chalk it up to mercy."

"To you? Have you been out trying to get money for my education? I'm not even sure I want to go to college."

"No, not me. I mean the mercy of God, Mick. Again. I don't mean to keep going back to what Joe said about Edna, but he's right. I'm not going to preach to you. And you're smart enough to figure this out. But Mr. Pop says most of his best lessons have come from the worst things—and you've been through lots. Every difficulty in your life has helped you become more thoughtful."

"Really?" Mick teased, leaning close for another kiss. "What else is so great about me?"

"You're good at sorting things out, and you have a kind heart and a good mind. All gifts from God."

Mick rolled his eyes. I swatted him.

"Don't do that," I said. "I mean it. And I'm not the only one who sees this: God's got His eye on you, trying to take care of you if you'll let Him. He's doing big things. Like He's doing in Joseph. And me. And all of us. Even Mr. Carmichael."

"Great. Next thing you know Mr. Carmichael and I will be shipping off to Africa to be missionaries together."

"You better watch out. I think God likes sass mouths even less than Mother does."

"Well," Mick said. "Maybe it's God Himself who gave me this mouth. Only trying to use it."

Mick leaned down to kiss me, but I pulled back. I wasn't angry. Actually, I loved where this was going. And though I didn't tell him, I guessed God maybe did too. But I could hear more folks heading out to their cars and I didn't want to get caught here with Mick. Even Mr. Pop would wonder where I was. We weren't trying to hide anything, but the fewer people we had to answer to, the better. So I grabbed Mick's hand, shivered a moment as my own hand took in the rough of his callouses and the strength of his fingers, and said, "Now why don't you head back down to Ellery's cabin before the girls cackle too much and our new hiding place is found out!"

"All right," Mick said, giving me a quick peck on the cheek. "See you tomorrow. We can talk more about how great God thinks I am."

Now I rolled my eyes at him as he laughed and ran off down the farm road toward Ellery's cabin in the woods.

Epilogue

I wiped the corners of my mouth. Laurel had pointed out the crumbs of scone that apparently rested there. This cafe had the best scones in New York, but neat, they were not.

"Better?" I asked.

"Better," Laurel said with a laugh. "So . . ."

"So what?"

"So you can't just leave the story there! Who paid for Mick's college?"

"*Mick's* college?" I raised an eyebrow at her.

"Sorry. *Grandfather's* college. When did he go back to school?"

"Laurel, my dear, *that's* your biggest takeaway from this story?"

"Well, that's the biggest mystery. At least, one of them."

"One of them?" I asked.

"Well . . ." Laurel said, flipping her long blonde hair behind her shoulders. Though Mick loved all his grandchildren, from the moment Laurel sprouted blonde curls, Mick was smitten in a whole new way. Never more so than when she'd sit on his knee and beg him to teach her Maliseet words. Every phone call to her grandfather began with a *tan kahk*.

"She could be the first blonde chief," he'd say, after hanging up the phone with her. "She's got—I don't know—*spirit*."

My eyes began to water at the memory of him.

"You okay, Grandma?"

"Fine, sweetie. Sorry, you were saying?"

"Oh, well, I mean, I've wondered for so long what it meant for me to be Maliseet. Daddy doesn't talk about it much, but I want to know more. But I also want to know what it means that I'm Paul

Millar's great-granddaughter. Seems like I should be equally proud of both."

"That's right."

"And that maybe there's lots more I should learn," Laurel said. "So maybe next summer . . . you could take me to Maine?"

"It's a date," I said, already planning the trip, the places we'd see, and the new stories I'd tell her and the mysteries I'd unravel.

The Maliseet Today and Local Aroostook County Farms

In 1973 Maliseet Indians were recognized as a tribe by the state of Maine. The state also recognized their aboriginal right to hunt and fish, and tribal members received free hunting and fishing licenses. This same year the state of Maine opened a regional office of the Department of Indian Affairs. Many of the needs of Maine Indians had been ignored and the Department of Indian Affairs stated in a memo that "to a striking extent, the history and problems of Indians in Maine parallel the history and problems of Negroes in the South."

In 1980 President Jimmy Carter signed the Land Claims Settlement Act, which, among other things, established the Houlton Band of Maliseets as a federally recognized tribe and it received $900,000 to buy five thousand acres.

The Maliseet today have a Tribal Administration building from which tribal issues of housing, health care, education, and other important issues are cared for. The tribe is led by its first female Tribal Chief, Brenda Commander.

Aroostook County potato harvesting looks very different today. Small farms gave way to larger, more commercial endeavors, and in the mid-1950s the mechanical potato harvester began doing the job previously taken care of by people. Today very few farms employ potato pickers, and while the Potato Blossom Festival still exists, with very few changes, to celebrate the county's farming heritage, harvest season 2012 was the first time that a significant number of schools did not take a harvest recess.

Acknowledgments

FROM ANITA:

Though my maternal grandparents passed away many years ago, they are always in my heart. My grandfather, Merle Nason, and his life as a farmer in Northern Maine inspired much of this story, as did my mother, Annette Nason Fore, who worked long, hard hours in the fields on that farm.

Special thanks to the following:

My coauthor, Caryn Rivadeniera, who said yes when I approached her about the adventure of writing fiction. Contrary to rumors, there were no bruises or bloody noses in the writing process!

My cousin James Watson and my mother, Annette Fore, who have written a small volume filled with Maine sayings and loaned it to me during the writing process.

The supportive women in my writers group.

The Houlton Cary Library and their archives of the Houlton Pioneer Times.

Brian Reynolds, Tribal Administrator, Houlton Band of Maliseet Indians, for answering my questions, loaning me a tribal history book, making time to be interviewed, and answering all my follow-up emails.

Richard Silliboy, Mi'Kmaq historian and owner of Brown Ash Baskets Made by Richard Silliboy. Richard opened up his home on the Mi'Kmaq reservation for a lengthy interview.

Houlton Farms Dairy, a great source of inspiration each time I consumed a vanilla Awful Awful with chocolate sprinkles on top.

My husband, Mike Murphy, who listened to my panic about

the book deadline and listened to my whining about working all day and writing all night. He is the best! My son, John, whose love for Maine is only eclipsed by his love for Civil War history. He embodies the word encouragement especially when I'm writing a book!

FROM CARYN:

First of all, thanks to Anita Lustrea for inviting me into her storytelling and for this amazing ride. That we not only survived writing a book together but had such a stinkin' good time (mostly) doing it is a testament to Anita's amazingness.

Thanks to the folks at Moody for suggesting that Anita write this story. To Deb Keiser for encouraging us from day one. To Pam Pugh for your meticulous editing and fact-checking (still laughing about some of the stuff we got wrong!). Thanks to the designer for your beautiful cover.

Thanks to Tim Fall for your legal wisdom (when you were on vacation no less!), to Sarah Pulliam Bailey for your New York City help, and to Ruth Pulliam for letting us "borrow" your apartment.

And of course, to my family: my husband, Rafi, my kids, Henrik, Greta, and Fredrik. Writing a novel was a joy but made me a tad crabby around the family from time to time. Thanks for your million shades of mercy to me. Love you!

FICTION FROM MOODY PUBLISHERS

River North Fiction is here to provide quality fiction that will refresh and encourage you in your daily walk with God. We want to help readers know, love, and serve JESUS through the power of story.

Connect with us at www.rivernorthfiction.com

- ✔ Blog
- ✔ Newsletter
- ✔ Free Giveaways

- ✔ Behind the scenes look at writing fiction and publishing
- ✔ Book Club

MOODY
PUBLISHERS

www.MoodyPublishers.com